CALL OF CTHULHU

Regency Cthulhu

SECRETS

&

SACRIFICES

CATH LAURIA

ACONYTE

ACONYTE BOOKS

An imprint of Asmodee Entertainment Ltd

Mercury House, Shipstones Business Centre

North Gate, Nottingham NG7 7FN, UK

aconytebooks.com // twitter.com/aconytebooks

CALL OF CTHULHU

There are realities other than the mundane one we perceive. Its places, people and occurrences are inexplicable to rational scientific thinking and antithetical to our existence. Ancient lore, monsters, forbidden tomes, and diabolical cults are just the forerunners of the unimaginable entities who dwell in the cosmic void. They are coming for us: our world and our very minds.

Exposure to such horrors can lead to madness, but some bold souls must make a stand against these seemingly insurmountable odds. Defeating them will save the world as we know it; failure will usher in the end times. Can you hear the Call of Cthulhu?

Dedicated to everyone who, like me, is thrilled by the intersection of monsters and manners. Here's to you, my friend.

PROLOGUE

Blensworth Manor, Corsham, Five Years Prior

It all had the air of the most delicious lark, right up until it didn't.

The theatre of these evenings was what Byron Wright enjoyed most – after the philological aspects, of course. Few things compared to the gratification he received from translating what had long been considered untranslatable. He was still humming with pride over the last sigil he'd deciphered, the one that would be necessary when the time came to... well, to perform the aspect of this "followers of Shub-Niggurath" bit that he wasn't looking forward to.

However, those dark times were far in the future, the distant, unknowable future. Byron never thought too deeply about the future, not when the past was infinitely more interesting. The revelations he'd learned about the Talliri, the sorcerers from whom he now could claim to be an ideological descendent, all in the name of protecting the nation; it was a heady affair, made even more so by the three glasses of brandy that he'd consumed earlier that evening.

"What is it to be tonight?" he'd asked his dear friend James over their second glass. "Another bird? A lamb, perhaps? You got *excellent* results with the lamb." The sacrifice of that poor, puling creature had been enough to win James his familiar.

Byron didn't care for the thing, personally, with its wrinkled face and shining pate, and the way it couldn't quite decide whether it wanted to be a rodent or a very small, evil-eyed mannikin. He had already decided he would decline if James offered to entice one out of the portals they opened for him. After all, he had the children to think of, and he wasn't quite ready to share his... revelations with them. He would have no hope at all of concealing such a creature within the manor, even if it was minded to obey him.

"I have a more... elaborate plan in place," James had replied, an easy, satisfied smile on his face. "I think it will win us a creature of significant power."

"A calf, then?" Byron hazarded. "Lord, that will be a mess to clean off the marble." As it was just the two of them in their little cabal so far, Byron knew the bulk of the work would fall to him, and he wasn't looking forward to it. They were friends, good friends, but rank was rank.

Then again, a calf was better than the other option. "Not a maid, surely," he murmured, laying a hand on James's arm. "We are not – the time is not yet right, is it? It cannot be, I *cannot*–"

"Byron." James gave his hand a quelling pat. "I would

tell you if it were time for *that*, never fear. I worry over this recalcitrance of yours, though. You know what the ultimate goal of our experiments is."

"Yes, but–"

"And you know I am determined to do my part for king and country, no matter how distasteful the path to victory might be."

Byron found himself sweating beneath his layers of wool and silk. The thought of watching a young woman die, of being a party to her death... surely it wasn't time for that. Animals were one thing, but the prospect of killing an actual person made all of this feel so much more real. "Yes, but, James, surely there are more things for us to do before that? We need more allies, we need to grow the Brotherhood before we can make use of such a... being."

"You're right, of course," James said, and Byron relaxed. He relaxed even further when James filled his glass yet again. "It is important for us to take measured steps, explore the different permutations of sacrifice and sigil. When the time comes, it would not do to be underprepared."

"Exactly," Byron said, his nerves settling. No, tonight would not be the night when he would have to watch what he feared he *could* not. Tonight would be black robes and chanting, sacred knives and blood rituals, dark portals and darker power... but it would not be an act he would find unbearable.

The altar was prepared in the far corner of the library when Byron came with the robes, the sacrifice lying under a thick layer of blankets. In the dim light, the shape of it was obscured, but Byron was satisfied that it could be a calf. Perhaps a yearling, it looked a bit big for–

James coughed lightly. "Brother Wright, if you would begin."

"Ah, yes." He picked up his chalk and began to draw the complex sigil on the wall that would open the portal to the other world. It was meticulous work and, after three brandies, rather harder than he had expected, but his many hours of practice had paid off. He was able to chalk and chant at the same time, and finally turned to James with a smile of triumph. "I am ready at your convenience, Brother Fraser."

"Excellent," his friend said. He raised his obsidian knife, pulled back the blanket, and stabbed the coachman through the chest, the knife slicing straight through his livery. "Damn these infernal ribs," James muttered, pulling the knife out with a hiss. "Look, it's chipped the bloody edge."

"James…" Byron said faintly, still not entirely sure what was happening. Surely this was not… it could not be… "*James, stop!*" he shrieked when his friend struck again, this time angling the knife differently. There was a *pop* sound as the blade broke through the thick muscle. *No no no…* Byron stared in frozen disbelief, while the coachman, unconscious though he was, grunted in agony as the blade penetrated his heart. Blood poured from the wound and down the altar, and as the poor fellow drew one last, shuddering breath, James laid his hand in the still-flowing blood, then pressed his handprint into the centre of Byron's carefully made sigil.

The symbol began to darken, the kind of darkness that came with a subtle glow of its own. Byron watched helplessly as the portal sigil did its work, faster and easier than it ever had before. A doorway to the other realm opened before his eyes, fed by unprecedented sacrifice, and within its darkness…

Death came to meet them.

"Good God, man!" Byron turned to James, his eyes as wide as saucers and his lips trembling. "You cannot – you – it isn't–" Those trembling lips were unequal to the task of describing the scene before him, but description was not what he desired. His heart desired explanation, reason, or better yet – rebuttal. *Tell me I am not seeing what I think I'm seeing. Tell me this is not real.*

James, who always seemed to know Byron's innermost thoughts, simply smiled as the creature within the portal drew closer. His smile seemed to say: *It is real. All of it is. Now, what will you make of it, my friend?*

In the seconds it took the spreading pool of blood to reach the tips of Byron's polished Hessian boots, his mind managed to turn itself over in such a frenzy that it was small wonder his sanity couldn't remain intact in the moment. He exploded away from the altar, dropping the chalk from his numb and nerveless fingers as he staggered back from the corpse and over towards the library door.

"Byron," James's warning voice called out from behind him. "This is not the time to let your tender sensibilities get the better of you. You knew this moment was coming."

"Not this moment!" he shrieked, risking a look back. A

long, black limb was emerging from the portal. It was bare and sinewy and had a five-fingered hand sporting truly horrific claws on each demonic digit. "One girl, that is all you said was required for Shub-Niggurath!"

"And what about my own requirements?" James snapped. "What about the power I require in order to make our world a safer place, a *better* place, for us and for our children? Surely you did not think this march would end with a solitary sacrifice. The needs of the future necessitate–"

"You murdered a man for *that!*" Byron pointed his trembling finger at the creature still making its way out of the portal. It seemed to be wrapped in shadows, obscuring the finer details, but when it lifted its eyes, they glowed with a vile internal light. "For a beast you don't even need! Send it back, James, *send it back!*" The more of it that emerged from the portal, the more intense was Byron's need, selfish and atavistic though it was, to run.

"There is no turning back now, Byron." James's voice gentled as he set down the knife and stepped away from the portal. "My dear friend, you know how much trust I have in you, how much *faith*. Our paths were fated to cross, and I truly believe that God himself saw what wonders you and I would create together in our quest to glorify his name and save our nation from invasion."

He reached for Byron's hands. "This is the greatest trial of your life, my friend. All of our hopes for the future, all our aspirations, the joining of our houses… it is all contingent on this moment. If you stay, our glorious futures are assured. But if you leave now, there will be nothing more I can do for you."

If he had been capable of rational thought, Byron *might* have been tempted to stay. It was not only himself he had to concern himself with, after all; his children were not all grown, and his eldest daughter Cassandra was newly engaged but not yet married to James's son. He was all they had, and he had been luckier than he deserved. If he ran, he was as good as throwing away their future prospects.

But those were the thoughts of a man in command of his wits, and Byron was many things – clever, devoted, and gullible beyond belief to name a few – but he was not accustomed to violence. The *pop* of the knife and the coachman's dying groan still echoed in his ears, drowning out every logical argument with pure fear. He quivered like a cornered fox as he met James's eyes for the last time. There was something there, something that might be construed as regret in a lesser man; in James, Byron only knew that it meant he had to run.

And run he did.

He burst through the doors and into the hallway. It was empty, free of servants who might trouble him or, worse yet, James's own family. His legs felt like they were encased in lead; every step was a massive effort, and his stride was as short as his breath, but he was moving in the right direction.

The door, the door… his carriage was waiting for him in the stable yard. He needed to get to his carriage, needed to get away from here, back to the safety of his own home.

Safe, safe… he needed to be *safe*, away from this madness, this utter insanity. He'd never wanted it to go this far, never, *never…*

"Ahh!" A sharp pain pierced his left heel, causing him to stumble into a rosewood side table, knocking the crystal vase of fresh flowers onto the parquet floor. Water spread like a wound, but worse than that was the shock to his system when Byron saw that the heel of his sturdy boot had somehow been penetrated right down to the flesh beneath it. He touched the ragged leather with trembling fingertips.

Were those… teeth marks? When he pulled his hand away, his fingers were painted with his own pulsing blood. Byron glanced from his hand back down to his foot, and that was when he caught the glint of tiny red eyes in the dark hallway, staring malevolently at him as their owner scuttled towards the open door of the library, where its master waited.

God save me!

Run!

Byron ran once more. He ran through the pain, through the slosh in his boot that meant his own blood was leaking out with every step, through the terror gripping his mind with teeth as sharp and biting as the creature that had attacked him. He ran out of Blensworth Manor into the cool air of a late spring evening, where finally the heat of his madness began to cool.

He was out. He was not yet gone but he was outside; out of that damned room, away from James's secretive company and this awful betrayal of their friendship and everything they were trying to accomplish together. He was free.

Byron limped towards the stables. He wondered that there were no servants about, no one to perceive his exit and fetch his carriage for him. Had they been warned off by their master? No matter, he could handle this well enough on his own. A dozen more yards and he would reach the gate, and–

A shadow peeled away from the manor wall ahead of him and placed itself directly in front of the entrance to the stables. Byron stuttered to another halt, staring in uncomprehending horror at the... the *thing* before him. Its shape was hard to make out on a night like tonight, when the moon was clouded over and there was only a single, feeble lantern by the stables to illuminate the way. If he had not been so closely focused on the door, he might have missed its movement entirely.

But he did not miss this ghastly thing's appearance – he had, after all, seen it emerge into the world mere minutes ago. He knew its presence like he knew his own name, and for the first time that night, Byron's terror gave way to despair.

"I be-beg of you," he breathed, voice squeaking through vocal cords so tightly wound every syllable threatened to snap them completely. "Let me pass. Let me *go*. I will say nothing to anyone, I want no part in any of this. L-let me go, for the love of God."

For a long moment, the shadow didn't move. Byron began to shift his weight to move away, but then the shadow straightened, reaching a height both towering and terrifying. Byron searched its features in the dim light, looking for any sign of humanity, of compassion.

All he saw reflected back at him were lantern-like amber eyes, and a gleam that could have been saliva dripping from bared fangs.

"*Run,*" the creature hissed.

Oh God, God Almighty, no, no, no!

The threads of Byron's hastily stitched-together sanity immediately frayed once more. He had no weapon, no stalwart companionship, no hope.

No hope. He knew it just as well as he knew it would be impossible not to run. Running wouldn't save him – nothing could save him now, and yet...

Byron turned with a strangled cry and fled towards the woods that abutted the manor. Losing the hint of moonlight reflecting from the opaque clouds was frightening, yet oddly comforting in a way. In absolute darkness, he and this beast were equal to one another. When no one could see what came next, then who could *say* what might happen? Byron had already looked upon what was to befall him, and no longer being tormented by the sight of the beast was a blessing.

Perhaps God would save him after all; if he ran all the way through the trees and out the other side he would come to a well-travelled road where he might cross paths with a coach pulled by fine, fast horses that could take him away from here, back to his dear children, where he would devote all his efforts to removing them from harm before–

A feeling like fire plunged through his wounded leg, and Byron screamed as he fell to the cold, loamy earth. He knocked his head against a tree root and lay there, dazed and confused, until he was rolled over onto his back.

The darkness above him stank of decay, and those hellfire eyes consumed his gaze. Something wet pattered against his face, dripping into his mouth, and it took a moment for Byron to realise that it was blood.

His blood…

"A poor hunt," the creature said with a sneer, but Byron didn't hear it. He didn't hear anything except the sound of his own soul shrieking in horror, so hideous and painful that he was fortunate enough to barely feel what came next as one long, sharp claw began to dig its way from beneath his jaw straight up through his mouth, puncturing palate and tongue as it sought a path to his brain.

By the time it scratched through his skull to the soft tissue within, Byron had already utterly lost his mind.

CHAPTER ONE

The old wagon creaked and rattled with every bump in the road as it made its way to Tarryford. Cassandra Wright, settled in the back atop her trunk beside sacks of winter onions and turnips, swayed right along with her conveyance. A proper young lady would be fighting to maintain her posture, but after nearly a week of travel by post Cassandra's fatigue had resoundingly won the argument it was having with her sense of propriety, and she let herself sway accordingly.

Truly, if she let herself do what her body longed to, she would be bent over with her head against her knees, sleeping instead of fretting about what was to come next. But her thoughts were not as exhausted as the rest of her, and try as she might to put her worries out of her mind, they tormented her ceaselessly.

A week on the road, plus lodging and food... she was already down more than half of what she'd saved. And she was only just arriving in Tarryford. She had yet to make her way to the manor, yet to find a way onto the staff. How long would it take her to do so? How long would it be before the other servants trusted her enough not to dog her footsteps? And how long could she possibly avoid the notice of the master of the house or his son?

Cassandra had more questions than answers and little patience for any of it at this point. Her legs and back ached, and her feet were practically numb from holding the same position for so long. She stirred herself and looked towards the owner of this vehicle, a farmer with a face like a wizened apple who had, gruffly but sincerely, offered her a ride into Tarryford that morning "since the post don't go that far out of the way, miss."

"I beg your pardon, sir," she called out, and the old man craned his neck back to look at her.

"Aye?"

"How much longer until we reach town?"

"Mmm." He thought about it for a moment. "Not been this way for some time, y'know, but we're near enough now."

Cassandra took hold of her impatience with both hands and shoved it away from her lips where it threatened to do the most damage. In a carefully calm voice, she said, "That is good to know. Is it possible, do you think, that I might walk the rest of the way and reclaim my trunk from you once I arrive?"

"Walk?" The man's thick, greying eyebrows rose so high they melded with his bushy hair, tamped down firmly by the broad straw hat he wore. "A lady like you, walkin' all by herself?"

She gave him a pleasant smile. "Indeed. The weather is mild, and the route seems safe enough." It was idyllic, even, if one disregarded the enormous burnt-out husk of a building on a hill to the west. Curious. She wondered how long it had been there…

Walking for a while would also give her a chance to gather her courage for the task ahead without worrying that she was being observed. The farmer had been nothing but kind to her, but she felt the weight of his eyes cast her way every few minutes. She knew what he saw, and she had undoubtedly heard every question he'd thought about asking her.

Seeing herself through his eyes, she knew that he saw her as a lady of some sort, if the dress was anything to go by. Simple white muslin, but good stuff; not overly worn and patched. A green silk bonnet, plain but finely made, with a matching pelisse and a silver hatpin. Dark gloves for the hands, and she must have decent enough boots if she was willing to walk.

But then there were the other things, less obvious but far more scandalous, to consider.

A woman her age out on her own with no husband, no children, no family at all. She had the look of a gentlewoman, but a single trunk – one trunk? What gentlewoman travelled anywhere with a single trunk? Was she running from someone? Was she traveling to seek employment, or catch up with a lover?

What was she?

This man, fortunately, was kind enough not to voice any

of the thoughts that were doubtless crowding his mind. He simply brought the cart horse to a stop with a low, "Whoa there," then dismounted and came around the back to offer her his hand.

Cassandra didn't need it – she had let herself out of more coaches and carriages than she could count now – but she accepted the offer in the spirit of friendly gallantry that had prompted it. Her knees nearly buckled when she hit the ground, but she held them firm with gritted teeth.

"Got business wi' the publican's widow, so ye'll find me at The Four Feathers," he told her. "I'll have your trunk there, safe and sound."

Cassandra smiled. "Thank you very much, sir."

"Ah, well." The old man's cheeks had turned a bit rosy – was he blushing? "Not a hardship, miss, not a hardship. Enjoy your walk." He briskly reseated himself and got the cart moving again, leaving Cassandra to stew in blessed solitude.

Cassandra waited until he was out of sight around the next bend to start her own walk. Her hips and knees informed her in no uncertain terms that she was twenty-five now, quite a distance from the lissom young woman she had been when she was last in the county of Wiltshire five years ago. It seemed like an age had passed since then; now she was in an entirely new county, heading for a town she'd never visited before. But today, in the sunlight, surrounded by thick, verdant hedgerows and familiar birdsong, she finally let herself indulge in a few cherished remembrances as she walked along.

From her birth until just after her twentieth birthday, Cassandra had lived the privileged life of a gentlewoman. Her father had been a wealthy solicitor, not quite of the social class he aspired to, but married to a gentlewoman who gave him access to the people he so admired. Her father Byron had been clever, affable, and capable, all while politely maintaining the distance of rank so many in the gentry deemed necessary for their very existence. It had made him quite popular with that set, and in time he had mingled among them as a friend.

With the benefit of hindsight, Cassandra could now look back and see that her father had been more of a loyal hound than a true friend to these people. Blinded by her own good fortune and youthful ignorance, she hadn't realised that so much of the care and condescension she had taken for granted was nothing but a courtesy that she wasn't entitled to, one that could be rescinded as easily as it was granted.

But what did that matter? She might be educated, better than most young women her age, but she would never have to put it to the test. Cassandra was to have been married – hopefully to a man of equal or greater social status as herself – and live a quiet, coddled life as a wife and mother. She had even gotten as far as securing a match when everything came crashing down around them, all thanks to that loathsome man…

"Mr James Fraser," she murmured, speaking the name aloud for the first time in years. Oh, she'd thought it often enough when she lay awake at night, exhausted from a full day of looking after the five young children in her charge, yet unable to embrace sleep.

James Fraser, the architect of her father's rise and fall; the man who had taken Byron Wright into his closest confidence, who had made much of their friendship and aided him at every turn, who had even approved of a marriage between his son and heir, Gilbert, and Cassandra herself… he had been the snake in the grass the whole time. And her father, her loving, clever, and occasionally stupidly trusting father, had offered himself up to be bitten.

The official explanation for his death had never made sense. "Self-inflicted wounds" did not describe the state of her father's corpse. Not that Cassandra had been allowed to see his ruined body, but she'd heard the servants mutter about it amongst themselves as everything in their home was broken apart and sold to cover debts to Mr Fraser that her father had never spoken of to her – if they even truly existed.

"Cored right out, he was, right up into the brain," she'd heard one of the stable boys say. "Nah, not a gunshot – that woulda taken off the top of his head, too, yeah? And how could a man knife himself like that? Why not slit his own throat and be done with it easy?"

On top of that, to think that her father's death was the direct result of him murdering one of Mr Fraser's servants … impossible! He would never! Her father couldn't even bear to watch a chicken be prepared for the dinner table, much less find it in himself to stab a man to death. The years hadn't resigned Cassandra to her father's supposed crimes, they'd only made her surer than ever that he had been greatly wronged.

Devil-worshipper. Occultist. A fellow better off dead. Rumours had abounded, all of them helped along by Mr Fraser himself. He had been "so troubled by it all, I can't believe Byron took me in so thoroughly." He had been "so sorry for how this affects you poor children, and yet I must have recompense for the wrongs your father has done me." He had been "so sad to see you go, my dear," and yet he had been the first to suggest ending the engagement between their families once her father was dead. And Gilbert, bless his silly head, hadn't uttered a word against it.

Ah, well. You wouldn't have enjoyed being married to Gilbert anyway.

"Marriage is not about enjoyment," Cassandra said quietly, indulging in a proper argument with herself now that there was no one else around to hear it. "It's about duty. Marrying him would have greatly elevated our family fortunes."

He was a pillock, as easily led as a calf with a rope around its neck. You would have been bored beyond imagining.

"Boredom is more easily alleviated by money than by the lack of it, and we would not have wanted for funds."

And would you have begged Mr Fraser for an allowance beyond what Gilbert was allotted? You know your father always said he was as tight as a drum.

"I would never have begged that man for anything."

Even when she'd been inclined to like Mr Fraser, Cassandra had always been faintly wary of him. There was something about him – a keenness in his gaze and a sharpness in his manner that left her on edge, feeling as though she were standing on a precipice that might fall out from under her at any moment. She had avoided him as best she could, never letting herself be alone with him. No, she would have sent Gilbert to beseech his father for funds had it become necessary.

Not that such an eventuality had ever come to pass; this was all pure fanciful thinking that would get her nowhere. She ought to be focusing on what was to happen next.

But she had thought it and thought it in circles! It was time to give herself a reprieve, for pity's sake. She needed to try to remember the good times she had back then, not just the bad. When her family was whole, when she had friends and entertainments and recitals to attend… and oh, the balls! She had loved the balls.

Dancing was one of the few outlets a woman could have for physical activity, and she had dedicated herself to the art of it. The music had called to her, a siren song impossible to resist, and not even the most oafish partner could diminish her pleasure at dancing. Next to spending time with her father, it had been her favourite thing to do.

And sometimes you were fortunate enough to land a most excellent dance partner as well.

While Gilbert was as good at dancing as he was at riding or hunting (which was to say, not very, despite his enthusiasm), his closest friend, Thomas Griffith, had been the most sought-after partner at every event. How could he not be, with a fine figure and innate grace coupled with the elegance of his movements and his stern but kind demeanour? Thomas had been besieged by young ladies – and occasionally by older ladies as well – requesting his time at every ball but he had always saved the last dance for Cassandra.

"What silliness," she whispered, pressing one hand against her cheek in an effort to dispel the heat rising in it.

Is it silly to seek enjoyment where you can get it?

"It is silly to do so at the expense of my own honour."

You never did a single dishonourable thing with Mr Griffith.

"No…" But that didn't mean that she had never wistfully considered it in the privacy of her own mind. Thomas had not been as objectively good a match as Gilbert; he was the second son of his household, not the heir, and more interested in the military than in frittering his time away on balls and the like. But if circumstances had allowed for him to ask her before she had been betrothed to Gilbert, and irrelevant of whether she considered him the best option, Cassandra would have said the most resounding "yes" in existence.

Ah, well. There was no use in thinking about him now; as far as Cassandra knew, Thomas had been busy with his family estate ever since his late brother's death recalled him from his military career. If he still happened to be within Gilbert's sphere, it was the season in London, and Mr Fraser's eldest daughter was due to be presented this year; the family would certainly be there right now, not out at their country manor, and where the Frasers went their friends followed.

Cassandra had very vague memories of the young Miss Frasers; they had been shy girls, neither as outgoing nor as oafish as their brother, and not inclined to make a fuss. Her sister, Elizabeth, had declared them – with all the wisdom and authority of an eleven year-old – to be "ex*tremely* tedious, and they are *obsessed* with ribbons! I will not play with them. I'd rather ride horses with Samuel."

Samuel, six years older than Beth and two younger than Cassandra, had been uncommonly generous towards his little sister, and indulged her often in riding and "swordplay" with two carved pieces of oak. He hadn't been part of Gilbert's set, and Cassandra had been glad of it when she saw how quickly she herself was ejected from the Frasers' society. At least Samuel was spared that pain, if not many others.

Stop being so pessimistic. He is doing quite well in the navy. She had not always been sure that he would. He'd entered the profession just a month after their father's death, and when he left his sisters behind on the rocky quay at Portsmouth, one of a dozen young men being rowed out to where his ship was anchored, he had looked so miserable it took everything Cassandra had not to break down in tears like Beth. The first few letters he sent were very carefully worded so as not to make her worry, which of course made her worry all the more. In time, though, it became clear he was finding his place on the ship, and even beginning to enjoy himself.

Indeed, it was Samuel's placement as a midshipman that had provided Cassandra with a path to employment, his captain being solicitous of their family's plight – as well as the plight of his own poor wife, with many children to tend and little help. As their mother's relatives were only willing to take in Elizabeth – and reluctantly at that – accepting a position as a governess in a rural Northumberland community was the best deal Cassandra was going to get, and she'd known it. Truly, it had been a stroke of good fortune, for she had been given honourable if tiring work, earned a small income on top of her room and board, and had the space to consider what to do next.

"Hold your luck close to your heart," she murmured. "It has carried you this far."

God willing, it would carry her further – to the truth about her father, a man who for all his faults had been as devout as any other and would never have allowed himself to be drawn into devil worship or the occult. Oh, he loved a good puzzle – his method of notetaking proved that – but he simply would *never* have–

A sudden rustle beyond the hedgerows drew Cassandra out of her musings. It wasn't a subtle noise, not like the birdsong and occasional skitter of a small animal in the underbrush was. This was a raucous sound, like something large bounding about. It came closer, making the hedges shake under the weight of whatever was drawing near.

Cassandra fought down her nerves as she reached up slowly and gripped the wave-like silver tip of the hatpin, ready to withdraw it and use its full eight-inch length to best effect should she need to. *Perhaps I should have invested in that dagger after all.* Hatpins were all well and good for deterring the wandering hands of overly drunk and indulged men, but this…

There was another rustle, then a growl and a straining crash in the bushes straight in front of her, and a moment later–

A massive hunting hound flipped itself head over heels as it tumbled to the road, panting from exertion. It was buff-coloured, with a white belly and a curling tail, and it had wide brown eyes. Cassandra kept a firm grip on her hatpin; this was no simple foxhound. This was a hunting hound whose head, she noted with an edge of fear, came up past her waist once it regained its feet. The animal shook itself off, looked straight at her, lunged forwards, and pressed its big, muddy face against her dress in an effort to make her acquaintance.

"Oh no," Cassandra lamented ruefully as she replaced her hatpin and attempted to push the dog back. "No, you great beast, I'll not look presentable at all now!" Another fruitless push resulted in her white gloves becoming as stained as her dress, and she finally sighed and gave in to the dog's attempt to solicit her affection.

"You overgrown puppy," she chided the animal as she scratched behind his ears. "What kind of brute are you, hmm?" He must be very young, or very poorly trained; no proper hunting animal would be so cosy with a stranger. "Not a brute at all. Just a baby, I think."

The baby proceeded to nudge her in the hip so hard Cassandra nearly fell over. She laughed for what felt like the first time since leaving her placement in the north, and briskly rubbed the dog's ears until his tongue lolled. "Shall we walk on to town toge–"

A horn sounding in the distance got the hound's attention immediately. "I believe you are being called home," Cassandra said. The horn sounded again, and the hound quivered but stayed by her side. "Go on then," she said, withdrawing her hands. The hound looked at her, its wide eyes almost human as it seemed to ask, "Are you sure?"

"Run along," she said just as the horn sounded for a third time. This time the hound gave in to the call and dashed off down the road so quickly clods of dirt flew from its heavy paws – Cassandra barely managed to dodge one of them. She watched the animal go with a smile on her face, then lost that smile as she glanced down at her dress. "Some lady you look." Still, it could be worse. Tarryford was a small place, a farming village really; surely they would not judge her badly for a few stains.

She'd find out soon enough. Cassandra set off once more, following the rutted tracks towards her destination – and, she hoped, her destiny as well.

CHAPTER TWO

The spire of the church was the first thing to come into view, paired with a few gothic-style arches that soared above the rest of the town. Cassandra used that as her lodestone, for surely the church was located in the centre of Tarryford. Where the church was, The Four Feathers had to be close by.

She admired the sturdy cottages she passed by along the way, all with thick stone walls and slate roofs. Several of the inhabitants stuck their heads out as she passed, clearly unused to seeing a young lady escorting herself into town. At the intersection of her street with another, a man holding a measuring tape in one hand poked his head out of what looked like a dress shop and called out, "Miss! Pardon me, miss, but are you in need of assistance?"

She wasn't really, but it didn't hurt to be sure about things, so she asked, "Could you tell me whether or not I am close to The Four Feathers, sir?"

"Quite close, miss. Proceed another hundred feet along this main road and the inn will be the first thing you see once you reach the town square." He looked slightly askance at her outfit. "Have you... walked a very long way?"

"Not long at all, sir," Cassandra assured him, doing her best not to take offence at the slightly impudent question. It was far from the first she'd received on her journey south. "Thank you for your assistance."

"I, ah – yes, quite, miss. Thank you!"

Cassandra held her head high and pointedly ignored all other expressions of interest in her person, verbal and otherwise, until she reached the intersection of that road and two others. It was the first busy place she'd seen in Tarryford, with a coach, numerous horses, and several carts either moved aside or vying for a place to disperse their wares. And there, she noted with satisfaction, was *her* cart, right outside a large building with a wooden sign in elegant script that proclaimed it The Four Feathers, with four rough feathers carved beneath the words for emphasis. A heavyset man with a florid face and a drink-pocked nose was slowly unloading the cargo, including her chest. *Good.*

Cassandra crossed the busy road and made her way inside the inn. It was dark and cool, and the air smelled like freshly baked bread and something savoury roasting nearby. She smiled with relief. Having worked up a surprisingly intense thirst on her walk, she headed towards the restaurant, which was set back a bit from the front door. It was a small room crammed with half a dozen wooden tables and several benches, as well as a bar where a young man with wild brown hair and a wide mouth was filling a glass with ale.

There was her farmer in the corner, drinking with several other men of similar dress and demeanour. He nodded to her as she made her way across the room but otherwise dedicated his attention to drinking. His companions were less sanguine, and rather unable to keep their thoughts to themselves; she heard them pelt her driver with all sorts of questions as she stepped up to the bar.

Once she got to it, she was surprised to realise that the young man pouring the drinks was a *very* young man – a boy, actually, he couldn't be older than twelve. When he saw her coming his way, he beamed at her. "Good day, miss! Welcome to The Four Feathers! Are you looking for a room, or perhaps a meal, miss? There's none finer to be had in town, I promise you that, better than anything you'd get from Salsmith or Banham's. My mum's been workin' in the kitchen before sunup, got a few chickens baked and plated, or a game stew if you want something heavier. Fresh baked bread, too, and there's a few jars of Mrs Pepperdine's strawberry jam left. Or she can do shirred eggs with chicken liver, or pigeon pie, or–"

"Thank you, that all sounds delicious." It truly did, as her stomach was now insistently reminding her, but first things first. "I'd like a room for the evening as well. Possibly for longer. I *would* like to dine here, but I'd prefer to eat alone in my room." The fewer people who knew about her presence here the better, although the way the men in the corner were jabbering about her right now, word was certain to get around. "If you can–"

"A moment there, miss." One of the other men in the room

stood up and ambled over, his demeanour cool. He was better dressed than the rest of the patrons, with a waistcoat that might be genuine silk – a tradesman of some kind? Someone older and established in the community, judging from the fineness of his clothes and the haughtiness of his expression. "Are you traveling in advance of your party?"

"There is no party," Cassandra said firmly. "There is only me."

"No party?" The man looked dumbstruck. "You are travelling by yourself?"

"I am."

"A lady, on her own?"

"Indeed, sir."

The man straightened imperiously. "I'm afraid that is highly improper."

The storm of impatience inside her whipped up again, pressing against her throat so hard that for a moment Cassandra could barely breathe. She swallowed forcefully, folded her hands, and said, "And yet, sir, that is my situation. I assure you that I have no intention of causing any sort of trouble for the duration of my stay."

"Indeed, you shall not, for you shall not be staying in this place. It would be scandalous in the extreme!"

"But Dr Parsons," the boy behind the counter protested. "She needs a room, an' we need a customer!"

"Young Garrett," the doctor said firmly, "I am not unmindful of the needs of yourself and your dear mother, but it is not proper to host young, single, and unaccompanied women in an inn, no matter how reputable."

Oh, this rot again. "Sir, I assure you, there is nothing improper about me," she said with a tight smile. The muttering in the corner got louder, with a few incredulous statements of "Ha!" standing out amongst the palaver, but she did her best to ignore it. "I am a wholly respectable woman and I only wish to employ this inn to house me for a few days, nothing more."

"Taking the word of an unconnected and unknown woman such as yourself would be the height of foolhardiness," the doctor replied, his nose in the air as he looked at her. Looked *down* on her, rather. "What sort of tales might a 'lady' like yourself concoct in order to gain a foothold in a place like this?"

A lady like yourself. A poor workaround for what he really wanted to say. So, it was to be like this, was it? He thought her the sort of independent woman who wished to set up "shop" in this tiny, ridiculous town, did he?

Fine. It wouldn't be the first time Cassandra found a person – usually a widow – to put her up who could use the funds, but she would be damned if she would ask this man for any assistance in finding one. Her impatience begged to be given free rein to tell him as much, but she was prevented by a raucous barking, punctuated by a man's shouts, filtered in through the windows at the front of the inn. Young Garrett took the chance to extricate himself from the argument and hopped over the top of the bar. "One moment, miss, if you please," he said as he headed for the door. "Just have to deal with this…"

Cassandra, ire still rattling around inside her, followed

the lad outside. She wasn't going to make a scene, but if she couldn't stay here then she would need to make new arrangements for her luggage, and find someone to ask about another place to stay, and–

Oh, Lord in Heaven help her. She gasped as she took in the scene, one hand rising to her mouth as her jaw quite literally dropped.

There was the hound she had met on the road, barking at the florid-faced man who had been unloading the cart. From this distance she could smell the alcohol on him, as though he carried his own personal distillery in his pocket. He was shouting at the hound, poking at it with a walking stick he'd grabbed. And there, not ten feet away, dismounting from a fine chestnut horse and striding over to take control of the situation, was a vision so fair that Cassandra might have conjured him straight out of her mind.

He seemed taller than she remembered, long limbs made stark by his riding clothes, but his hair was as dark and curling as ever, and the look on his handsome face was one of indulgent exasperation that felt a bit too close to the caring expression she had held close in her dreams for the past five years.

Cassandra's traitorous heart skipped a beat, and she pressed a hand to her chest in an attempt to quell it. She should leave. If she turned around now…

"Merlin, stop that at once," Thomas Griffith said, and the hound immediately turned towards him and sat down, a perfect picture of obedience. The scene was too charming; she couldn't pull herself away. "Oh, you're not getting away with your bad behaviour so easily," he muttered. "You–"

"Yah!" The man with the stick poked the hound – Merlin – hard in the back, making him yelp, then turn with a growl, prepared to defend himself.

"Drop your weapon," Thomas said very firmly to the drunkard.

"I'll not!" he slurred, although a moment later he as good as dropped it when he had to lean on it in order to stay upright. "Tha' dog of yours's been … been … been *hounding* me all day, *ha!* Runnin' where it shouldn't, making a mess of the– the barrel where I likes to sit in th' shade, bein'… loud." He scratched his head. "A man can't sleep wi' all tha' noise, sir!"

"You shouldn't be sleeping at all, Old John!" Young Garrett snapped. "Ma hired you to assist our guests, not catch yourself a catnap whenever you like." He turned to Thomas. "Terribly sorry for the mistake regarding your dog here, sir."

"If he were my dog," Thomas said with a hint of a smile, "he'd be much better behaved, I assure you. Still, I–" As his eyes were idly tracking the front of the inn, they finally lit on Cassandra.

You silly thing! You had your chance to escape his notice and you bungled it!

But perhaps it wasn't too late. There was always a chance he wouldn't recognise her, and–

"Miss Wright," he said in a voice more breath than sound. "You're… you're here."

Well, damn it.

Cassandra put on a pleasant expression and dropped into a curtsy. "Mr Griffith," she said, heartened to find that her composure didn't wobble at all. She'd been half convinced she wouldn't even be able to speak to him. As Plato wrote, necessity was the mother of invention.

"Miss Wright," he said again, looking at her in a daze. Old John, taking his opportunity to exit with far more alacrity than Cassandra had, lurched off towards the aforementioned barrel where, fouled or not, he was more than happy to collapse in a heap on it.

"Ah!" The boy looked between Cassandra and Thomas with a growing smile on his face. "Do you know the lady then, sir?"

"Oh, he–" Cassandra began, but then faltered, unsure of how to go on. What was he to her? Nothing, anymore, and never better than an admired acquaintance even at the height of their association. And now…

"Indeed I do."

Cassandra dropped her gaze in the hope that no one was looking at her right now, for she was not at all sure of the expression she was making. She ought to explain, to defend herself against those who might think she was here to "ply a trade," and yet she couldn't tell him the real reason she had come to Tarryford.

"I've been expecting her," Thomas said after a moment. "For I engaged Miss Wright as a companion for my sister, who will be arriving within another week or so. Unfortunately, Harston Hall does not have the space in which to house her–" which was certainly a blatant lie given the scale that these places tended to be built upon, but it was a lie which was acceptable to all parties for reasons of their own "–so I asked her to seek lodging here. Which I will, of course, be paying for," he added, and Cassandra finally found the strength to lift her head.

Indignancy filled her chest – she had saved for this very purpose! She did not need some overbearing gentleman with a pretty mouth full of lies to come to her rescue at this *very* late hour. This was not, however, the place to argue about it. And at least it would quash any objection from Dr Parsons. If a gentleman like Thomas Griffith himself was paying for the room, then it couldn't be improper for her to stay here. "You are too kind, sir," she said, a trifle coldly. Thomas narrowed his eyes at her, but Young Garrett seemed immune to the tension between the two of them, too eager for a sale or too inexperienced with the world to care.

"Right, then! I guess this is one of your trunks, miss?" he asked, pointing to her well-worn but sturdy luggage. Thomas looked between it and her a few times, and his eyes narrowed even further. Was he assessing her dismal state of affairs? Was he perhaps wondering whether his act of unasked-for gallantry had found an undeserving recipient?

"It is," she said. "And there is but the one."

"Ah. Right, I'll get Old John to–" He stared over at his snoring employee with a look of mild dismay. "Oh. Never mind. Me an' one of the lads in the stables will get this to your room, miss. Won't be a moment." He walked away, leaving Cassandra and Thomas standing next to each other on the side of the busy street with the eyes of dozens of people upon them, some discreetly, some blatantly.

Cassandra opened her mouth to say something – what, she hadn't quite put together yet, but she hoped it was suitably ladylike yet cutting at the same time – when the dog, Merlin, decided he was done with being good. Much like he had in the road, he lunged towards her enthusiastically, forcing her to spread her hands in an effort to keep her balance.

"Merlin!" Thomas went to grab the massive dog by the scruff of his neck, but Cassandra got there first.

"Merlin," she said in as serious a tone as she could muster, "stop that at once." To her delight, the dog immediately obeyed. She rewarded him with some very generous attentions behind his ears. "Naughty puppy."

"I see you've already made Merlin's acquaintance," Thomas said.

"Did the dirty nose prints on my dress give it away?" she asked, belatedly recognising her reply as too forward. He didn't seem to mind, however.

"A bit, yes." It was only his third address directly to her, but he had mastered his surprise admirably. He sounded cool and composed, the perfect picture of a young gentleman. He must be… twenty-nine, now? Thirty? He had aged quite well; the years seemed to have hardly touched him. He had the same dark, curling hair she remembered, held back by the black top hat on his head. His white linen shirt was contained by a dark green waistcoat beneath a rather severely cut black coat that should not look so well as it did, and complemented his silver-grey cravat quite nicely. His fitted riding breeches reached the very tops of his leather boots, which stopped just below his knees. Utterly fashionable, perfectly handsome.

She wondered what he saw when he looked at her, and whether he was assessing if her looks had withstood the test of five years. Cassandra was suddenly quite glad for her gloves, however stained, since they hid the callouses and little scars that years of hard work had created. Her figure was thinner, less rounded than it had been before, and the dress which she had deemed perfectly adequate for travel seemed woefully unsuitable for facing Thomas.

"I–"

"How is your–" They both paused, mildly embarrassed at trying to speak over the other. After the silence lingered a little too long, Thomas took the lead, stepping a bit closer and lowering his voice.

"I was not expecting to see you once more in Tarryford, of all places."

Cassandra imagined he wasn't. "Nor I you." A terrible thought struck her. "Oh, please tell me that you didn't come here with Mr Fraser?"

"No, of course not. He's still in town."

Cassandra's eyes closed briefly in thanks at her unexpected reprieve. Except… "Then you came with his son?"

"I did." Another pause descended upon their conversation, this time broken thanks to the return of

Garrett along with another stout lad, who helped him hoist Cassandra's chest off the ground.

"Right, if you'll follow us upstairs, miss, I'll take you to your room," he said.

"Thank you very much," she replied, then turned back to Thomas. "And thank you for your generosity, sir. I do appreciate it." She leaned in a little closer, lowering her voice to a whisper. "I pray you… if you could keep my arrival here to yourself, I would greatly appreciate it." Cassandra was fairly sure she could hide her presence from Gilbert even while working on his staff. Gilbert had never bothered to attend to the names and faces of the people who served him, preferring to save all his attention for the pretty ladies and dashing men who made up his coterie.

"I will do so," Thomas said, and Cassandra felt a surge of relief that was nearly blissful. "But I would be most obliged if you would take dinner with me this evening, so that we might renew our acquaintance."

And so that you might explain yourself, his expression communicated rather effectively. *Ha!* As if he had the right to expect such a thing from her. He might fancy himself a saviour, but Cassandra did not agree that she was in need of saving. And if he thought she was going to let him swan in and take over all her months – no, *years* – of planning simply by raising one supple eyebrow at her–

"That would be acceptable," she said, cutting off her embarrassing thoughts as quickly as possible. If she couldn't put him off, she might as well get the inevitable over with. "Thank you again." She dropped another curtsy, received a gracious bow in return, and patted Merlin one last time before following her host and the stable boy back into The Four Feathers.

CHAPTER THREE

This time around they skirted the restaurant and headed up a dark stairwell to the second floor.

The room Young Garrett led her to was a surprisingly comfortable one, easily some of the pleasantest accommodation she'd had on her trip so far. That was the power of money and a man's voice. Or perhaps it was simply all they had left. Either way, Cassandra was gratified to have it, even though she was far from pleased to be beholden to Thomas Griffith for it. She thanked the lad for his assistance and informed him of her dinner plans, then graciously shooed both him and the other boy out of the door.

As soon as it closed behind them, Cassandra leaned her back against it with a sigh and let her eyes fall shut. To be alone, at last, was positively blissful. Never mind that in some ways she felt far less alone now than she had at any time on her journey to Tarryford.

Thomas had seen her. Had spoken to her. Had *helped*

her, the way almost no one had been moved to help her for these past five years.

Cassandra let herself have one minute to wonder what things might have been like if she had reached out to Thomas after her father's downfall instead of allowing herself and her siblings to be chivvied away in the night like a group of thieves. He had always been rather gallant, far kinder and more attentive to nuance than many of the young gentlemen he kept company with. She knew he had grown up in a troubled household and sought the military at a young age to escape it. Had he learned his great ability at forbearance there, his patience hard-won on the battlefield? Or had it been earlier experiences, such as when he sought to evade the heavy hand of his patriarch, that had made him so understanding to those in trouble?

Perhaps she would ask him.

Or perhaps you will limit your discussion to polite nothings and not give him a chance to stop your plans.

Cassandra moved over to the bed in a fugue, stripping off her gloves and pelisse and finally setting her bonnet and pin aside as she came to grips with the very unpalatable situation she now found herself in.

Gilbert, she was confident she could fool with frumpy clothes and a ragged bonnet. He so delighted in *being* a fool, after all, that he made it quite easy. With his father still gone, her original plan could indeed work ... except now, Thomas knew she was here. And Cassandra had no doubt that while he'd been easy enough to get rid of this afternoon, he would prove far more stubborn with regards to her business in Tarryford when they met for dinner tonight.

You may have to be honest with him.

"Heaven forfend," Cassandra murmured before letting herself fall back onto the bed. It was delightfully soft, the comforter filled with down. The material itself was coarse, but she still wanted to snuggle into it and take a much-deserved rest.

But no. Now she had reached Tarryford, it was finally time to respond to the latest letters from her dear siblings, a task she'd promised herself she would attend to as soon as she was settled in one place for more than a single night. With a sigh, Cassandra forced herself back onto her feet and over to her trunk, whose key she kept on a slender chain draped around her neck. She unlocked it, then reached into its well-ordered contents for her writing materials… and, upon reflection, her best gown.

Her desire to look well for her meeting with Thomas tonight was no mere act of vanity. Rather, it was an act of pure practicality; she needed to convince him that she was no damsel in distress, no princess to be rescued from a dragon. Cassandra had spent her time chained to the rocks, but she had freed herself. Thomas might argue he should be allowed to aid her – indeed, he already had before knowing the slightest hint of her circumstances – but he might just as readily try to dissuade her from her objective. That could not be allowed.

So she would look fine tonight, and dine well, and pay for the meal herself. She would tell him as little as possible of her plans, and if he attempted to tell her no… well, she would set him straight, as she had with numerous gentlemen on her journey thus far. She would be sure to keep her hatpin handy, just in case.

Get your mind back on the task at hand!

Cassandra set the writing supplies on the dressing table, which was complete with its own little chair, and removed her sister Beth's latest letter from the envelope in which she had been keeping all her correspondence. It had come well over a month ago; Beth was not the most faithful of writers, but when she *did* write, she always sent pages and pages stuffed full of news.

In this one, she was full of laments over the stupidity of the season, her utter distaste for balls, and how she'd gotten in terrible trouble for stealing their uncle's finest bone-handled hunting knife and learning to throw it hard enough to stick in the plaster in her room:

> *But I covered the holes up with a ghastly painting of our Great Aunt Ghiselle so he would never have known about it if not for the fact I stupidly neglected to properly clean the blade before putting it back. It did not take long for him to trace the plaster dust back to me. As a punishment, I have been forbidden from balls for the rest of our stay in London. Happy day! Unfortunately, he has also forbidden me from riding Percival, so I am left to wander the house like a ghost all alone.*

"Oh, Beth." Cassandra could so easily picture the distaste on her sister's face. At sixteen, Beth was in many ways still a child, unwilling to step into a woman's role or cease her youthful games. At the same time, Cassandra had to admit her sister's odd focus on martial exercises was something she now wished she shared. It was all well and good to be a delightful dancer, but she would have felt better if she had the faintest idea of how to defend herself past the deft deployment of her hatpin.

She wrote back, keeping her story as vague as possible. If she let on that she was travelling, Beth would surely go mad for details, and when Cassandra had to confess that she wasn't coming to London – at least, not unless she had to in order to catch her prey – her sister would be heartbroken. Better to tell her the family was retreating to the country for a bit, and that she would be out of touch for a time as a result. She *did* add in her experience with Merlin without mentioning Thomas, knowing that Beth would enjoy that.

Receiving her brother's letter had been more of a close call. If Beth's letters were rare by dint of personality, Samuel's were rare due to lack of proximity. He was near-constantly at sea, ever at work fighting the French navy – and the Spanish, whenever diplomacy failed to keep things polite – and when letters did arrive, they always came in a pack, many delivered all at once. They tended to be short and to the point, but Cassandra still treasured them.

Rather oddly, this one had arrived all by itself, and just a day before she left. She felt fortunate to have received it in time, but its contents were truly mysterious to her.

For one, there was the censorship. Cassandra knew

better than to expect that her brother's letters had not been read by others; he was an officer in a ship of the line, and while espionage in such a situation was difficult, it was not unheard of. The Admiralty had to be certain their sailors weren't spreading information that could be damaging to the English fleet, but in this case, there was far more blacked out than simply his location and the relevant weather.

Half the first page was smeared over with ink, entire paragraphs cut down to a single innocuous line or two.

Can't say as I miss the salt pork, but– followed a
bit farther down by *–patching more holes in sail and
splicing more rope than ever before. My hands are
beginning to blee–*

It was the final line that she was allowed to read that really bothered Cassandra, however. It was the last line before her brother wrote his loving farewell, and though to some it would be a meaningless platitude, Cassandra was intensely disturbed by it.

Pray for me, sister.

Samuel had always been devout, the only one of the three of them whom their parents had never had to cajole to get ready for Sunday services. Cassandra had been half convinced that the clergy lay in his future, before his future was so fatefully dashed.

In every single letter, Samuel had always signed off with:

*I will pray for us, or I pray for the souls of those
poor dead men we sent to the deeps, or even once*

I'm just praying the rain stops long enough for my smallclothes to dry.

Never, ever before had he asked her to do the praying. It smacked of a sense of hopelessness on his part. Cassandra would have scoured the letter for more clues as to why he felt that way, but when the letter was an inked-up mess, that was close to an impossibility.

In the absence of any real insight into Samuel's situation, all Cassandra could do was ensure she did not add to his anxieties. He, more than any of them, needed to keep his nerve.

Although right now, Cassandra did rather feel like she was girding herself for battle.

But such news was not for Samuel. He got niceties, generalities, and every assurance of her love and affection.

I shall pray for you (she added before the postscript), *as I pray for us all, but know that I believe God has a plan for you greater than anything you might expect right now. Even the darkest night is followed by the dawn, and no matter what, you are not alone. Beth and I will always be here for you.*

At least, she hoped they would.

Cassandra stared into the small mirror in her room, touching the dark curls that framed her face and wondering for the fifth – or possibly tenth – time whether she ought to have tucked them back, pinned them up, or otherwise hidden them. Her hair, thick and shining as it was, was also of a type to have a mind of its own, especially on a damp night like this. Rain fell in a thick curtain outside, and for a moment she wondered whether Thomas would be able to keep their dinner engagement after all.

It would be better if he could not. She could more easily ignore him then, with the advantage of affront on her side, and work her way into the good graces of whoever was hiring at Harston Hall.

That was the logical position to take. Cassandra was quite irritated that her disobedient, incomprehensible heart nevertheless lightened when she heard a familiar shout as Thomas called out to the stable boy.

He came. Of course he had. He had always been reliable, the opposite of his favourite friend, Gilbert. How often had Cassandra been left waiting at some party or engagement, wondering when her betrothed would arrive? How many times had she been rescued from that lonely awkwardness by Thomas? Too many for her to properly remember. She was grateful to him for that... and yet she would hold firm tonight. Now was not the time for fond reminiscences and light conversation. Now was the time for her to tell him, plainly, that her business here was none of his concern.

She took the maid's announcement that her companion had arrived with equanimity, and after one last look in the mirror and a furtive pull to one of her curls for luck, headed down the stairs. Cassandra was very conscious of the swish of her pale blue satin dress, how the fabric reflected the light and complemented the elegant lapis lazuli necklace she wore. She wore gloves but had foregone a jacket, and as she was led into the semi-private room attached to the pub where she and Thomas would be taking their meal, she wondered if she should go back up and get a shawl. It was chilly down here and damp from the rain, and the fireplace in the corner did little to warm the space up.

Then she saw Thomas waiting for her and immediately felt much warmer. He had changed from riding breeches to proper white trousers, but otherwise his outfit was the same. The look on his face when he first caught sight of her was the same, too: disbelief coupled with something much more intimate, something Cassandra did not dare put a name to.

They greeted each other formally, sat in their respective chairs, and hardly spoke a word until dinner was brought out and the servants dispersed back to the pub, which was much fuller now. Cassandra took a sip of the glass of wine, a rather robust madeira, and was grateful she'd drunk plenty of water earlier. Thus fortified, she opened the conversation before Thomas could attempt to pin her down.

"I greatly appreciate your assistance today, but you should know that it was not necessary. I might not be a woman of means any longer, but I am no charity case." There. Plainspoken and upfront, as she always attempted to be these days.

"I was simply surprised to see you standing on the street here in Tarryford and reacted without thought," Thomas said, sidestepping her pronouncement with an agility that vexed Cassandra. "I don't believe you have any family in the area, do you?"

"No, I do not."

"Do you have some sort of engagement bringing you here, then?"

Cassandra arched one eyebrow. "Like being employed as a companion to some gentleman's younger sister?"

Thomas had the grace to look a bit abashed. "It was the first thing I could think of that seemed plausible."

She decided not to push it. "Indeed, I have had ready occupation as a governess these past five years, so I would be well qualified for it. However, from what I remember of your sister Francine, she can have no need of tutoring. She was determined to study every other young lady into the ground, and most of the young men as well."

"We are not here to talk about Francine," Thomas said irritably, pushing his plate forwards and setting his elbows on the table. "Miss Wright, I must know what you are doing here."

And *there* was the bluntness she knew Thomas best for. Seeing it levelled at others had been a highlight of many a dull party when she had been a member of the gentry. Having it turned against her now was less than ideal. "Respectfully, and with renewed thanks for your assistance today," she said with icy stiffness, "that is none of your concern."

"You are alone in a town where you have no connections or friends, to my knowledge. There are no distinguished features of natural beauty here, and if you were interested in seeking a husband you would be in London with the rest of them." His brow furrowed briefly. "And I think I know you better than to imagine that you came here to attempt a renewal of your former affections with Gilbert. So, what *has* brought you here?"

No friends and no connections. Yes, that described her very well, as hard as it was to hear. Only moments ago, she'd thought she could count at least one friend in Tarryford, but apparently he didn't see it that way. "It is a private matter, Mr Griffith."

"A private…" Thomas's face suddenly blanched. "Cassandra, are you here because you're chasing a man? Has someone abandoned you?" He lowered his voice, but the softer volume did nothing to disguise the horror in it. "Has someone *violated* you?"

"No!" she cried out, shocked that he even thought of asking. The noise in the pub dimmed momentarily, and Cassandra was forcibly reminded that although they were in another room, there was in fact no door to help conceal their conversation. "No, it is nothing like that at all," she continued much more quietly a moment later. "I assure you, I am well in every regard. It is simply that the time has come for me to undertake a new sort of… occupation, that's all."

Thomas's eyes narrowed. "What sort of occupation are you referring to?"

"That is none of–"

"My concern, yes, I realise that's what you think, but let me tell you what *I* think, Miss Wright." He leaned forwards, his bright eyes focused unflinchingly on her face.

"I think that you are one of the cleverest people I have ever known. I think that when your family was ruined after the scandalous details of your father's behaviour came to light, you took it very personally. I think that you are resourceful, dogged in the pursuit of the truth, and would do anything to preserve the memory of the man who raised you as you thought him to be rather than we were all told he truly was. I think you are here on a mission, and that the Frasers are a part of it." He sat back but didn't look away. "What do you think of my suppositions?"

I think you are perilously close to a truth I don't want you to know.

"Mr Griffith… please," she said. "Do not inquire any further. My presence is nothing that need concern you, or anyone else in Gilbert's party."

"It is far too late to tell me not to be concerned," he said. "If you decide not to tell me of your own volition, my honour and concern for your welfare will only be satisfied by accompanying you about your business from morning till night, so that I may see for myself you are well and safe."

Cassandra barely resisted the urge to roll her eyes at his overbearing announcement. Who did he think he was, speaking of concern for her welfare five years too late for it to make a real difference? "That is *not* what I need!"

"But it is what you'll get unless you tell me the real reason you're here!"

"Fine!" They glared at each other in silence for a moment, then Cassandra shook her head. "Fine. I suppose

I should have known better than to try and get around you. If I could be called dogged, then you are like a hound after a fox."

"I would never cause you any harm," he assured her.

I do believe that. She shook her head slightly, paused for a drink, then said, "I am here to recover my father's journals from Mr Fraser's household. Before you ask, yes, I specifically saw Mr Fraser take them as our home was being picked apart by the crows of imagined reparations. I think that they hold the truth about my father's associations with Mr Fraser and, ultimately, why he died."

Thomas steepled his fingers and tapped them against his chin. "You don't believe that he killed himself, then."

"No, I do not," she said firmly. "Nor do I believe that he killed anyone else. Such a despicable act would go against every aspect of his character." She paused, prepared to counter what she knew would be Thomas's next argument. "I cannot deny that he was close friends with Mr Fraser. However, I believe if *anyone* in that set was inclined towards such dark acts, it was not my father."

"Are you suggesting that, of the two of them, it is Mr Fraser who is the murderer?"

And an occultist, and more. So much more. "I think the clues that will lead me to the truth about my father and his relationship with Mr Fraser can be found in my father's journals. I think that is why they were taken, and I am determined to get them back."

Thomas sighed. "What makes you think he even still has them?"

"Mr Fraser is not the sort of man who throws anything away that might be of use to him," Cassandra said with more bravado than she felt. The truth was, she could not know for sure the journals hadn't been burned or thrown into a midden heap somewhere, but they were all she had to go on. "Either way, I must know for sure."

"Then allow me to look for you."

Oh, she should have seen that offer coming. Cassandra allowed herself a few seconds to feel astonished before retaking control of herself. "I thank you, but I don't believe you'll be able to properly identify them."

Not to mention you would look inside them and see nothing but gibberish. Then he would surely think her mad.

"Give me a chance."

"My chances of success are far greater."

"Your chances of success are non-existent!" Thomas insisted, slapping the table with one hand. "Or do you not think it will be strange for you to walk up the road to Harston Hall, knock on the door, ask to be shown to the master's private library, and actually expect his servants to not only allow you entrance, but to refrain from reporting on your actions to Mr Fraser himself?"

"Which is why I will be disguised as a servant," she snapped, stung by his rebuke. Did he think her a complete fool? She'd thought of all of this. "And not even disguised! For I intend to seek employment at Harston Hall in the morning."

Thomas shook his head. "Absolutely not."

Oh, how dare he. "You are neither my husband nor my

father," Cassandra said coldly. "You have no right to dictate my choices, and this is one I am determined to make."

Thomas's tongue seemed to stumble for a moment, but he rallied quickly. "You could be whipped or worse if you were discovered trying to steal from that household. Besides which, there is no world in which you could ever be mistaken for a servant."

Cassandra laughed. If it came out a trifle bitter, hopefully it was only detectable to her ears. "Never mistaken for a servant?" She reached for the fingertips of her right glove and began to remove it. Thomas stared at her, unable to look away from her unveiling. Once the glove was off, she held up her hand palm out. Even in the dim light of the fireplace and the candles set about the room, there was no mistaking the thick red callouses that lined her flesh.

"Since we last met, I have been washerwoman, seamstress, and cook, not to mention governess to a household with five young children. The duties of a servant are very well known to me, Mr Griffith. It is not an occupation that I place myself above."

The frustration inside her boiled against her lips, and this time she let it out. "You are not meant to be here!" Cassandra dropped her hand back to her lap so she would not point at him. "*None* of you are meant to be here. It is the middle of the season, you are all meant to be away in London. Mr Fraser ought to be shopping Gilbert around for a wife, not letting him idle away his days at their country estate."

To her surprise, a quiet laugh escaped from Thomas's lips.

"What?" Cassandra demanded. "What have I said that amuses you, sir?"

"It is not you," he assured her, a smile still on his face. "It's just... you have as much understanding about Gilbert's prospects as I would expect of someone so clever. How the two of you ended up eng–" He stopped, then began again a moment later in a more sedate tone of voice. "The truth is, Gilbert is better sold by his parents without his presence to disrupt the proceedings. He has been engaged twice more since your... departure, and both times the match has fallen through. The country is the safest place to manage his prospects from, and given there is an actual reason to be hunting here right now, it seemed like a good chance to occupy him.

"And as for me..." He looked away. "Indeed, I had not meant to accompany Gilbert here, but my business in London was finished quickly this year and returning to my estate was... not what I wanted."

It is none of your business... And yet she couldn't resist asking, "Is it so lonely being there?"

"On the contrary," he replied drily. "It is far too full of company. Ever since my brother's death, my extended family has taken it upon themselves to attempt to... *renegotiate* their dealings with the main branch, of which my sister and I are the last representatives. I am, quite simply, fatigued from their many requests. When Gilbert issued his invitation to me to join him here for the hunt, I took it gratefully." He smiled, but it looked a bit resigned. "I will be surprised if the silverware survives my absence."

Now it was Cassandra's turn to laugh. "Such trials and tribulations you have faced, sir."

"I understand now that they are nothing compared to yours." He was back to looking straight at her. "And that is why I cannot allow you to put yourself at risk by seeking employment at Harston Hall. The chances of discovery and punishment are far too great."

Oh no, he didn't. "Mr Griffith–"

"No, please, do not try to convince me otherwise. I am very determined about this."

"And I am equally determined to find a way into that household and retrieve my father's journals by any means necessary," Cassandra said, holding herself straight. She would not be dissuaded. She would *not*. "Whether I make my way as a servant, a thief in the night, or by some other means, this will happen."

Thomas stared at her penetratingly. "Are you open to other means, then?"

"I am," she said cautiously, wary of any suggestion that might entail delay. She had delayed her attempt to prove her father's innocence for too long already.

"Even if they throw you into company you might prefer to avoid?"

She stiffened. "I will not beg Gilbert for a place at his table."

"There would be no begging involved," he assured her. "Perhaps some well-justified shock from the rest of the party, but I am sure it is nothing that would cause you to falter given your convictions. And no matter where you have been these past five years, or how you have conducted yourself, I cannot imagine you as anything less than poised."

Oh, sweet Thomas. He had not seen her weeping into her pillow late at night, especially in the early years as she spent too much time reflecting on everything she had lost and missing the comfort and safety of her parents' presence. He had not seen her cradle her reddened hands as they stung from using caustic soap for the laundry or soak her aching feet in a basin of cold water after a day spent running around after her charges. Cassandra had been very far from poised many times in these past few years, nothing like the confident young woman she barely remembered.

But he does not know that, and I would have him keep some illusion of me.

"I do not see any other way," she said at last.

"Consider this, then."

As he told her his suggestion, Cassandra's mind stopped working. It was not a voluntary reaction; she wished to say something, anything, but instead she was frozen in amber, her internal voice finally silenced as a wave of heated incredulity swept over her. It took far more attempts than she liked to regain her ability to speak, and even then she was unable to properly articulate the impossibility of his notion.

"That is not… you cannot… it is simply…"

"I can and I shall. You need an excuse for being in Harston Hall, and I need you to be safe. This is the perfect compromise."

Cassandra found her voice. "It is a compromise of your reputation! And think of how it could damage your friendship with Gilbert!"

Thomas shook his head. "Our friendship was damaged years ago. It has limped forward this long on the strength of our school day companionship, but over time even that has frayed." He leaned forwards and stared at her with an intensity she found almost unbearable, yet impossible to look away from. "You have always been kinder to me than I deserve, but believe me, I fear nothing from this. To have you seeking a solution on your own would be a far worse eventuality."

Cassandra opened her mouth to object once more, but found that, in fact, there was nothing that she could honestly say in the face of Thomas's pronouncement. The truth was, having his assistance would make things a great deal easier for her, even if it ended up being absolutely mortifying. "Then… I accept your help, Mr Griffith."

The tension seemed to run out of his body all at once, and he sat back with a smile on his face. "Thomas, please," he told her. "After all, we are engaged now."

Engaged. What a ridiculous farce!

It was so ridiculous, in fact, that Cassandra had to laugh. Once she began it was hard to stop, as if now that her trampled sense of humour had been given an outlet it was taking full advantage of the situation. She buried her face in her hands as she sought control of herself, and finally was able to raise her head again to look at Thomas.

His mouth was slightly open, his eyes set firmly upon

her. The way they glistened in the firelight lent them an air of vulnerability and affection that she could not help but wish was real.

That would be too much, even for him. Be grateful for what you have.

"Thank you, Thomas," she said at last.

"It is my pleasure, Miss Wright."

"Cassandra," she corrected him gently.

Was that a blush upon his cheeks? "Cassandra," he agreed, and then the main course was brought in, and the moment was broken.

But perhaps… perhaps it was not entirely lost.

CHAPTER FOUR

Despite her belief that this course of action was the best she had available to her, it did not prevent Cassandra from falling prey to a fit of nerves half an hour before she was due to meet Thomas downstairs the next morning. She had managed to occupy herself for the earlier part of the day – exercise was a sovereign cure for nervousness, she had found – and had taken herself for a tour of Tarryford, walking the border of the town and noting the places of interest.

It was truly a charming little place, with a more interesting collection of shops and shopkeepers than she'd first imagined. The blacksmiths, for example, were a pair of brothers who were as charming with their words as they were deft with their hammers. The bakery was delightful, and a trip to the fabric store, followed by another to the dressmaker, left Cassandra assured that she would at least be able to avoid embarrassing herself with the limited number of garments she owned by the time the ones she'd ordered were ready.

It was all thanks to Thomas's largesse, of course. It made her feel slightly guilty to be spending his money on things for herself – after all, she was not truly his betrothed – but he had been very insistent before leaving her last night, and the truth was… well, the truth was that she *wanted* to feel beautiful again.

Cassandra knew better than to place all her value in her appearance, but she also knew the power of costume as a shield against rumour and supposition. With the purchase of a few ready-made things to accent her wardrobe, she would at least be able to look the other ladies in Gilbert's party in the eye when she was presented to them tonight, rather than feeling outshone by their finery, a common wren to their goldfinches and kingfishers.

Even she could only walk for so long, though. After a light repast, she spent an excessive amount of time getting ready, creating curls to frame her face and putting on the last thing she had of her mother's: a small gold cross on a fine chain. It rested just above her decolletage, which felt daring after so many years affecting a servant's modesty. She tucked the chain with the key to her trunk into her bodice; travel had made her wary of letting it leave her person.

"You will be all right," she assured her wavery reflection in the vanity's mirror. "You will be fine. You have waited for this for so long. What is the fear of society compared to the culmination of your plans? Nothing," she said, but her voice was unaccountably breathless. "Nothing at all."

Just like you.

The voice in her head sounded suspiciously like Mr Fraser's

when they last spoke, when he had made it oh-so-clear that she was to have nothing further to do with his family.

"No." Cassandra would be condemned to hell before she allowed that man to dictate anything to her now, especially in what should be the safety of her own mind.

"No," she said again. "No." She said it to her wavering courage and years of painful memories, a firm rejoinder against the insidious vision that was trying to drag her down. She would be dragged nowhere. She was here, she was alive and strong, she even had an unexpected ally and friend to help her through her stay. No, she would not give in to these fears. Not when her chance had finally come.

A sudden knock on the door broke Cassandra free of her reverie. She took a deep breath, got to her feet, and opened the door to see Mrs Copeland, the widow who owned The Four Feathers and Young Garrett's mother.

"Mr Griffith is here for you, miss," the friendly-faced woman said. She had introduced herself that afternoon, and assured Cassandra she was welcome here no matter what "*some* people'd like to say, I tell you." Having her support had strengthened Cassandra's will immensely.

"Thank you," she replied. "I will join him at once."

"Of course. Might want to take your shawl though, miss," Mrs Copeland added as Cassandra began to exit the room. "It's cold out tonight and the curricle he came in is open."

Cassandra nodded. "That's a good thought, let me get it." It was the work of a moment to add the shawl to her ensemble. It didn't match the dress, but perhaps that would not matter so much.

Who are you trying to fool? Everything about you shall be judged by these people, right down to the hems of your clothes and the stitching of your shoes.

Cassandra pulled the shawl even more tightly around her shoulders as she followed Mrs Copeland downstairs. Young Garrett was at the front door, speaking eagerly with Thomas about some sort of hunt – ah yes, Thomas had mentioned something about that yesterday, hadn't he? She had never got around to asking what they were hunting, but she could remedy that tonight.

Thomas was listening to the boy's enthusiastic prattle with a slightly long-suffering look, but he turned towards her the moment he heard her footsteps on the stairs. He didn't say a word about the fact she was wearing the same dress this evening that she had for their dinner the night before. He simply bowed, then held out his arm. Cassandra hoped the sudden shiver of delight that coursed through her wasn't visible. This was a charade, nothing more, and yet seeing him waiting for her, in formal eveningwear and a blue ascot that brought out the colour of his eyes, was enough to make her feel slightly giddy.

"Miss Wright," he said cordially.

"Mr Griffith." She slipped her hand into the crook of his elbow, nodded at the innkeepers, and left the confines of The Four Feathers with him. Out front, Old John was holding the reins of a horse attached to a two-wheeled curricle, looking like he was about to topple over at any second.

"Thank you," Thomas said, pressing a small coin into the man's hands before helping Cassandra up into the little gig.

"God bless ye, sir!" Old John said enthusiastically, dropping the reins to give a bow. The horse shied, and it was all Cassandra could do for a moment to keep her seat as Thomas lunged for the fallen leads. "An' may he bless yer hunt as well," the drunkard continued, completely oblivious to the accident that he'd nearly caused to happen.

Thomas snapped the reins and they were off a moment later, heading down the torchlit street and north, out of Tarryford. Silence reigned between the pair of them for a while, threatening to become awkward before Cassandra homed in on a point of conversation.

"What sort of hunt are you participating in, exactly?" she asked. "You mentioned it was special, but I'm not sure what that entails."

"I'm not entirely sure myself," Thomas said, easily guiding the horse along the road and avoiding the worst of the ruts. "Then again, no one is. For the past year, this area has been plagued by a series of brutal attacks on livestock. I saw the aftermath of one such incident on a heifer a nearby farmer owned. The animal was eviscerated, parts of it thrown as far as–" He paused, and if Cassandra could have seen his face in this faint light, she would have guessed he was blushing. "Forgive me. I forget my manners at times. This is not a proper conversation to be having with a lady."

"I did ask about it," Cassandra pointed out. "And I would be much obliged if you would finish the story. For an entire cow to be torn to pieces, there must be more than one animal at work, mustn't there?"

"One would think," Thomas said after a moment. "I

would have guessed a pack of wolves myself, if such things still existed in this part of the country. Since there are no wolves here now, I assume it must either be a pack of feral dogs, although no one in the area admits to losing their animals, or perhaps something more exotic."

Cassandra leaned in a bit. "Exotic? What do you mean by that?"

"Have you heard much about the previous owners of Northlake Hall?" Thomas asked.

Cassandra had heard nothing of them, but a thought occurred to her. "Is that the home on the hillside? The one that burned down?"

"That was the estate of the Northlakes, a family that had lived in this county for many generations," Thomas said. "They had a sound reputation overall, but several years ago there was a series of events – none of the locals are quite sure what, and those who were directly involved are either dead or fled – that resulted in, well… what you see left. It is said that upon discovering the body of his eldest daughter, Sir James went mad and set the house afire himself." Thomas glanced in that direction grimly. "None of the family remains, and the suddenness of their ending suggests that they were involved in things that they should not have been. It is not impossible to think that they may have smuggled one or more beasts of some kind into the country that would be capable of doing this sort of damage on its own."

Cassandra shook her head. "What, like lions?"

"Or a tiger. Or a bear, one of the massive ones you find

in places like Svalbard," Thomas said, and his grimness gave her pause. Heavens, he was *serious* about this. The scene he'd come across must have been a truly grisly sight.

"Whatever it is," Cassandra said after a moment, "it has only gone after livestock so far, though."

"We would be hunting it down with a great deal more alacrity if it was killing people," he confirmed. "But the attacks are coming with greater frequency. And the carcasses… these animals are not being killed out of hunger. Too much meat is left behind for that. They are being killed for sport."

"For sport…" Cassandra tightened her grip on her shawl. "That is a distressing thought. It was good of you to come and help Gilbert track down this beast." *It is good of you to help him focus long enough to actually complete something.*

"I do my best," Thomas said, something of a smile in his voice. The rest of the ride passed with lighter conversation about hunts he'd been on before, and by the time they arrived at Harston Hall, Cassandra's nerves were nearly forgotten. It had always been this way for her. She could work herself into a fit given too much time to contemplate, but when confronted with the object of her disquiet, she never quailed.

Hopefully her heart would stand firm with her this time as well.

CHAPTER FIVE

Cassandra did not remember much about her mother, Phaedra. The sad and simple truth was that the elegant, loving woman had died giving birth when Cassandra was only nine years old. Her beauty stood out in Cassandra's mind, but beyond that there were few conversations she could specifically recall, unlike the many years she spent learning by her father's side. But there was one incident that had stayed in Cassandra's mind quite vividly during a visit to her mother's parents.

Cassandra and her little brother Samuel had received a rather lukewarm welcome from their grandparents, and their cousins had refused to play with them. Their father was barely tolerated as well. Through it all, every snub and pointed glance from the "gentry" side of the family, Phaedra had been poised, calm, and dignified. She had also made a point of keeping her children at her side once it was clear they weren't going to be welcomed elsewhere, forcibly including them in the family discussions and ignoring every hint that she ought to turn them outside to amuse themselves.

It had been, in all honesty, a very dull visit, but it had taught Cassandra a lasting lesson: you could not always change how others treated you, but you could control how you reacted to their efforts, and how much you let it affect you. She never saw her grandparents again after that, but she had been assured without a doubt of her mother's affections and pride in her children. That was the attitude Cassandra was heading into Harston Hall with tonight.

It was not an easy state to maintain. Riding up to the house – a handsome and expansive structure, well-lit and well-tended even in this season – Cassandra felt her nerves begin to flutter again. It took every bit of her will to keep her hands folded carefully in her lap rather than giving in to the urge to clench her shawl so hard it wrinkled. She knew she looked well – well enough to get by, at any rate – and it was not as though she had come here as a beggar. She was with Thomas, who was without a doubt a cut above any and all of these people.

That thought helped. Having his arm to support her helped even more, such that when they were finally announced and entered the drawing room together, Cassandra was able to respond to the sudden gasps of several members of the party and the rude stares of *all* of them with equanimity. She smiled, sphinx-like, and dropped a curtsy in her ex-betrothed's direction.

"Mr Fraser," Cassandra said politely. "It is lovely to see you again."

Gilbert was unable to manage the same level of pleasantry. He gaped at Cassandra, then at Thomas. "What the devil?" he demanded at last, a red flush appearing on his doughy cheeks.

The past five years had not been as kind to him as they had to Thomas; he had gained probably two stone, and it showed in his face and neck more than anywhere. His reddish-gold hair looked a bit thinner than before, and the high-waisted, tight fit breeches that were currently in fashion did not flatter him. He looked almost nothing like his father, the other Mr Fraser, which was the only reason Cassandra was able to look him in the eyes.

"I did mention that I would be bringing someone with me tonight," Thomas said with perfect composure.

"You didn't say it was going to be *her*!" Gilbert flung an arm towards Cassandra. "What is she even doing here?"

"You might ask her directly," Thomas replied, his voice gone cool. "And I beg of you, mind how you speak to my betrothed. Everyone, this–" he looked around the room "– is Miss Wright."

"Be-betrothed?" One of the women, sitting on a chaise in a blue velvet dress with a headdress so elaborately feathered it looked like an entire parrot had been stuck on there somehow, pressed a gloved hand to her cheek. "Captain Griffith, you cannot be *serious.*"

"I am, Mrs Humphrey," he replied. "Completely so. And," he added with an air of frustration, "I have already asked you to forego the use of my former rank, so please abide by my request."

"Ah, but–" Her hand fluttered above her chest, as though not sure where to press for best effect. "Mr Griffith, then, but… how terribly rude of you not to let us know of her sooner! Goodness, Miss Wright, you are such a…" Mrs Humphrey paused to look her up and down. "Such a *surprise*, aren't you!"

"*Terribly* surprising," one of the other ladies agreed. "Why, I feel faint just looking at you."

"Probably because you're on your third glass of sherry," the man sitting closest to her said, and the couple devolved into bickering.

"Miss Wright, is it?" another woman interrupted, so smoothly that it scarcely seemed like an interruption at all. She stepped forwards from where she had been standing beside the piano, a serene smile on her face. She was tall, taller than Cassandra by several inches, and wore a patterned muslin dress in a more conservative style than any of the other ladies. Her face was well favoured, and there was an air of dignity to her that made Cassandra want to stand a little bit straighter. "What an unexpected pleasure. I am Mrs Cross."

"Pleased to make your acquaintance." They curtsied to each other, and then Mrs Cross looked at Thomas.

"I see that it never pays to underestimate your ability to surprise people, Mr Griffith."

"I did not bring her here to provide this company with entertainment," he replied stiffly.

"No, of course not. Nevertheless, you have done so, and for that I'm very grateful. A party such as this can get so stale over time, and here you are sweeping in with your beautiful betrothed like a breath of fresh air. Miss Wright," she continued. "You must be thirsty. Would you care for a drink?"

"I would, thank you."

Mrs Cross's turn at playing hostess gave Gilbert time to collect himself. He set his drink down on the mantel, shook his arms and shoulders out in a bit of a flapping gesture, then plastered a hearty and utterly false smile on his face before striding across the room.

"Thomas, you rascal, I ought to whip you for surprising me like this but I'm far too pleased to see Cassie again to do it. And Cassie!" He stopped in front of her and stared. His mouth worked silently for a moment before he finally finished, "You look very well. It is… it is quite good to see you again, after so long apart."

"Indeed." She offered her hand, and he took it and bowed over it like a true gentleman. Cassandra, meanwhile, was grateful she was wearing gloves. It was hard enough to look at him while keeping her composure; actually touching his skin would surely make her own flesh shudder and crawl. "You seem to be doing very well, sir," she added.

"Oh, yes, well enough, well enough – and what is this 'sir' business?" He forced a hearty laugh. "Come now, we were once quite… I mean, good friends. Call me Gilbert, eh?"

It was quite the presumption for him to "allow" her this largesse when Cassandra had every reason to disregard him, but she knew the nicer she was to Gilbert, the more likely it was that the rest of the party would accept, or at least resign themselves to, her presence.

But must he call me Cassie? Ugh.

"Gilbert, then."

"Right, right!" He swivelled his attention to another subject as quickly as possible. "Thomas, you look like a man who needs a fresh drink. Come, join me." Gilbert took his shoulder and hauled on it, but it wasn't until Cassandra nodded that Thomas acquiesced and went with him. His courtesy warmed her, and she was able to join the ladies at the card table in the corner with more composure than she'd thought she'd be able to muster.

It was a good thing Thomas was warm, too, for with the exception of the cordial Mrs Cross, the rest of the ladies seemed inclined to freeze her out. There were Mrs Humphrey and Mrs Kildeer, both of them quite a bit older than Cassandra and accompanied by their husbands, as well as Miss Getty, who was not married but who was the sister-in-law of Mrs Humphrey. Four ladies, almost all of them attached… heavens, with Thomas now "engaged," Gilbert was the only single gentleman of the lot. It must be a strange circumstance for him.

Do not let your easy heart forgive him before time. He's scarcely a child.

Miss Getty, it seemed, would be more than willing to remove Gilbert's status as a single man. She was the most elaborately dressed woman of all of them, even outshining her sister's fancy feathers, but it seemed that there was no level of costume that could redeem her rather strong chin and flinty gaze in Gilbert's eyes. It became quite clear as they moved from the sitting room into the dining room that, while she was actively courting him, he was just as actively avoiding her, even going so far as to change the seating arrangement and put Cassandra beside him with the explanation of, "Old friends, you know, we ought to catch up!"

If looks could kill, the daggers from Miss Getty's eyes would have turned Cassandra to mincemeat by now. She was grateful to have Thomas on her other side, helping her deflect the incoming barrage of pointed questions from the rest of the party.

"Have you been long in this part of the country?" Mrs Kildeer asked as she speared a piece of roast on the end of a very sharp-looking silver fork.

"Not very long at all," Cassandra replied. "I only just arrived yesterday."

"Hmm. How curious, Mr Griffith, that you did not let the rest of us know you were expecting your betrothed to join you here!"

Thomas didn't even bother to look up. "As I did not know the exact date she would be arriving, it seemed presumptuous to share incorrect knowledge."

"But you knew she *was* coming! If you had given us even an inkling that her arrival was expected, we could have prepared better for her charming company."

One of the men – Mr Humphrey, perhaps, it was hard to tell them apart between the haze of the candles and the high collars – snorted derisively. "What sort of preparation does any woman need when it comes to company? Worse than a flock of starlings, you are, always chittering and going on no matter who you're with. What would you have done differently, hmm?"

"It would have been the gentlemanly thing to do," Mrs Humphrey icily informed her husband. "But I suppose for a former military man such as yourself, Mr Griffith, the finer points of polite society often elude you."

"Am I to understand that you find military men uncouth, then?" Colonel Cross asked with a half-smile before glancing at Cassandra.

"Oh, I don't mean you, dear colonel, of course not!" Mrs Humphrey exclaimed. "You are as elegant as a swan. I simply meant–"

Mr Humphrey barked a laugh. "Elegant as a swan! You mean he's a honking, flapping, mean-spirited bastard who'd as soon bite you as look at you?"

"That is not what I meant at all!" Mrs Humphrey tossed her napkin on the table in a fit of pique. "Oh, you do go out of your way to vex me, sir!"

"It is the sole joy of my life, given our regrettable lack of children."

"I do *not*–"

"Miss Wright," Mrs Cross interrupted in a slightly-too-loud voice. "How was your travel down from … where was it again?"

"Northumberland," Cassandra said, grateful that someone else was interested in staving off what looked to be a well-trod argument between the married couple. "It went very well, thank you. I enjoyed seeing more of the country."

"Northumberland." Gilbert grimaced and shivered dramatically. "Good God, that's too bloody cold, if you ask me. What on earth could have carried you so far north, Cassie?"

"I went to stay with friends there," she said as generally as she could.

"What friends?" he asked with all the social grace of a pregnant sow. "Your family didn't have any friends up there from what I remember."

"Friends tend to pop up out of the unlikeliest places when you're destitute, don't they, Miss Wright?" Miss Getty said with a hard smile. "And how did you occupy yourself amongst these dear friends of yours?"

"I assisted in tutoring their children," she replied.

"Ahhh, a minder of children! What excellent work for a young woman such as yourself," she sneered. "Yes, you look just the type to be well-suited to such things. Very... bookish."

"You did always have a book in your hand before," Gilbert said with perfect blindness to the brutal nuances of the conversation. "I could hardly tear you away from them sometimes! Thomas, you're going to have your hands full keeping Cassie from whiling away a whole day doing nothing but reading. Who will manage your estate then, eh?"

"I would never tell her how to spend her days," Thomas replied as he picked up a dish of potatoes and held it out to

Cassandra. "I am in the fortunate position of being assured of the character of the woman I am to marry, and it is of the very highest quality. Nothing she does will ever cast a poor light on myself or cause her to neglect her duties." When he looked at her with a soft smile on his face, Cassandra genuinely felt her heart skip a beat.

Oh dear.

"You are too kind," she said, meaning every word of it.

"You *are* too kind," Mr Kildeer said from where he sat near the end of the table. "Ladies of quality are a fine breed, but like any other form of livestock, they need to be carefully managed or else they'll run helter-skelter, and you'll never get anything done."

"Livestock!"

"Breed!"

"Mr Kildeer, honestly!"

Cassandra simply took her next bite. Yes, there were *certainly* parts of society that she had not missed, and that attitude was one of them.

I am not relegated to being an elegant broodmare for a man, and I pray to God that I never shall be. I have a purpose here; I have a goal.

And I shall accomplish it, no matter whom I must go through.

CHAPTER SIX

The rest of the dinner passed with all the ire thankfully diverted away from Cassandra, which she was grateful for. It gave her a chance to catch her breath and actually eat some of the sumptuous food that had been laid out for them. She couldn't remember the last time she had dined so well, despite always eating with the family she'd lived with up north. The quality of the menu, the creamy splendour of the tablecloth and napkins, the gleam of the fine china plates and the crystal glasses... it was like something out of a dream... or rather, a nightmare.

How much of this splendour was stolen? How much of it came from the lives of other people that Mr Fraser had destroyed on his ascent to the top of the ton?

Cassandra knew without a doubt that her father was not the only one to be treated as disposable by the man. His reputation might be flawless on the outside, but she had heard plenty of murmurs about Mr Fraser's callousness after her family's ruin. He would be your best friend, your closest companion, as long as you had something he wanted. And once he had acquired it … well, as with staring any viper in the eyes, you would be lucky to survive the encounter.

After dinner Cassandra had been hoping they would break into separate groups – it would be much easier to evade just the ladies and make her way to the library – but apparently this was a tradition that Gilbert had no interest in implementing. Perhaps, she thought uncharitably, he preferred maintaining the company of individuals he could pretend superiority to instead of solely surrounding himself with his fellow men. They all returned to the sitting room, where more drinks were passed around and the subject matter turned to the hunt, which had apparently been going on for nearly a week without success.

"Honestly, it seems quite a waste of time," Mrs Humphrey said disconsolately before upending her glass of madeira. She had drunk heavily at dinner as well, and now swayed slightly in her seat, only held upright by years of practice maintaining her posture. "There hasn't been a killing for days now, an'… and it's just so *dull* here. Reggie–" She turned to her husband, who raised an eyebrow at her. "Shall… shall we not return to the city? There's so much more occupation to be had there. How shall my dear sister ever find a husband if we don't go back to London?"

"A good point," her husband said dryly. "As I am inclined to marry off your *dear* sister as soon as possible, this is the best argument you could make on the subject."

"Oh, Reggie!"

"Brother, honestly!"

"You ladies are welcome to leave at any time," Gilbert said, looking a bit relieved by the prospect. "These things can be tricky, you know. Beasts have a feral intelligence that can make a mockery of the best hunters at times."

"Simply imagine what it is doing to you," Mrs Cross murmured just loudly enough for Cassandra to hear. She hid her smile with a sip from her own glass – a small one. She had not drunk so much wine for years, and it wouldn't do to lose her head now.

"We'll find it soon enough," Mr Kildeer put in. "Gilbert, I've brought a capital gun from Purdey and Sons with me with a bigger bore for heavier game, none of this birdshot business. I'll pull it out tomorrow and we'll see what we can do against this beast of yours, eh?"

"We have to find it first," Gilbert said disconsolately. "Hopefully it'll rip up another cow tonight and give us something to go off."

"What if it goes for a person next, eh?" Mr Humphrey asked with what Cassandra thought was an unseemly amount of interest. "Now *that* would be a creature worth going after! I hear France is full of all sorts of man-eating beasts these days. *There's* a proper place for a hunt. Can't scarcely go out at night for fear of some great beastie snatching you off the road."

Gilbert frowned. "I thought that was the cultists they've got there. Loads of the blighters, aren't there, colonel? Practically running the show, from what I hear."

Colonel Cross shook his head. "I believe that the concept of evil cultists in the French military are greatly exaggerated. There may be a few here and there, but there's certainly no one snatching people off the streets and sacrificing them to some imaginary god. As we all know, there is but one God." He raised his glass. "And he is firmly on the side of England."

"To England," all the men said before drinking. Cassandra drank as well, but given her brother's letters, she couldn't be so sanguine about the prospect of French cultists being few and far between.

"We ought to make a plan, though, regardless of whether or not there's another attack tonight," Colonel Cross went on. "The town is counting on us to solve this problem for them."

"Peasants," Mrs Humphrey said disdainfully. "Their expectations should not have any bearing on what you, as *gentry*, do." Now her disdain found its home yet again with Cassandra as she turned to her and said, "Although I suppose you would prefer to see the little people rise up and overthrow the lot of us, hmm?"

Heavens, but Mr Humphrey ought to take his wife away and sober her up. Cassandra had never been in close quarters with a woman who became so thoroughly intoxicated so quickly before. "I am many things," Cassandra said, "but I am not a revolutionary."

"But surely you–"

"Gentlemen," Gilbert interrupted, and Cassandra actually felt grateful to him for a moment, "let's head for the study, eh? Talk about tomorrow like Cross suggests. And ladies, you can…" He waved a vague hand. "Um. Do something else."

Cassandra sighed. It looked like there would be no chance at the library tonight. She met Thomas's gaze and he seemed to understand her immediately.

"It is getting late." He stood up and held his hand out to Cassandra. "Allow me to take you back to Tarryford."

Insightful and agreeable… I could not ask for a better conspirator.

"Nonsense, man!" Gilbert protested. "What d'you think I've got coachmen for, eh? I'll have one of them take her back. We need you to stay and help us plan our next move."

"I would much prefer to accompany Cassandra," Thomas said stiffly.

"Oh, but it's hardly appropriate, is it?" Mrs Kildeer said. "For you to be spending more time in each other's company while only being engaged. Unheard of! I daresay her father wouldn't allow it, if she had a proper family."

I do have a proper family, you–

"I shall accompany her," Mrs Cross said, setting her glass aside and rising to her feet.

"Oh, I am sure that is not necessary, Mrs Cross," Cassandra demurred, not wanting to spend any more time alone with any of these people. "I will be fine on my own."

"Nonsense," she said with a little smile. "I daresay your betrothed won't hear of it, and besides, I could do with a bit of an airing out. It has gotten rather stuffy in here." Her look invited Cassandra to share in the joke, but she couldn't quite bring herself to smile back. Instead, she looked at Thomas, who nodded reluctantly.

"I will come and get you tomorrow," he said firmly as he took her hands and helped her to her feet.

"Such gallantry." Mrs Humphrey cast a disconsolate look at her husband. "Reggie, why are you never gallant towards me?"

"Gallantry would be wasted on a goose."

"Reggie!"

"Brother, honestly!"

"Until tomorrow, then," Cassandra said over the clamour. Thomas retrieved her shawl and handed it to her, and then she and Mrs Cross were being shown to the front of the house, where a carriage was brought up almost immediately – a proper carriage, enclosed for protection against the night's chill, with two gleaming grey horses and a dour-faced coachman who nevertheless bowed low for them.

CHAPTER SEVEN

"Well," Mrs Cross said once the two of them were ensconced inside the carriage and it was on its way. "I daresay that is the worst of it over for you, my dear."

"I'm not sure what you mean," she replied, doing her best to keep her voice steady despite how her heart suddenly began to pound. What was Mrs Cross hinting at?

"The reunion, my dear. Confronting your past in such a public way. It must have been quite hard for you."

Cassandra shook her head. "There is little in my past that pains me." Nothing she cared to share with a woman she barely knew, at least. "Certainly nothing associated with Gilbert."

"Ah. Yes, you did not have the look of a slighted lover when you saw him," Mrs Cross said sagely. "I would venture to say, in fact, that you might look upon your current circumstances as an improvement over the engagement you shared with Gilbert."

"I would never express such a–"

Mrs Cross tutted. "Of course you would not. You are a well-bred gentlewoman, but one would be a fool not to see that Mr Griffith is the better catch by far."

Cassandra allowed herself a small smile in the dark. "I do not believe that Miss Getty shares your opinion."

"I cannot say that Penelope is not occasionally a fool," Mrs Cross said, amusement clear in her tone.

Cassandra laughed despite the fact that she felt a bit torn. On the one hand, she appreciated Mrs Cross's incisiveness and slightly cutting sense of humour. It would serve her well to have a friend among Gilbert's set beyond Thomas, and this lady seemed to be offering herself up to serve the function. On the other hand, Mrs Cross knew nothing of Cassandra. She had every reason to be suspicious of her, like the other ladies were. Why was she going out of her way to be accommodating instead? Her unusual generosity of spirit did not sit well, but that didn't mean Cassandra couldn't make a small gesture of her own in return.

"Please, call me Cassandra," she said, and was gratified when Mrs Cross smiled at her. "As for Miss Getty, perhaps she sees something in Gilbert that we do not."

"I daresay," Mrs Cross replied. "And you must call me Jane. But I think that–"

Whatever she thought, it was lost as the carriage suddenly, violently jolted to the side. Caught off guard, Cassandra fell off her seat and into the door, grabbing desperately at the frame to keep from putting too much weight on the thin piece of wood separating her from the ground. The horses whinnied desperately, and there was a harsh scraping sound against the surface of the carriage. Mrs Cross quickly got to her feet and stuck her head out of the window, and a moment later the carriage stabilised once more.

"Heavens, sir, are you drunk?" she called out to the driver. "Go more carefully!" She took her seat once more with an air of irritation.

"What *was* that?" Cassandra asked, energy flooding her body and making her shift restlessly in her seat. Her hand strayed towards her silver hatpin.

"Simply the result of poor driving," Mrs Cross assured her. "The coachman put us straight into a rut."

"But the scraping sound!" Cassandra protested. "That was no rut."

"The fool nearly managed to drive us into a tree as well," Mrs Cross said. "Never fear, though. We shall be in town shortly, and I will make sure that Gilbert knows his man was quite irresponsible with his precious cargo."

Cassandra, who remembered the route quite well thanks to the open nature of the gig she and Thomas had taken to get to the manor, opened her mouth to point out that there were no trees close enough to the road to scrape along their carriage like that. She swallowed her own words.

Something was going on here; something strange was at work. Cassandra chided herself for not expecting things to become odd; any venture connected to Mr Fraser was bound to be more than it looked at first. After another moment of consideration, she decided against mentioning her concerns to her companion. Mrs Cross might be innocent of any involvement, but it was better not to tip her off in either case.

The rest of the ride passed uneventfully, and soon the coach was pulling to a stop in front of The Four Feathers. The coachman hopped down to open the door for Cassandra, but before she could exit, Mrs Cross put a hand on her arm.

"I take you to be a young woman of some insight," she said frankly, her eyes surprisingly bright in the dim light of the carriage. "Therefore, I know that when I tell you to tread carefully at Harston Hall, you will understand my words to be not a remonstration, but a fair warning."

"What is it you feel that I need to be warned about?" Cassandra asked quietly. Perhaps she had been wrong about Mrs Cross's apprehension of the potential risks they faced. She was suddenly very aware of the listening ears of the coachman and the restless shiver of the horses, who seemed to still be spooked.

"I daresay you will find out, if you remain in Gilbert's company long enough. The Frasers are a powerful family, but you might find it wise to limit your exposure to them. I am sure that your betrothed would oblige you." She gave Cassandra's arm a light squeeze, then leaned back in the seats. "Congratulations again, I must say. He is a most active man, and not without his fair share of charms. He reminds me of my own dear husband ten years ago, when the war had not yet wrought such great changes in him."

What changes? Cassandra wanted to ask, but she knew that to do so would be wildly impertinent. She inclined her head, then stepped back from the carriage so that the coachman could close the door.

As soon as Old John let go of the horses, the coachman used the whip to get them going at such a speed that Mrs Cross must have been holding on to the seat for dear life inside. The carriage raced back down the road and out of sight, but not before Cassandra saw the sharply delineated scratch along the far side of it, one that seemed to cut far too deep to have been made by an errant branch.

What happened on the road?

Had they been attacked by the beast the party was here to hunt? Surely the coachman or Mrs Cross must have seen something, if that was the case. Or perhaps there was some aspect of this that she didn't comprehend – a creature that could conceal itself so well in the shadows it was impossible to make out. It seemed like something out of a legend, but given what the men had described at dinner tonight, they might very well be dealing with something legendary.

Cassandra shuddered and drew her shawl more tightly around her shoulders. If she'd fallen through the door, would hitting the ground have hurt more than being found by the beast that made that scratch? She would have to tell Thomas as soon as she saw him next.

"Oof, miss," Old John said, shaking his head. His hair, interlaced with straw here and there and as wild as a summer dandelion, glowed in the torchlight like an orange halo. "Awful late to be gettin' back, in't it, miss? S'not safe to be on the road with th' beast around, eh?"

"Have there been any issues with the beast appearing on

the road?" Cassandra asked. Gilbert and his friends hadn't indicated any such thing, but there was an entire class of people whose experiences they preferred to be ignorant of.

Old John nodded so hard he almost fell over. "Noises," he said slyly, trying to lay a finger alongside his nose but missing and nearly poking it into his eye instead. "Awful growls and snarls and the like. It never comes into the light, though – got folk puttin' lanterns on every corner o' their wagons, just in case. So far it works, but…" He shrugged with the air of a man for whom nothing had ever worked for very long.

"How disturbing." Cassandra wondered if her companions back at Harston Hall had heard of these precautions. How much did the hunting party really know about the beast they were after? And was it possible that some of them, like Mrs Cross, knew more than they let on?

How could she, though? More likely she didn't want to scare me. But Cassandra didn't scare that easily.

"S'like the bad old days with the Northlakes and the Williamses," Old John kept on. "Hard time for the town then, it was. All kinds of people skulking around the town, and that mess with the sleeping sickness…" He made a face. "Bad business, infecting the *ale* of all things. Too many dead… and now this…"

"Where do you think I would be able to find a record of the events that happened here before?" Cassandra asked. She knew she could simply inquire of people, but then she would have to trust they weren't going to pass on her questions to someone she didn't wish to know about her curiosity.

"Oh, well…" Old John scratched at the front of his rather stained shirt. "Upper Tarryford Church is bound to have notice o' the deaths, at least. Not sure about the rest of it…"

Of course. She should have thought of that herself. "Thank you," she said. "I appreciate your advice."

Old John's face split into a grin. Half his teeth were missing and he stank of booze, but there was nevertheless something innocent about the man, almost childlike in a way. "My pleasure, miss, my pleasure. On in wi' ye, now." He gave her a very tilted bow, then ambled back over to the haybale where he'd apparently been taking his rest.

Cassandra took his last bit of advice and entered the inn, pensive, exhausted, but also exhilarated. The hardest part was over; she had re-entered society and survived the experience thanks to Thomas's assistance. From here on out, things would be easier.

Her next trial to overcome would be gaining access to the library. She could already see that Gilbert's companions were not the most erudite of company; she would have to come up with a viable pretence to gain entrance to it.

Thomas would help. Of that, at least, she was certain.

CHAPTER EIGHT

The second day was easier. Slipping back into the persona of a gentlewoman was like slipping on an old pair of boots Cassandra had not worn in a long time. They were terribly stiff at first, rubbing her raw in places, but after a bit of walking in them they softened and became well-worn once more. It helped that Thomas came to get her himself the next day. He wore a lighter jacket in a shade of blue that set off his eyes marvellously, and handled the gig with the ease of someone accustomed to command, whether it was with horses or his fellow men.

"Miss Wright." He dismounted and looked at her a bit anxiously as she dropped a curtsy to him. "You look... very well this morning."

"You sound surprised, sir," she noted with a little smile as he helped her up into the elegant, two-wheeled carriage.

"Mrs Cross returned with a slightly alarming tale last night."

"Oh, I imagine she did," Cassandra said dryly. "Something to the effect of the coachman nearly driving us off the road and an incident with a tree?"

"Exactly that," Thomas said, taking the reins from the stable boy. Old John appeared to still be sleeping on his barrels and hay; Cassandra could hear his snoring from twenty feet away. They turned and headed north out of town, and only once they were on the open road did he continue. "I assume you disagree with her."

"The coachman may have been drunk, that's not something I can speak to, but have you seen *any* trees close enough to this road to leave such a terrible scratch in the side of the carriage?"

"Hmm." Thomas narrowed his eyes. "I didn't see the carriage this morning. Gilbert was worried one of its wheels had been damaged, so he had it taken to someone in town to be looked at."

Cassandra shook her head. "I did not see any damage to the wheels, but I would be surprised if the carriage isn't freshly painted the next time you inspect it."

"You think you were attacked? Truly?"

"I cannot say for sure, but I've heard talk that locals are afraid to travel at night."

Thomas grimaced. "Then we must count ourselves fortunate that you managed as well as you did last night. We also need to get on with the *actual* hunt, rather than simply talking about it."

"Do you share Merlin's frustrations with being locked in all day?" Cassandra teased him, and Thomas surprised her by laughing. She stared, transfixed, at how the smile reshaped his face from handsome into something much more dangerously dear.

"I suppose I do have something in common with that hound other than a clear preference for your company," he said, and… oh, heavens. Now she couldn't look at him; she was blushing too profoundly. Cassandra cast her mind about for another topic of conversation and remembered, with a hint of shame, why she was going along with this in the first place.

"Do you think I will get a chance to see the library today?"

Thomas thought for a moment. "I believe the plan is for the ladies to enjoy a picnic on the green just behind the house while the gentlemen ride to hounds. It should not be difficult for you to find the chance to be alone for a time. The library is on the ground floor, the second door on the right along the west hall."

"Thank you," Cassandra said gratefully. "But… what shall I do if the ladies won't leave me alone?"

Thomas shook his head. "I do not believe that will be a problem."

His meaning became clear as soon as he and Cassandra entered the manor. Gilbert was all blustering enthusiasm, the awkwardness of their reunion forgotten in exchange for forcing them into a state of normalcy, however false. The men followed his lead, and Thomas would not have allowed them to be rude to her regardless. The ladies, though…

"Oh, here at last!" Mrs Humphrey exclaimed from where she was leaning back in a chair, one hand already occupied with a glass. It might have been punch, but judging from the unnatural brightness of her cheeks, she had already moved on to more elaborate drinking. "We were beginning to think poor Mrs Cross had lost you last night."

"Now, Hillary," Mrs Cross said from where she was sitting at a nearby table patiently stitching a silk ribbon onto a bonnet. "I told you quite clearly that I got Miss Wright back to the inn safely, despite our little adventure. I must apologise once more for that," she added with perfect earnestness to Cassandra. "I would never have agreed to step in that carriage if I had known the driver was drunk."

"What a damn fool," Gilbert agreed, puffing his chest out like a pigeon. "I let him go this very morning. No more worries about being tossed around by a fellow like that!"

"What a relief," Cassandra said, not quite meeting Mrs Cross's eyes. After their strange interaction in the carriage last night, she wasn't sure what to make of the woman. The thought of cultivating another ally was tempting, but Cassandra wasn't sure she could trust her yet. "Thomas tells me you gentlemen are going on the hunt today."

"Indeed we are!" That began a monologue from Gilbert on the subject, part self-aggrandising and part nerve-racked, if the way he kept looking to the other men in the room for validation was any indicator.

Heavens, he had scarcely changed at all. It had been exhausting being his betrothed, always delivering the encouragement Gilbert seemed to require as much as he did air.

How fortunate I am to have avoided becoming his wife.

"And will you be joining us on our outing?"

Miss Getty's question brought Cassandra back to the present. "Ah, I'm afraid that I am a bit fatigued from last night," she said, pressing one hand delicately to her chest.

"Too fatigued to sit on the grass sipping tea and eating cakes?" Mr Kildeer said incredulously. "Women. Truly fragile creatures. It's a wonder the human race has managed to survive this long."

"Then you should stay inside and recover yourself," Thomas said swiftly, coming over to where she sat and taking her hand. "I've no doubt that Mr Fraser will ensure the servants know not to disturb you while we're out so you may take the opportunity to rest."

Gilbert stuttered into effusive agreement a moment later, playing the part of gallantry to poor effect. Cassandra let herself revel in the feel of Thomas holding her hand, his touch so warm and comforting, and ignored the acrid wordplay happening around her.

Soon enough, the party was packed up, and Cassandra was directed to rest and recuperate her strength while they "basked in the sun," Mrs Humphrey said with an air of real enjoyment. "Oh, that's what I miss the most when I go to town, just sitting out in the fresh air and sunlight without the shadow of so many grand buildings around me. I love the sunshine – I swear I would move to France and enjoy it all the time, if we weren't at war with them!"

"If ever I wished I was capable of stopping a war, now is the time."

"Reggie, really!" They departed, the couple sniping at each other while Miss Getty fixed herself smugly next to

Gilbert, who hardly seemed to know what to do with her as he walked away. Before being the last to leave, Thomas sat down beside her and put his lips close to her ear.

"I will make enough trouble for the servants in the main hall to send them running for the next few minutes," he whispered. "Hopefully that will give you enough time to get there and begin your search. Explaining your way back will be easier if you are seen than being stopped on the way."

"Thank you," she whispered back, shivering slightly as she contemplated the nearness of his body to hers.

Thomas pulled back with a concerned look. "Are you cold?"

No, just foolish.

"Griffith! Come on, man, we're wasting the day!" Gilbert hollered.

"And whose fault is that?" Thomas muttered, but he got up and, with a final smile for Cassandra, left the room. He shouted orders like a little lordling, sending servants scrambling with every few steps to "–find my riding gloves, check my room and if you can't find them there check the luggage, and I need you to run and get my hat, and you – ensure the proper saddle is on my horse, I've no interest in falling off when I …" His voice gradually faded away, and at last Cassandra was left in silence.

She wasted no time, immediately getting to her feet and hurrying over to the parlour door. She was but two hallways away; she could do this. Quiet as a mouse, she slipped out onto the beautiful marble floor and, grateful she'd worn her slippers instead of her boots today, hurried towards the main hall.

She almost turned the corner but ended up doubling back a few feet when she heard footsteps running down from upstairs. "Proper bloody gloves," a man was muttering before he left through the door a moment later. Cassandra waited another moment, then darted across the main hall and into the west wing of the manor. Two more doors down, and...

The door opened with a faint creak, and she slipped hurriedly inside. *Well. That wasn't so bad.* Now to make sure she'd come to the right place. It was a large room, and very dark. Cassandra carefully made her way around barely seen obstacles and to the windows. She pulled back the drapes, and...

Oh, yes. Yes, this was the library. That it doubled as a study for the senior Mr Fraser was clear by virtue of the large desk in the corner, complete with its own drinks cabinet. She could hardly blame him for wanting to set up shop here, so to speak; apart from the enormous windows that looked out on unspoiled green fields and fast-moving grey clouds, the room simply smelled right. There was something inimitable about the scent of paper and leather, of thousands of words sitting idle, just waiting for a curious mind to open the pages that bound them and set them free. It felt like the place that used to be home, although Cassandra was surprised to find Mr Fraser didn't have half as many books as her father had.

There were numerous full floor-to-ceiling shelves, though, and she let her hands trace over the nearest titles as her eyes roamed over the others. Many of the classics, which she'd expected, but none in their original languages. Novels, a few travel treatises, a book on keeping a household from the sixteen hundreds – how droll – and–

Ah, but here was a Latin title mixed in with the English. Cicero's *De Officis*... but... where had this been printed? The text on the spine should have been done in gold ink, and this was black. Frowning, Cassandra pulled the book out and opened it to a random page, then nearly dropped it.

She was looking at a picture, one so all-encompassingly black it nearly devoured the entire page. In the very centre of it was a ... she peered at it, trying to make out the details of the shape, but they eluded her somehow. From one angle it looked like a tree limb; from another it could have been the tail of a snake, or perhaps the tentacle of some sea-faring beast or other. "What on earth?" she murmured, turning the page.

The script was not one she was familiar with, its runic-style letters both confounding her and tugging at her memory. She'd seen something similar before, once... *the one book Father wouldn't let me look at. I remember; he slammed it shut when I got close to him that day, told me I was better off with something more accessible.* Cassandra hadn't thought much of it at the time; her father taking on a new language was nothing new. She assumed she would have a sufficiency of time to procure the details of his new pastime.

How wrong she had been. One week later, he had been dead.

A thought struck her, and Cassandra replaced the book on the shelf and began to scan the titles again. One supposedly Latin text, not even next to its translation – *On Obligations* was three rows up and two books over – was perhaps all the guidance she needed to find what she was looking for.

Lucretius's *De Rurum Natura* confirmed that she was on the right track; it had the same runes inside, and the ink stank dreadfully. It wasn't until she opened Plato's *Politeia* that she struck gold. This had neither runes nor the Latin text she would expect from the cover. This book contained her father's handwriting, a flowing cursive script that spelled out a series of nonsense words that no one would be able to make sense of... no one but Cassandra, that is.

Seeing his writing was like hearing his voice in her ear once more or feeling his hand on her shoulder. She was warmed all the way through; her heart eased in a way she hadn't imagined possible before now.

This was it; this was what she needed! She should take it and go, except–

Scritch-scritch-scritch!

Cassandra shoved the book back onto the shelf and whirled around to look at the rest of the room. Even with the curtains pulled back, the corners were still dark, especially now that it had started to rain. Ah, well... no matter. She reached for the book again, but–

Scritch-scratch-scritch. There was that sound again, closer this time. It had to be some sort of animal, likely a mouse. Or perhaps a rat, if its nails were that noisy against the floor.

Something pattered right over her foot. Cassandra shrieked, biting the noise back as soon as she could so it came out as more of a whimper than a shout, but it still sounded terribly loud to her. She ran away from the bookshelf to the enormous globe standing in the centre of the room, casting her gaze every which way to see what had just crawled over her. There, at the end of the shelf… was that a tail vanishing behind the chair? It was thick and meaty, almost more like a dog's tail than a rat. Something red gleamed at her from beneath the chair, and Cassandra's hand rose to her hair before she realised she wasn't wearing the hatpin.

That is not a mistake I will make twice. Her mouth dry and her hands clenched into shaking fists, she was preparing herself to run when she heard footsteps sounding in the hall. Instead of darting for the door, she quickly settled herself beside it so that if it opened, she would remain hidden.

And open it did, just a foot before whoever was behind it suddenly stopped. "Where're you off to, then?" the servant on the other side of the thick wood said, sounding annoyed. "We're meant to ready this one for that doughy bastard when they get back!"

"It can wait! The way the rain's coming down now, all those ladies'll be soaked to their skin. Get more towels!"

"Oh, for the love of…" The hand left the door and the footsteps trailed away, taking a string of curses with them. Cassandra waited another moment to be sure they were gone, then crept into the hall. She made her way down to the main entryway, which had several servants laying out towels, then squared her shoulders and stepped into the hallway quickly enough that she hoped they would not know where she'd come from.

"Ah, miss!" A lady who Cassandra took to be the housekeeper caught her eye. If she was annoyed at being distracted from her preparations, she hid it well. "Is everything all right?"

"Quite all right, thank you," Cassandra said. "I merely wished to greet everyone on their return."

"You're the one what's engaged to Mr Griffith, yes?" one of the younger maids asked. Cassandra nodded. The maid laughed and fanned herself.

"Sarah!" The older woman looked like she wanted to take a swipe at her with a towel. "Mind your manners. An' they'll be pretty rough coming in, miss," she added to Cassandra. "You might wish to wait for them in the parlour, or I've heard Mr Fraser is of a mind to open up the library today if you prefer."

She ought to go back and get the book, this was the perfect opening, and yet… Cassandra reflexively squinched her toes up in her shoes as her mind conjured the feeling of scrabbling claws on her foot. "I will be in the parlour, then." She turned and left, getting out of range of the returning party as quickly as she could. She could hear Mrs Humphrey going on about the wet ruining her shoes already.

It was a much damper and more downtrodden group that joined Cassandra soon thereafter. The men had returned as well; apparently the rain was too much for Gilbert to tolerate. She ignored the complaints and jabs of the ladies and met Thomas's eyes instead. He raised one eyebrow in question, and she gave a little shake of her head. So close… she had been so close…

"You said you had a local history of this place in the library, didn't you?" Thomas said, speaking to Gilbert even as he came over to stand by Cassandra. The rain hadn't changed his looks, apart from curling his hair a bit more.

"I – yes, supposedly," Gilbert said from where he was pouring himself a fresh glass of wine. He didn't look bothered to be back inside, although the other gentlemen were grumbling about giving up the hunt too soon. "My father mentioned something about acquiring one soon after he bought this place, but I haven't bothered to find it."

"Perhaps we ought to take a look, see if there are any mentions of similar events from before," Thomas said. "Besides, it's a smaller room, if I recall, and the fire will have warmed it considerably." He glanced at Mrs Humphrey, who alone out of the ladies hadn't gone to get into a different outfit. "That ought to improve your comfort, madam."

"Nothing can improve my comfort now except a complete change," she huffed, brushing a sodden feather back from her face. "But all that is left are two incredibly odious gowns that should never have been packed in the first place! So now I am *stuck* in this one until it dries." Miss Getty, who had hastened back downstairs in a much simpler gown and sidled as close as she dared to Gilbert, nodded with sympathy for her sister.

"See to the packing yourself next time rather than leaving

it to the maids, then," Mr Humphrey groused. "And if you're going to fuss so much about odious gowns, get rid of them rather than hoarding them."

"Hoard them!"

"Brother, really."

"The history is a good thought," Gilbert said, but he didn't look too enthusiastic about going to hunt for it until his eyes fell on Cassandra. "Actually, why don't you accompany me to look for it, Cassie? You love books, do you not? You always liked them so well before. It was all I could do to pry you away from them at times."

"Oh, I–" She did need to get to the library again, but going there with Gilbert alone seemed like the least desirable way to do it. The last thing she needed was to be accused of further impropriety after coming here "engaged" to his best friend.

"I will go with you," Thomas said immediately, stepping over and offering his arm to Cassandra to help her up. "Another pair of eyes can only help."

"I will go as well!" Miss Getty said, standing up and walking over to Gilbert's side with her imperious nose in the air. "I simply *adore* libraries."

Mr Humphrey snickered. "You only like books with pretty pictures inside them, Penelope."

"Reggie, honestly!"

Gilbert, for his part, had gone from looking eager to morose in the space of just a few seconds, but there was no gracious way out of it for him now. "We had better get on with it, then," he said, and led the way from the parlour down the hall, following the path that Cassandra had crept along herself just minutes ago.

"I know where to find it," she whispered to Thomas under her breath as Miss Getty, who had latched very firmly onto Gilbert's arm, was regaling him with her love of poetry, of all things. The conversation was rather intimidating to him, given how he was leaning back from her face. "All I need is a moment to hide it away. I should have brought my pelisse," she added with a frown. She had had it sewn with a pocket on the inside that would easily hide a small book such as this one.

"I will aid you as best I can," he said, pressing his free hand to hers where it was wrapped around his arm. Cassandra let herself lean into the embrace a bit – what did it matter if anyone saw them behaving as though they were in love? The better to sell her story and get her what she needed. "You feel cold, my dear," he added. "Allow me to offer you my coat." He had it off and over her shoulders before they reached the library door.

The outer layer was still a bit wet, but the inner layer was warm from his body heat. She pulled it more firmly over her shoulders, delighting in both the warmth and the ease with which he had devised a way to go along with her plan.

The library door was open this time, and a fire blazed in the hearth along the eastern wall, away from where the precious books were shelved. Cassandra walked towards them, arm in arm with Thomas, but found their steps dogged almost immediately by Gilbert.

"Griffith," he said heartily, having somehow dislodged

Miss Getty's tenacious grip on him, "I'm desperate for a drink after all that work this morning. Go and pour us some, eh? My father keeps a few bottles over by the desk."

Thomas frowned, but Cassandra smiled to let him know it was all right before letting him go. "Of course," he said, and headed briskly for the drinks. Miss Getty, meanwhile, had pulled up as close to the fire as she could, and cast a gimlet glare at Cassandra as she saw her in Thomas's coat. Apparently, the woman could not be satisfied, or perhaps she just bore Cassandra a particular ill will.

"Cassie," Gilbert said quietly but quickly as he joined her by the bookshelf, which was the last place she wanted him. "I just wanted to say that… that I feel very bad over what happened between us before."

"There is no need for that," she replied, turning to peruse the books for the history he was ostensibly looking for. "I have quite moved on from those unhappy events."

"I have not," Gilbert said, completely ignoring her cues and stepping even closer. "I've often thought about them as the years went by, and – and I wish it could have all gone so differently. You were never to blame for your father's actions, and my own father, well… he has a tendency to allow his anger to overrule his good sense at times." He focused on her face, his gaze turning wistful. "And do you know, no lady I've ever met has ever been able to quite compare to you."

There was an outraged *"hmph"* across the room, but Cassandra was far more concerned with the awful blush she knew had to be spreading across her cheeks right now.

This was incredibly inappropriate, and Gilbert had to know it. "What's done is done," she said, gentle but firm. "Please do not make yourself unhappy over it, Mr Fraser. I–"

"Do call me Gilbert," he said with a pout. "Or can you not bring yourself to use my Christian name once more?"

It was a terrible intimacy, and yet… Cassandra sighed. "Once more, perhaps," she said, realising that if she did not want to relive this conversation over again, she would have to be very clear. "But no more after this. Gilbert–" he beamed at her, and her heart panged, but she pressed on "–five years ago you were a part of my happiness." A vague, bland part of it, but a part, nevertheless. "When the end came, I was deeply saddened, but I also recognise there was no other way things could go. We could not be together, and I do believe now that we were not meant to be together. You will find a lovely wife to live out your life with, and I have Thomas."

Gilbert's nostrils flared with emotion. "Yes, Thomas. I don't – I have to say, I am surprised the two of you ever came together. You never spoke to him much before."

Because I could scarcely bear to look him in the eyes, I was so worried about giving my own feelings away. "Time has wrought changes in all of us. Meeting him again was pure serendipity, but I count myself fortunate to have won his affections, and there is no one dearer in my heart now than he – other than my siblings, of course."

"Of course," Gilbert said with a dejected frown. "Yes, of course, but–"

"Your drink." Thomas appeared from behind Gilbert and

thrust a glass into his hand. Gilbert looked away, and – oh, this would have been the perfect time to grab the journal except that Miss Getty was staring with such dire intent at Cassandra that she could not.

There was a sudden *click-click-click*, and a moment later Miss Getty began to scream.

"A rat! A rat crawled right across my *foot*, how *disgusting*, it was *huge*–" Gilbert ran to her side and Cassandra quickly reached out, grabbed the journal, and tucked it away safe in the sleeve of Thomas's coat.

"Well done," he murmured in her ear, then looked over at Miss Getty, who was flapping her hands so frantically that Gilbert couldn't actually get close enough to attempt to soothe her. "We had better go," Thomas said loudly. "Let the servants know about the rat, and we'll come back for the history some other time."

"Indeed, indeed," Gilbert said, finally latching onto one of Miss Getty's arms. "Let's get back to the parlour, hmm? You can stand by the fire there just as easily," he soothed as he led her out of the room.

Cassandra and Thomas followed, Cassandra casting a backwards glance at the room to see if she could spot the rat that had caused her and Miss Getty so much consternation, but there was nothing. The rest of the afternoon passed in a haze of condemnation of the housekeeping, complaints over the weather, and copious application of smelling salts and wine for the sake of "nerves."

It was a day Cassandra was quite glad to see the end of when Thomas finally brought her back to the inn. He did not help her down immediately, though; rather, he paused and then, in a torrent of words almost as awkward as any delivery of Gilbert's, said, "Is that all, then? You have the journal now; is that every service I can render you?"

Was he asking if she was done with him? Cassandra baulked at the very thought of it, but why? She had indeed recovered a journal of her father's, something that could very well give her the insight she needed into the truth behind his death. And then… then she would be alone with that knowledge, with no real means to apply it, and justice would be as far away as ever.

Unless she continued the ruse with Thomas. Unless she continued to use him for her own ends.

No, it is not like that. I am not so mercenary.

Perhaps she was fooling herself, but when she shook her head and saw him breathe what seemed to be a sigh of relief, Cassandra let herself wonder for the first time if there was more to this ruse than met the eye. "This is a start," she said, "but it may not hold all the information I need. If you would be so kind as to continue to aid me for a while longer…"

"Of course," he said. "For as long as you need."

Cassandra chose to interpret Thomas's offer as his generous spirit shining through. Doing otherwise would only distract her. "You are all kindness, sir."

"I am not, I assure you." And with that cryptic statement, she had to be satisfied.

CHAPTER NINE

It had been some time since Cassandra had had the opportunity to read anything in her father's coded writing. Once, she would have been able to breeze through it without pause, but now, after a long day of intrigue and in the light of a guttering candle, she found she lacked the energy to properly decipher his words. It would take a concerted effort to get back the ease she'd once had, and all her effort, it seemed, was spent for the day.

Still, she barely let the book out of reach as she washed up and readied herself for bed. Cassandra stared at the cover as she brushed out her long, dark hair, which was somewhat unruly thanks to the dampness in the air. If there were nothing of import in it, surely Mr Fraser would not have kept it. But what sorts of things would she find in there?

What unfortunate role had her father played in his own downfall?

She recalled the last time she saw him, just before he

left their home on the evening of his death. He had been distracted, losing a glove, then forgetting his coat entirely. Cassandra had helped him steady himself and asked him what was wrong. "It's just a dinner with Mr Fraser," she'd said, idly straightening his cravat. "You have them every week."

"Indeed, yes, but… this one promises to be a bit more interesting than usual." He was trying to sound his usual bombastic self, but Cassandra was never one to be fooled be her father's facades.

"More interesting in what way?" she asked carefully. "He… he is not *compelling* you to some action, is he?" Cassandra's mind had automatically flown to a potential marriage – her father was an older man, but far from his dotage; he would be a good prospect for certain women. She wasn't sure how she felt about the idea of her father remarrying. If it made him happy, though…

"Compulsion, my darling?" His laugh was positively jocular, and it was quite disturbing. "No, not at all! This is merely a dinner amongst friends, as you say." He patted her hands, then stepped back.

"I've no need of another wife at my age, Cassie," he told her firmly. "All will be well. But…" He paused, his eyes curiously blank as he looked at her before finally refocusing. "No, never mind. All will be well, of course it will. And soon enough, I won't be going to the house simply to visit Mr Fraser, I'll be going to see you, hmm?"

"Father," she had scolded him mildly. "The wedding is still three months away."

"So it is, so it is. Still, we shall have to make the most of the time we have left, perhaps take a trip with your brother and sister to the coast. Would you like that?" He capped his ensemble off with a tall, elegant hat. "I would like that," he murmured, already turning towards the door. "To get away for a time, clear my mind… yes, that's what I need." Cassandra had let him leave without any more questions, but in her heart she had been troubled.

"And I was right to be," she whispered to herself. Finally, she put her brush away and lay down in the bed, the book within reach. How fortunate she had been to get it.

Not fortunate. I sought it, I found it, I spirited it to safety. With Thomas's help, of course.

Cassandra shut her eyes tight, willing away the image of Thomas standing so close to her, the feel of his arm beneath her hand. He had done so much for her, gone out of his way to assist her. It had been a very long time since she'd been able to allay her worries and share her burdens with another.

She would miss him desperately once this was all over.

I could ask for more.

Even speaking the temptation in the quiet of her own mind was enough to make her turn her face into the pillow with embarrassment over her own longing.

Impossible! Ridiculous! Thomas Griffith was no more meant to be hers than Gilbert Fraser was – and at this point, you could not *gift* her Gilbert Fraser. She did not care a bit for him and wondered that she had somehow convinced herself otherwise five years ago. They were too dissimilar, and she knew now that she would never have been truly happy with him. But Thomas was clever and quick-thinking, active and bold; every moment that passed served to make him more pleasing to her.

There was no future for them, and yet perhaps, in her own mind, in her dreams tonight if she was fortunate enough, she would be able to envision one anyway.

Cassandra woke the next morning with no clear memory of what her dreams had been like, but the dried tear tracks on her face informed her that they likely *weren't* the sweet and loving ones she had hoped for. She got up and scrubbed her skin briskly, feeling a renewed determination come over her. She would not allow herself to be distracted from her goal, not by anything. Not even by Thomas's regard, heady as it was. Cassandra gave herself a moment more to bask in the thought of it, then readied herself for the day.

She didn't wear anything particularly fetching, just one of her less mended gowns. Today, she hoped to make a great deal of progress on the journal. She remembered the cipher well enough, but writing it out would help her get her mind onto the right track. Then she could–

The knock at the door jolted her out of her thoughts. "Begging your pardon, miss!" the now-familiar voice of Mrs Copeland called through the door. "But Mr Griffith's come to see you!"

Come to see her? So early? The room had no clock, but Cassandra would be surprised if it was past eight yet. "Please tell him I shall join him presently." With a longing look at the journal, she got up from the table and tucked it beneath some clothes inside her chest, then locked the chest once more. She laid the key chain around her neck, grabbed her shawl, inspected herself quickly in the mirror, and headed downstairs to the room which had become their de facto meeting place since her arrival at The Four Feathers.

Thomas was indeed there, with a breakfast spread on the table behind him, but his expression was not one of congeniality. Rather, he looked quite grim.

Oh no. Gilbert discovered my thievery. Thomas is here to spirit me away – or would he spirit me to him instead? No, surely not... Half a dozen terrifying ideas swirled through her mind before Thomas finally spoke.

"The Beast of Avon Vale struck again last night."

"Is someone dead?" she asked, dread already gripping her heart.

"No."

Oh, thank God!

Before she could express her relief, though, Thomas continued, "But it was a near thing. A farmer was heading into Tarryford and one of the wheels on his cart broke. It was late, already dark. He was in the process of unhitching his horse when the beast attacked. It wounded him, but knocked over one of the lanterns on his wagon at the same time, setting it on fire. The fire was apparently enough to drive the beast off." He looked at Cassandra solemnly. "The farmer who was injured is the same man who brought you to Tarryford."

Her hand flew to cover her gasp of shock. "Where is he now?" she asked.

"He was taken to the doctor's home for treatment. Dr Parsons sent word to the house early this morning about the attack, and to essentially demand that we do what we came here to do."

Cassandra nodded. "Hunt it down."

"Yes."

Hunt down a beast that was bold enough to attack a man on a well-ridden road, even if he was all by himself. Hunt down a beast that could rend a cow in two. Hunt a beast who had eluded all attempts to find it so far. She wished she could do more to help than listen to his plan to find it.

"How will you even know where to start?" she asked.

"Oh, we have an idea of where it's gone." Thomas shook his head grimly. "We set the hounds to track it and they led us straight to Ferris Woods."

Ah, it made sense. That was the pretty little forest between the hall and the house, and the source of the "tree" that Mrs Cross had attempted to convince her was behind the attack on their carriage.

A bold beast indeed. "Then today will be spent hunting."

"With the ladies along to watch."

Cassandra couldn't help casting her eyes towards heaven. Naturally the women of the party were desperate for distraction, but if they distracted their menfolk in turn, such a thing could be fatal to the hunters.

"I know," Thomas said, a new bit of humour injected into his voice. "It's a bit ridiculous, but the hunt *is* the whole reason we came here in the first place. They want to see their men bring down the beast, or at least bring its carcass into the light, and none of the gentlemen are interested in arguing the point."

Cassandra saw where this was going. "And I am expected to join them, I suppose."

Thomas hesitated, then reached out and took her hand. "I know you would prefer to stay here and work," he said in a low voice, "but we must also keep up appearances with Gilbert and his set. For you to be the only lady missing from the party would be–"

"It's quite all right," she assured him. Truthfully, there *was* something rather appealing about the thought of watching Thomas ride out in search of the beast. She decided not to examine that aspect of herself too closely. It might prove too embarrassing to face head-on. "I do not mind joining you. Allow me to get my pelisse and bonnet and we can be on our way."

Thomas shook his head. "Ah, but first." He gestured to the table. "I must see to it that my lady is fed."

Cassandra laughed. "Yes, I suppose it would be inconvenient for me to faint of hunger whilst you're off hunting a monster."

"I would drop everything in a moment and come to you," he said with the air of a promise. He leaned a bit closer to Cassandra, and she found herself mirroring the action, closing the distance between them as she swayed nearly close enough to brush their bodies together.

A sudden shouting from outside fractured the building

intimacy, and a moment later Young Garrett came running into the small dining room, an eager light in his eyes. "Begging your pardon, sir," he said without even a glance at Cassandra, "but your dog is barkin' up a storm out front, and some of the horses don't like it."

"Merlin," Thomas groaned with the air of a man who was at his wit's end. "He ran behind me the whole way here. He is the least biddable animal in the whole kennel."

Cassandra bit back her smile. "You'd best go and handle him, then," she said. "I will join you in just a minute. And," she added when he looked a bit recalcitrant, "I will eat something before I do."

"See that you do, madam," Thomas said with mock gravity before turning and walking briskly out of the inn.

"Is he off to hunt the beast?" Young Garrett asked her, all excitement as he stared after Thomas's exit.

"I believe that is the plan today, yes."

"Do you think they'll get it? They have good guns, and dogs, but the beast's got to be awful fast to have lasted so long." Garrett barely paused for breath. "I ain't seen any of its dead yet, but my ma says that Mrs Harper says that her husband saw the last cow it took out, and it was spread all over the yard!"

"How ghastly," Cassandra said, barely restraining herself from teasing the excited lad. "Not the sort of thing most would care to see, I think."

"But I've got to, miss!" he insisted. "Got to know what we're dealing with if I'm going to protect my ma and my sisters all right, don't I?" He puffed his chest out a bit. "I'm the man of the house since my pa died. It's my responsibility now."

Cassandra smiled at him. "Your mother is fortunate to have such a devoted son."

Garrett ducked his head. "Thank you, miss. Oh, you're to leave – shall I pack some of this food up for you?"

"I will manage, but thank you for the offer," Cassandra said. She took a piece of toast, spread it with jam, then headed back upstairs to gather her things.

The journal would wait. The hunt had to come first for now.

CHAPTER TEN

Four hours later, Cassandra was beginning to rethink her assurance to the publican that she had no more need of food. By the time she and Thomas had arrived at the house, breakfast was long since over and done with. The men were gathered outside, readying themselves with guns and hounds and horses, while the women were piling themselves into a landau drawn by a matched pair of beautiful white mares.

"Oh, you two are come after all!" Mrs Humphrey exclaimed the moment Thomas pulled the little gig to a halt beside them. "I thought we might have lost you to the charms of Tarryford," she said to him with a sly smile.

"I have brought its greatest charm along with me," he replied rather shamelessly. He helped Cassandra out of the gig but was immediately swept off by Gilbert, who needed a great deal of assistance, it seemed, getting himself together enough to mount his horse.

"And you, Miss Wright," Mrs Kildeer put in. She was the

oldest lady in the party and tended not to say as much as the others, but when she did speak it was with no lack of polite venom. "I suppose *you* are come to celebrate this hunt as well."

"That is my intention, yes," she said.

"Ah, but unfortunately, this carriage is only big enough for four." Mrs Kildeer frowned dramatically. "So I am afraid you will not be able to join us. We all know how you prefer to sit around inside anyway, likely chattering with the servants. It must make you feel quite at home! Never fear, we shall cheer on your dear Mr Griffith on your behalf." She leaned back, looking satisfied with herself, while Mrs Humphrey and her sister giggled behind their fans. Only Mrs Cross looked slightly uncomfortable.

Cassandra considered her choices. She could kick up a fuss and insist upon joining them in the carriage, but in truth, it *was* rather narrow for four people. Five would be uncomfortable, and she would sooner walk than be relegated to sitting on the floor. Walking was no good option either, for she would be quickly outpaced. She *could* use this opportunity to get back into the library and see what else she could find amongst the books, but this hunt was important. Thomas had not outright said it, but she could see that it was important to him, just as it was to the people of the town. Gilbert might be treating the whole thing like a lark, but Thomas was not, and she was meant to be his support as much as he was hers. If the other ladies were going, it would not speak well of her connection to her "betrothed" if she did not find a way to join them.

At the very least, she might find a way to keep her contemporaries from swanning into danger behind the men.

"Never fear," Cassandra said, turning a placid smile on the ladies in the carriage. "I would never importune you in any way, but neither will I be satisfied to wait at home while our gallant gentlemen hunt down the beast." She turned to the coachman sitting in front of the carriage, who was watching the whole encounter with avid interest. "Would you be so kind as to saddle a horse for me?"

"A horse?" Mrs Humphrey laughed. "What, do you want to ride into action with them? Shall we get you a gun as well? For I see that you already have a dog of your own." This was true enough; Merlin – who had run alongside the gig all the way back to the manor – had attached himself to Cassandra's side the moment she was handed down. He looked up at her in adoration, nuzzling her hands every now and then in an effort to solicit scratches.

"I think a dog and a horse shall be enough for me," she replied, then turned to the coachman. "See it done, if you please."

"Aye, miss." He shouted over to a stable boy to "bring a horse for the lady!" which got the attention of the rest of the party.

"A horse?" Colonel Cross raised one eyebrow in polite incredulity. "You ride, Miss Wright?"

"I have not in some time, but I'm certain it will come back to me quickly," she said. Riding was one of the few acceptable hobbies she could have away from her family, and had been a treasured opportunity for some time to herself – with a groom at a respectful distance, of course. Riding was decidedly preferable to being stuffed into the carriage with the other ladies.

"Oh, right," Gilbert put in with the air of a man who was just remembering something. "You *did* do a lot of riding before, didn't you? Not so much as your brother and sister, but you had the prettiest mare. What was her name again?"

"Penelope," Cassandra said, and had the pleasure of seeing Miss Getty's face go bright red. "After Odysseus's wife," she added for clarity.

"Right, right…"

"Are we talking or hunting?" Mr Kildeer snapped, already mounted and ready to go.

"Hunting! We're hunting," Gilbert said. "Give me just a moment. I seem to have lost my hat."

It was not a stable boy, but Thomas who brought a sedate-looking gelding over to Cassandra a moment later. "I am sorry for this inconvenience," he said, truly looking it as he helped her into the saddle. "I did not think they would go so far as to exclude you in such a manner."

She did not want him discomfited on her behalf. "I daresay I will be more comfortable on horseback than I would be in that carriage," she murmured. "Do not worry for me."

"I am afraid I cannot help myself," he confessed. "Cassandra…"

Her chest tightened with anticipation. "Yes?"

"Griffith!" Gilbert shouted. "We're leaving, come *on*!"

Another moment broken. Thomas exhaled heavily then headed for his own horse, whistling Merlin over next to him. The gentlemen rode out in a pack, not unlike the dogs they hunted with, leaving the ladies' carriage and Cassandra to follow behind at a more sedate pace.

Cassandra had, indeed, once been a very capable horsewoman, and this animal was as gentle a mount as she could ask for. Still, after the first hour she found herself beginning to sway in the saddle a bit, muscles unused to holding this position growing sore. Her body, it seemed, was no longer accustomed to sitting side-saddle, and her hips and thighs were making their complaints known.

The ladies twittered like birds in the carriage, passing around food and drink, but none was offered to her, and Cassandra, in a moment of pique, declined to ask for any. She would not be beholden to these women for anything if she did not have to be.

They finally stopped the carriage in the shade of a small copse of trees a little way out from the deeper forest. Cassandra dismounted onto unsteady legs, then patted her pleasant bay gelding on the neck. "You are doing a wonderful job," she assured him softly, listening to the baying of the hounds in the distance. Were they getting close? Were they homing in on the beast even now?

"Miss Wright."

Cassandra whirled around, nearly stumbling in surprise before she realised it was only Mrs Cross, a cup in one hand and a tiny smile on her face. "Oh, you startled me," she said.

"Forgive me for that. It was unintentional." She held out

the cup to Cassandra. "I thought you might enjoy some tea."

Well, as long as she was offering. "Thank you." She took the cup and drank it down in one long, delicious swallow. It was still warm on her tongue, and she could not suppress a sigh of satisfaction as she handed the cup back.

"Goodness." Mrs Cross took it back with a frown. "Would you care for another cup? It seems as though you could use it."

"Thank you, I am quite refreshed," Cassandra replied. She was a trifle hungry, but she could bear that much better than thirst. "I am much obliged to you."

"Common courtesy is no obligation," Mrs Cross said. "Although you would not know it, given the company I sometimes keep."

"Why do you keep their company, Jane?" Cassandra asked, emboldened by the distance between them and the carriage. "How do you even know Gilbert? You and your husband seem to be rather... not the sort of people he usually seeks out."

"I believe I will take that as a compliment," Mrs Cross said archly, smiling a secret little smile. Cassandra had never liked her better. "The truth is that like many of young Mr Fraser's companions, we were at first introduced to the society of his father, not himself. The elder Mr Fraser is making himself into a rather important man in town, seeking to gain allies in all areas of society."

The brief moment of companionability fell apart. "I daresay he is," Cassandra said, not capable of keeping the ice entirely out of her tone. "He seemed to me to be quite practiced at making friends."

If Mrs Cross was put off by Cassandra's new mode of address, she did not show it. "Indeed," she said, looking down across the swathe of bright green grass stretching ahead of them. The road was a few hundred yards distant, easy to look upon from the height of the little hill the carriage and horse had climbed. "He is a man with a vision for the future of our country many find to be very compelling. There is so much happening in the war with France… so much that is being hidden from everyone."

"What do you mean?" Cassandra asked cautiously, but in truth she was afraid that she already knew. The things her brother wrote around, so many blacked-out lines, his request for prayers… yes, a great deal about the war was being hidden.

"Only that this is a war not only being fought between armies of men," Mrs Cross replied, her gaze distant. "I have travelled enough to see evidence of that myself, but my John… he was posted to Barfleur at the beginning of this war, along with a troop of French defectors against Napoleon. They were tasked with retaking the town and creating a safe port for English ships to disembark from, so we would have a foothold for making further progress into France. The things that happened to him there…"

Mrs Cross turned to look straight at Cassandra. "Men are monsters to other men in times of war. That is a sad truth, but an expected one. Where great ambition goes, death inevitably follows. But this… the weapons that are being used in this fight are so much darker than cannon and shot."

She spoke with rising passion, transfixing Cassandra with her fervency. "This is about more than pitting man against man, Miss Wright. This is about pitting mankind against creatures that are darker and more powerful than you would ever believe. Creatures capable of devouring whole companies in one great bite, creatures so dark and merciless that there is no point in fighting them directly. They can only be overcome by being *swayed*. Our priests, our scholars, our armies... they need to adapt to a new reality. Do you understand what I am saying?"

Knowledge Cassandra didn't want to acknowledge crept in at the edges of her mind. She recalled bits and pieces of conversations overheard between her father and Mr Fraser – philosophical meanderings, she had thought them, but perhaps there was more to it. Perhaps there was a great deal more. Discussions of fundamental good versus evil, of two wrongs making a right, of the means with which one could wield the power to shape nations. Dark means, for a glorious end; did that not make those means glorious as well?

"I..." Her voice stalled. "I do not know," she managed at last. It was the truth – an incomplete one, but a truth. "I cannot imagine that of which you speak."

Mrs Cross nodded grimly. "None can until they themselves are presented with it. All I ask is that, while you are considering Mr Fraser and those of us who have aligned ourselves with him, consider the greater good. It is a sad fact of life that virtue alone is not enough to save us, especially not in this age of modern warfare. When one is confronted with the unknown, and defeated by it, the only path to salvation lies in turning the unknown *into* the known."

She looked down at the ground for a moment, then back up at Cassandra. Her face was placid again, eyes calm and composed. It was like their strange conversation had never happened. "Shall I fetch you some more tea? Truly, you are looking a bit unwell."

"No, thank you," Cassandra said, and Mrs Cross nodded and walked back towards the carriage. Cassandra was struck by the sudden urge to follow her, to grab her shoulder and swing her around and demand answers to the questions she was suddenly *sure* Mrs Cross knew full well about. A friend of Mr Fraser's, someone versed in the sort of darkness that might result in a good man's death – she had to know something! Cassandra even took a step forwards, determined to do just that, when–

A growl erupted from the trees behind her, low and menacing. Cassandra's gelding shied wildly, knocking her to the ground with its sudden sidestep. She fell flat on her back, barely managing to hold onto the reins, and immediately rolled to avoid being stepped on. As she fought to regain her feet, her heart already pounding wildly, one of the ladies in the carriage screamed – a genuine sound of fear, rather than a performative one.

"Go, go!" the woman shrieked. Cassandra regained her feet just in time to see the carriage racing off towards the road, three of the ladies in it screaming while Mrs Cross stared back at her, consternation on her face.

Cassandra had to get out of here.

CHAPTER ELEVEN

Cassandra turned to her horse, ready to mount up, but the animal was staring into the darkness of the forest, unmoving. All its earlier energy seemed to be bound somehow, locking its muscles in place. It shivered and sweated profusely, signs of the horse's terrible fear, but no matter how she pulled at the reins it did not move.

What did it see in there? What had it so fixated with fear? Cassandra was tempted to look herself, but some atavistic instinct warned her that even a second's delay could prove fatal. "Look at me, come away," she begged, but the animal resisted all her efforts to turn it.

Perhaps if she was mounted… Cassandra rounded the side of the gelding to get to the stirrup, but then the horse was jerked away from her. Literally *jerked* – the energy with which it flew through the air was an impossible thing for her to conjure from her own imagination. The leather of the reins burned her right hand as it slipped from her grasp, finally disappearing into the darkness along with the horse. The sounds that followed were…

Dear God!

Cassandra had not known that horses could scream like that. She clapped her hands over her ears as the hideous shrieks of pain threatened to bring her to her knees.

Run, run! She should run, she knew it, and yet she also knew she would never be able to outrun whatever was within those trees. She wouldn't look, she *couldn't* look, but–

Wetness flew out, spattering her face and hands. A tremulous glance showed her the specks were red.

Blood.

The screams cut off quite abruptly, and a moment later her horse's head thudded to the ground just a yard away from her feet.

Only its head. Half of its face was missing. Cassandra shrieked before she could stop herself, then clapped a hand over her mouth so hard it felt like a slap.

The growl started up again, and Cassandra knew without a doubt she would be next.

Cassandra couldn't think, all she could do was react. She lurched to the right, where a large branch lay fallen on the ground. She felt drunk on terror and yet strangely clear-headed, as though she was watching her own impending death from outside her body. She hoisted the branch up and held it ready over one shoulder, staring into the darkness from where the beast was watching her. It was too late to run, and her hatpin would do her no good here. Better that she saw what was coming and did her best with her poor weapon than die in ignorance. Slowly, the darkness began to resolve into a discernible shape.

Its body was dark and lanky, a perfect blend for the

shadowy trees, and while she could not make out the details of its face, she could see its eyes quite clearly. They gleamed in two different shades, yellow from some angles, red from others as the beast twisted and turned its head, taking in her paltry defiance.

This was no animal, no mere beast. Cassandra had never seen anything like it before, had never even *heard* of anything like it before. This creature seemed the perfect embodiment of malice, and she could have sworn that its mouth was twisted into a rictus-like grin. It reached a massive, clawed hand towards her as it emerged from the underbrush…

BOOM!

It was just as well Cassandra was too rigid with fear to startle, or else the close-quarters crack of the gun going off just to her left would surely have made her jump. The monster in the shadows stumbled and withdrew into the darkness with a pained snarl.

It was not dead yet, though. If they did not kill the Beast of Avon Vale now, it was going to vanish and reappear all over again, hungrier than ever for death. She knew it somehow, knew it by the murderous gleam in its eyes, by the way it toyed with her mount before killing it for sport.

Cassandra turned, frantic, and immediately fetched up against Thomas's chest. He clutched her close with one hand, the other still holding his smoking weapon. At his feet, Merlin growled fiercely, barking like a mad thing at the creature in the woods.

"Fire again!" Cassandra pleaded, desperately relieved

and desperately afraid at the same time. "It is still in there, still moving – fire again!"

"Are you hurt?" Thomas demanded, ignoring her plea in favour of checking her over for wounds. "Did it injure you?"

"I am fine," Cassandra insisted, not quite feeling as well as she professed. Why was it so hard to catch her breath? "But please, you must send the pack in after it before it escapes again. Where… where are the others?"

"Distracted by the other kill," Thomas said grimly. Something moved in the thicket; Thomas dropped his long gun and immediately pulled his sword. "Stay behind me," he said, letting go and stepping in front of her.

Other kill? What – and Thomas, no–

The thought of him imperilling himself for her made her sick with fear, yet she could not move away.

"We're here!" That was Gilbert, shouting from a distance, but she could hear the hoofbeats of horses, and suddenly she and Thomas were no longer alone. Her relief was short-lived as Merlin apparently lost what little control he had over himself the moment the others arrived and, snarling wildly, darted forwards into the woods.

"Merlin, stop!" Thomas called out, but it was too late. The dog was gone.

A second later, the other four men fired after him.

"No, you'll hit Merlin!" Cassandra protested, but it was too late to stop them. She could only hope the dog had avoided the shots, just as she knew the monster who had attacked her had surely managed.

"Ha!" Gilbert, rather fuller of vigour than usual, stepped

forwards as though he were going to run into the woods himself. "That'll show you, you blagga – oh, *ugh*!" He had stepped directly into the pool of blood flowing from the horse's head. He saw it, then saw the remains of the rest of the horse beyond it, and his voice broke into a high-pitched scream.

"Gilbert, for God's sake!" Colonel Cross caught him by the shoulder, spun him round, and slapped him fiercely across the face. "Get a hold of yourself, man!"

"It killed my horse!" Gilbert moaned.

"It almost killed the rider, too, you silly fool." Colonel Cross looked over at Cassandra, who had moved close enough to Thomas to feel the tension radiating from his back. "I'm gratified to see you well. What happened, Miss Wright?"

"You expect her to be able to recount it now, after what just happened?" Thomas demanded.

"I can do it," Cassandra said. She laid her hand on Thomas's shoulder and squeezed gently, letting him know that she appreciated his defence of her, then stepped forwards. There was little enough to tell, after all, and she did not want to have to relive the experience again later. From the way she was trembling, and how her mind seemed to be unable to stop fixating on the beast's face, she already knew she would be reliving it in her dreams.

"A bear," Mr Kildeer said once she'd completed her tale. "It must be a bear. One animal, doing all this damage? Someone has set a great northern bear loose in these woods."

"I have never heard of a black tiger before, though that

might be possible," Mr Humphrey said. "A panther, perhaps?" They seemed more entertained by the notion than dismayed.

"It did not look like a bear," Cassandra said, wanting to be understood on this point. If this was her only chance to convince them of her story, then she needed it to be accurate. "It was very tall, and it had no pelt, just skin, and–"

"How would a woman have a proper idea of what a bear looks like?" Mr Humphrey asked, dismissing her protestations out of hand. "There have been none in this country for centuries."

Cassandra felt the very unladylike urge to start shouting at this arrogant man's utter dismissal of what she'd just seen with her own two eyes. "Exactly, which is why I am sure it must be some other kind of–"

"Surely it's dead now," Gilbert interjected, finally able to speak in a normal tone of voice. "Five shots, hell, at least one of us must have hit it. It has run off into the woods to die."

"And took Merlin with it," Thomas murmured. Tears welled up in Cassandra's eyes at the thought of such a dark fate for their silly hound.

No. He was never mine, poor thing. She went to wipe her cheeks dry, then hissed in pain.

"What is it?" Thomas asked immediately.

"My arm," Cassandra said. Now that the terror had ebbed, the aches and pains of her body were making themselves known. She was sore from riding, but the sharpest pain by far came from her upper arm. She inspected it and, sure enough, there was a gash in the cloth there.

When had that happened? Had she grazed a rock when

she first fell to the ground? Had she done it to herself with the branch? Had ... had the monster made contact with her somehow?

"We must get you back to the inn," Thomas said immediately.

"No, surely Cassie will be more comfortable at the house," Gilbert objected. "I can send for a doctor to treat her there."

She could think of few places she would be less comfortable at right now than the hall. "The inn, please," she whispered in Thomas's ear.

"You tend to the other ladies," Thomas said, sheathing his sword and gently taking her good arm in his hands. "I daresay they're in need of it. I will ensure Cassandra gets help at the inn. And someone needs to track down the rest of the dogs," he added with a grimace. "I do not think it would be worth it at this point to go in after Merlin."

It was at that moment, after holding herself together through what Cassandra would objectively call the third-worst day of her life after the respective deaths of her parents, that her control finally shattered. Tears welled up in her eyes and spilled over, flooding her cheeks with heat. She covered her mouth with her hand to keep any noise in, but the heaviness of her breathing certainly gave her away, because a second later Thomas swept her up in an embrace, letting her tuck her face against his shoulder to hide it.

"May we leave?" she whispered as best she was able to under the circumstances. "I want to leave." She didn't want to be on display like this, a "weak woman" breaking apart in the face of adversity.

"Of course." He made just enough space between them to lead her over to his horse, then helped her up onto it. Cassandra stared down at the animal's neck for a moment before her stomach lurched alarmingly, imprinting the image of her sweet mount's bloody neck on top of this one. She closed her eyes and turned her head away, and a moment later Thomas was behind her, one arm secure around her waist as the other reached for the reins.

Cassandra wasn't looking, but she heard another of the party approach them. "Ride carefully," Colonel Cross – his voice was the deepest among them, easy to identify – said with an air of gravity. "And do not stray into any shadows along the way."

"I will," Thomas said. "And I will be sure to warn the people of Tarryford as well, once I have seen to Cassandra's comfort."

"Good man." The colonel looked like he wanted to say something else, but whatever it was never made it beyond his throat. A moment later, Thomas turned his horse and took them from a brisk walk to a canter so fast that Cassandra barely bounced with the transition. She kept her eyes firmly closed, and made shameless use of Thomas's strength to keep herself upright as well.

Shameless indeed. Ridiculous. You have spent five years doing everything for yourself, with no need of anyone else to support you. Now, less than a week in his presence, and you're already allowing yourself to fall back into old habits. He is not yours! You are not his! To give in to sentiment would be the greatest of follies.

Cassandra hated when her conscience was right. She

sighed a shuddering sigh, then forced her eyes open. Heavens, they were already back in town! People were staring, whispering about them behind their hands; what a sight she must make.

Thomas stopped in front of The Four Feathers and dismounted quickly, then helped Cassandra down. She just barely kept herself from leaning into him once more, but stiffened her spine and her knees at the last moment.

"Innkeep! Ah, Garrett, you–"

"God Almighty, milord, what happened to Miss Wright? Did the beast get her? Did you kill it? Did you–"

"Get me hot water and clean cloths," Thomas said with authority. "Her injury needs tending."

"I'll fetch Dr Parsons," someone said.

"I am perfectly capable of–"

"Sir." This was Mrs Copeland, speaking in a gentle but firm voice. "I understand that you two are engaged, but as you are not yet married, it would be… inappropriate for you to tend to her injury."

Ah, yes. The wound was high on her upper arm. She would have to pull her dress down, exposing the bare skin of her upper back. She would have to be handled quite intimately, and, no, this was not a thing she could ask of Thomas, no matter how badly she desired to, no matter that she'd rather submit to his ministrations than someone else's, especially Dr Parsons's. She hadn't forgotten how the older man had been determined to think the worst of her the moment she stepped through the door of The Four Feathers.

"I can tend to it myself," Cassandra said, forcing herself to pull back from Thomas. He looked pained, his hand still extended towards her like he wished to reel her in once more.

Mrs Copeland looked searchingly at Cassandra before smiling in understanding. "Garrett, fetch Ma Hughes instead," she called out. "She's our local midwife," she said as explanation, "and a dab hand at fixin' up little things like this. I am quite sure everything will be all right," she added for Thomas's sake. "Come with me, miss, and we'll get you ready for her."

Cassandra nodded and followed Mrs Copeland into the inn, turning back only once to see Thomas staring after her. She willed herself to smile at him, but whatever expression crossed her face, it only seemed to make him glower harder. A question from one of the thronging men drew his attention, however, and a moment later he was replaying the events of that afternoon to a captive audience.

"Up you get, Miss Wright," Mrs Copeland said firmly, ignoring the shouts and excitement from outside. Cassandra nodded and made her way upstairs to her room, where Mrs Copeland took the liberty of unlocking the door and letting her in.

"Ma should be here soon," she said, opening the shutters to let in some light as Cassandra gratefully sat down on the end of the bed. "Till then, let me help clean up some of this mess." Her hands were firm and dispassionate, just what Cassandra needed to give herself the space to regain her composure. If it had been Thomas helping her, she knew full well she would have dissolved into tears by now.

"Miss Wright," Mrs Copeland said once she was done helping prepare her for the midwife's attentions. It was the first time she'd sounded uncertain since taking Cassandra in hand. "Is it true, what your betrothed is saying about the beast attacking you?"

He is not my man. No matter how she wanted him to be. "It's true," Cassandra replied. "It happened in Ferris Woods, not two miles from the edge of town."

Mrs Copeland crossed herself, her face a greyish white colour. "Oh, God help us all, not again," she whispered.

"Again?"

But the lady was already gone, leaving Cassandra alone with the pain of her undressed shoulder and far too many questions. The beast, the reactions of the townsfolk, God, the *beast*…

"'Ello there!" The door opened again, this time to reveal an older, heavyset woman who somehow managed to wear a smile that didn't seem out of place despite the circumstances. "You're the lady that got a bit roughed up today, hmm?"

"Yes," Cassandra said. "But I don't think it's bad."

"Well, let me take a look, eh?"

In the time it took her to cluck over Cassandra's wound – not much more than a scratch, but deep enough to merit bandaging after she washed it out with the hot water – and put her back together again, Cassandra had made up her mind. Today had proven that there were dark things going on in the vicinity of Tarryford. Given what Mrs Cross had alluded to earlier, it was even possible that Mr Fraser was the source of this darkness. Whether such mysteries came from Mr Fraser or not, however, she could not in good conscience leave them unsolved.

Talk to Thomas about it. He would help you figure it out. He is clever and brave and loves a challenge.

And perhaps… perhaps she would. Perhaps the time had come to do more than let him assist her in little things – although saving her life, as fortuitous rather than planned as it had been, was no little thing. Perhaps he would help her figure out the provenance of the beast that had nearly ended her life today, and–

Her heartbeat picked up speed, and Cassandra resolutely pinched herself hard on the thigh. She needed to think about something else, something that did not frighten her out of her wits. She needed to focus on her good fortune – that she was still alive – and leave the fear behind for now.

She knew there was no use in trying to avoid confronting her fear forever; that sort of thing led to a terrible dependence on alcohol, from what she'd seen of the uncle of the children she'd tended in Northumberland. But for now… for now, she had an afternoon to herself, and an old mystery to attend to.

It was time to delve back into her father's journal. She hoped it contained the information she needed.

CHAPTER TWELVE

Opening the journal up felt like shaking the hand of an old friend. Better than that, even. If she leaned in close enough, Cassandra could still detect the faintest whiff of her father's pipe smoke, a horribly strong tobacco that lingered in the air for hours. She had chided him about it as a girl, disliking how the smell permeated the books, but now the scent brought tears to her eyes. New cover or not, this journal was a piece of home.

Cassandra stared down at the symbols drawn inside with a little smile on her face. Her father's earliest interest had been history, not law; he had been a great fan of runes and hieroglyphics, and fancied himself something of an artist as well. The letter system he had personally created was a curious blend of the two, cryptic enough to baffle those who hadn't been introduced to it, but then on top of that he had instituted a transposition cipher in all his personal writings. Cassandra remembered her mother asking him once why he bothered.

"Because it amuses me," he'd replied with a huge grin. "I do not write what I do for posterity, dear heart; I write it because these are things that I do not wish to forget."

Cassandra didn't wish to forget it either, but it had still been quite a long while since she'd tried to decode any of it. She'd begged as a child to learn her father's "secret language" and he had, after making sure she was in earnest, taught her the cipher. It had been fun to write each other notes that puzzled the rest of the family; it was something they alone shared and held a special place in her heart.

Let's see… This symbol is always a double letter, and when laid next to this symbol, those letters are always the same… This symbol means that I must reverse the order of the two following it, but have no need to move around the letters themselves… The first page was painstaking work that eventually required her to get out a clean sheet of paper and her ink in an attempt to rewrite it.

It took three tries to create something legible, but once she had that, it was far easier to write out the next few pages, and once *that* was done, she was able to translate the following three without having to write anything down at all.

She was glad she did not need to write those pages down.

The first page was dated almost exactly a year before her father's death. It all began so innocuously, with the sort of grand philosophising that her father had been prone to.

There comes a time in every man's life when he must weigh the comforts of his current existence against the necessity of discomfort in creating a better future for the ones he loves. No human eye can cut through the

*dark and impenetrable veil of what is yet to be, but
I am assured by my dear friend James that, with the
aid of devices newly come to light in the battle against
France, that restriction is potentially one of the past.*

"And you thought that a good thing?" Cassandra murmured, dismayed by her father's blatant naivete.

*That I put myself in danger by assisting him in his
arcane research, I am duly – even readily – resigned
to. He has need of my philological expertise, which is
something I am happy to share. The texts he has me
read... they are quite mesmerising things, with runes
so complex that at times they seem to dance across
the page, defying even the sharpest eye to pin them
down and hold them steady. Even in my recreations,
inaccurate though I know them to be, they are oddly
slippery characters.*

Below this was a... rune? It seemed it could hardly be called a simple rune, more like some elaborate character that had been stamped onto the page, then stamped again slightly beside that, then *again* a bit up and to the left. It was not Eastern as far as she could tell, although Cassandra could claim no fluency in languages like Chinese. Nor was it from any other alphabet that she could readily name.

Cassandra had to tear her eyes away from the rune after a few moments; staring at it was making her feel a bit dizzy. She took a few deep breaths, then looked back down at the page, resolutely avoiding the strange sigil. Her father had more to say and she needed to know what it was, no matter how painful she found it.

*This is but a small sample of the many symbols
I have been tasked with mastering. Their use, in
connection with certain artefacts and necessary
actions, such as the use of his ancient obsidian knife,
will create the opportunity we need to reach into
another world. There are beings there, James assures
me, that can truly tell the future – for a price. It is
a price that we, the Brotherhood of the Black Goat,
must find a way of paying if we are to maintain
England's sovereignty and power in this new and
rapidly changing world.*

*Shub-Niggurath is this being's name, and the
price for her assistance is sacrifice. A single human
sacrifice – the existence of one young woman of
upright and gentle standing to be her vessel in the
world. She will provide a conduit to the other realm
that allows us to see into, and change, the future as it
has been laid out. In this way, we will–*

Cassandra could read no more. She had to stop. She
pushed away from the table, stumbling in her haste to
put some space between her and her father's journal. She
moved over to the window, desperate for fresh air to help
rid her of the sick feeling that had lodged in her stomach
after reading her father's words.

How could he think such a thing? How could he possibly
imagine that such dark activities would be of greater
benefit than the cost asked for them? To sacrifice a young
woman – and Cassandra knew she was not mistaken in
thinking that such a sacrifice would result in that woman's

death, even if her body lived on – for access to such dark and evil power... it was sheer folly. A gross overestimation of the skills of the people who would wish to have it. It was un-Christian, it was against the natural order of the world, it was *cruel* in a way she had never imagined her father capable of being.

Was she wrong? Was it possible she was mistaken about the cause of her father's death? Had he died as a result of his own arrogance, sacrificed to this awful Shub-Niggurath in an effort to enact some sort of material change on the world? Or had Mr Fraser taken that decision out of his hands and made do with the sacrifice of an old man instead of a young maiden? What about the coachman who had died, whose murder her father had taken the blame for? What had *he* been sacrificed for? Perhaps his death bought a beast like the one that had attacked her for its master. Had her father known it was going to happen?

You cannot judge him yet. Not fully. Not until you know the full story. But in her heart, Cassandra already knew that no matter what she read next, she would never be able to think of her father the same way again. The man who had cared so tenderly for her, who had taught her right from wrong and protected she and her siblings against the world... that man was no more than an illusion.

Byron Wright as Cassandra had imagined him, a pure-hearted, over-trusting victim of circumstance, was truly dead to her now.

Cassandra wanted to mourn him anew, wanted to lay out her grievances to a willing ear and a tender heart and seek reassurances that not everything in her life was a lie, and yet… there was no such person she could turn to.

I can never let my brother and sister know.

It would destroy them. Her brother idolised their father, holding him up as a model for how men should behave in the world, with care and righteousness, while her sister still thought of him with the easy affection of a young girl whose parent could do no wrong. She could not take that from them, but neither could she keep all her bitter disappointment locked in her chest. She could already feel it poisoning her veins, leaving her cold and disillusioned.

What was the point of being here, of humiliating herself in front of her former betrothed and his guests, of staring down a beast that might literally have come from another world, all for the sake of a man who had known what he was getting himself into? Should she risk herself for any more terrible truths involving him? Had any good come of her efforts at all?

Yes, there has been good. You have met with Thomas. You have his support, his understanding. You have his respect.

The thought, far from setting her nerves aflutter as it had every time she had entertained such notions so far, served to settle them instead. Yes, she did have Thomas. Moreover, aiding her had been his idea entirely, and he had acquitted himself of it admirably. And today… Cassandra let her eyes close, let herself relive the moment of sheer relief that she'd felt when Thomas appeared, gun in hand, to save her life. If he had arrived but seconds later, it would have been too late for her.

Could she abandon him now to this terrible place, this awful hunt, suspecting what she did – that Mr Fraser himself had brought the Beast of Avon Vale into existence? Could she leave, knowing that he would face something truly evil, without doing everything in her power to stop it? Could she abandon this town, filled with people who seemed regrettably familiar with such dark arts, when she might be able to help? No, it was impossible. She needed to see this through – if not for her father's sake, then for Thomas.

You care for him too much. You could lose your heart if you stay.

Or perhaps she had lost it already, dropped it irretrievably down the well of her regard for Thomas Griffith. If so, it was a loss over many years in the making, and she would not regret it, no matter what came of it.

She would talk to him about this tomorrow, she decided. He needed to know about the horror they were facing, and she needed to share her burden with the only person in her life who she knew could listen without being overwhelmed by pain or guilt. When he came for her in the morning, she would share what she knew with him, perhaps show him the journal, and together they would make a plan. Yes… yes, but until then…

Until then, she had a journal to read. Cassandra straightened her back and nodded firmly to herself, then returned to her place at the table and began to read once more.

It was a bit easier to distance herself from the words now that she had taken a moment to collect herself. Cassandra read all about what sort of person this young woman needed to be: beautiful and virginal, among other things, a proper blank slate that Shub-Niggurath would enhance even further with power and charisma. She would become a being who could entice others into doing her bidding, all while securely under the control of the brotherhood of occultists her father was a member of.

And all of it was for the sake of fighting Bonaparte, of course. Once the French tyrant was defeated, once his armies were laid to waste and the creatures he summoned out of darkness were sent back to the realms from which they had been pulled, then everything would change. There would be no more need to use the navy as a human shield between England and the rest of the world, no more need to risk their brave soldiers and sailors against such dire opponents. The Brotherhood wouldn't need their intimate connection with the black goat god any longer, and would:

–*gently end the life of the young initiate, severing her connection with Shub-Niggurath and allowing her the dignity of an honourable death.*

"Disgusting," Cassandra muttered.

We have not yet reached the point of choosing who might be a suitable vessel, of course. There is much work yet to do to ensure that our ritual contacts the correct god – a mistake in this arena could be fatal to all involved. I have given the issue solely into the keeping of James; he has a larger acquaintance than I, of course, and will be better able to discover the most

*appropriate candidate. Beauty, gentility, cleverness –
ha! It is just as well that my dear Cassandra is
betrothed to Gilbert.*

"Yes, because that *worthless* fool would have been sure to save me," she snarled, discomfited by the very thought that her father could have considered her for the role of sacrifice, even jokingly.

The first entry ended there. Following it were pages upon pages of notes, most of them details of various runes and sigils. Sometimes her father expounded on origin, meaning, or how to activate the symbols and shut them down again, but mostly he simply copied them, faithfully, over and over again until Cassandra felt as though the imprint of the first one in particular was burned onto her eyes. It had to be the rune that the Brotherhood of the Black Goat planned to use to connect with their dark god.

It all seemed such incredible folly to her. How could a mere mortal hope to contain, to control, a being with the power these people ascribed to Shub-Niggurath? How could they think there would be no repercussions for it amongst themselves? How could her father have been so incredibly blind to the risk he was taking?

Oh, he had acknowledged it in a cheeky, "there but for the grace of God go I" sense, but wasn't that just perfectly him? So willing to think the best of himself and his friends, so determined that all would be well even when every sign indicated otherwise.

The latter entries, she was both gratified and sickened to read, did indicate that her father was coming to the realisation that he might have been wrong about some, if not all, of his early assumptions.

Blood is needed to open the portal to the other realm. Of course, I should have realised as much – blood seems to be the necessary ingredient in so many of these dire rituals. Tonight we experimented with killing a rabbit and laying it on the altar. Our efforts were unsuccessful.

I did not know before tonight that rabbits could scream.

Two weeks later, they tried a lamb to greater effect. Apparently, it had enabled a portal to be created, but not one large enough for Shub-Niggurath to enter the world through. Something had exited the portal, though – something that her father declined to describe in great detail. Was it the Beast of Avon Vale? Or was it possible that he referred to the small, red-eyed creature that had run across her foot in the library? Heavens, how many times had they done this ritual?

Whatever they'd produced, her father was apparently rather disgusted by the result, although he had been careful to hide his disgust from Mr Fraser.

He tells me that we need all the assistance we can get for this endeavour, and that as we have found the sigil that allows him to exercise control over the beings which come through the portal, their assistance is assured and perfectly safe. James would not lead me astray in this. He has my full confidence, my full support.

The very last entry was dated a week later

I do not know what this evening will bring. I hope it
to be success, and good news for our brotherhood and
for all of England. I suspect that James is prepared
to bring something else through the portal tonight. I
don't know why – he already has his mannikin, but
if he thinks a second would be helpful then I must
support him. Our discoveries thus far are already
enough to change the fates of everyone we love for the
better, if applied correctly, so how can I do otherwise?

James is my greatest friend, and I flatter myself that
he listens to me more than anyone else. We are on the
cusp of fantastic progress, and I am excited to see what
the night brings, so long as no one is hurt."

Far from making her feel better about the situation,
these words only made her loathe her father's memory
more. "Changing fates, ha! You were more than ready to
condemn some innocent young woman to a fate worse
than death," she snapped, slamming the journal closed and
shoving it away from her.

The movement made her shoulder twinge painfully, and
she winced even as she got up to pace, eventually walking
over to the window and opening it up to give herself some
fresh air.

CHAPTER THIRTEEN

Cassandra was a good, God-fearing woman, the same as any in England. She had always gone to church and said her prayers and believed, however vaguely, in the promise of a deity who looked after those who prayed to him. She had never witnessed a miracle firsthand, however, never seen the blessing of the Lord play out before her very eyes. Now, to be confronted with the fact that not only were there beings out there who responded to pleas when they were accompanied by *death*, of all things, but that her father had essentially been worshipping one of these monsters...

It seemed impossible, like the sort of thing that should not be allowed. Why should they be allowed to influence the affairs of humanity so readily? Why should these eldritch creatures be so easy to sway and influence, when God himself was not?

He would not be much of a god if He were so easily controlled, Cassandra reminded herself. She was no curate, trained in philosophy and religion and capable of understanding the Almighty. She was just a woman. But knowing what she knew now, she had renewed faith in her purpose. There would be no leaving Tarryford now. Being made into an unholy avatar was not something she could allow, even passively, to happen to another person, some unsuspecting girl who was lured in by Mr Fraser's charms and enticements only to give up her body and likely lose her soul to a dark god. Standing up to Bonaparte? Ha, these rituals weren't for a noble purpose; they were merely that insufferable man's best hope of gathering an immense amount of power and influence to himself, and damn the rest of the country. And her father – her clever, trusting, *stupid* father – had fallen hook, line, and sinker for that man's lies.

To be fair – which Cassandra was far from inclined to be right now – she was guilty of the same crime. Oh, she had not fawned on Mr Fraser the way her father had, but she had encouraged his son's attentions even when she knew she did not love Gilbert. She had set herself up to gain a position of respectability and comfort without regard for the dark murmurings about the family she was marrying into. Murmurings which had swelled the longer their acquaintance lasted. Mr Fraser had sent his own wife and daughters away a month before Cassandra's father was killed. Had he done so to protect them from his eldritch rites, or from the growing rumours about his own conduct?

But this was getting her nowhere. Cassandra sighed and sat down on the bed again, fatigued as though she had run from Harston Hall to Tarryford today – or rather, as though she had been on the verge of being bitten in two by a beast which she was sure was not of this world.

Mr Fraser could have set it loose here. But why? To amuse himself? To terrorise the people of Tarryford? What good can come of such a thing, especially when his hunters do not appear up to the task of triumphing over it? Can such a thing even be killed by mortal means?

Her father's writings seemed to indicate that the dark god, at least, could be driven back to its realm with the death of its vessel. If he wasn't a complete fool – which Cassandra couldn't say with any certainty now – then perhaps this was similar. Perhaps…

Cassandra stifled a yawn against her fist, then wondered why she had bothered when there was no one around to see her.

It would be an early night for her. That was what she needed, rest – although how successful she would be at gaining it, she did not yet know. She sighed, then stood up and headed for her door. She would ask Mrs Copeland for water for a bath and to have her supper brought to her room tonight, and…

She had barely cracked the door when she remembered the journal laid out on her table. Truthfully, Cassandra could barely stand to look at it right now, much less handle it. Yet she could not risk someone innocent, such as Mrs Copeland or the maid Molly, coming across it when they came in to clean. Biting back a grimace, Cassandra grabbed the journal, shoved it into the bottom of her trunk, and locked the whole affair up once more. She tucked the key about her neck, then headed downstairs to negotiate for what she needed.

The bath that followed was wonderfully scalding, and when Mrs Copeland offered her some tea by the fireplace in the private dining room, Cassandra gratefully accepted it. She read by herself for a bit – a novel, rather than anything as salacious as what she had stowed away upstairs, and by the time she returned to her room she was feeling much more sanguine.

It was at last full dark, and Cassandra shivered as she realised she had left the window open. The room had gotten quite chilled, but she found she still craved the fresh air; any hint of staleness or foulness reminded her too much of the beast in the wood. She left a small gap in the window, brushed out her hair one last time, then stared at the object she had laid on the vanity and wondered how foolish she was being at wanting to keep it close.

There is no one here to see you being foolish but you. As long as you don't mind it, then suit yourself.

Sound advice, Cassandra reasoned. She slipped the comforting thing beneath her pillow, pulled the heavy down comforter over her body, then blew out her candle.

The only light left in the room came from the sliver of moon that peeked around the edges of the window. The wind was light but persistent, keeping the air moving in a way that soothed her spirit. After a few minutes of deliberate relaxation, Cassandra began to drift off to sleep…

Click. Click click click.

Something was in the room with her.

Click click click click…

Something familiar. This was a sound she had heard before, at the hall. Too heavy to be a mouse or rat, but too loud to be a cat. What was it? Another rampaging beast, or something more sinister?

How had it found her?

What did it want?

Click click click… She heard it pace around the room, shuffling objects as though it were searching for something. What did it want? The journal? She had first encountered this creature in the library – perhaps it was the guardian of those tomes. Perhaps she had offended it by making off with one. Would it attack her? God, had she not weathered enough attacks for one day? Something so small shouldn't make her heart race like she was facing down the beast again, but the sound of her own pulse seemed as loud as a drumbeat. If it came close enough, it might hear her pounding heart and realise that she wasn't asleep.

What would she do if it did?

She heard the creature natter to itself under its breath, a faint, whispery noise that almost sounded like speech. Perhaps it was scolding itself for not finding whatever its prize was. Perhaps it was working itself up towards a confrontation. Perhaps…

It crawled closer, slinking across the vanity and onto the bedside table, carefully peeking around every corner as it went. Now it was hard for Cassandra to maintain her ruse of sleep; her legs trembled beneath the comforter, the movement only hidden by virtue of its thickness, and her breath was too shallow and fast. She would not be able to fool the creature for long.

You do not need to fool it. You only need to strike first.

She cracked an eye open to watch its progress. As soon as the thing put a foot on the edge of her bed, Cassandra moved. She grasped the long hatpin she'd tucked beneath her pillow, reared back like she was about to throw a proper punch – *thank you, Samuel* – then stabbed the silver needle forwards with all her might.

The pin sank deep into the creature's belly, so deep that Cassandra's knuckles brushed the chilled, furless flesh of the little beast not two feet in front of her.

It screamed, a shrill animal sound, but even in the dim light Cassandra could see that this was no simple animal. It was just slightly larger than a rat and had the same hunched posture, four paws, and long, worm-like tail, but there the resemblance ended. This creature's head was round, almost humanoid, and its beady red eyes caught the dim light just like she remembered from the library as it grasped the hatpin and slowly pulled it out of its body, then threw it onto the ground.

Blood dripped from its wound, but the rat-thing seemed too furious to care about the damage it had already endured. It bared two rows of sharpened teeth, spread its clawed, hand-like front forepaws, and leapt at her face.

Cassandra jerked away as she grabbed her heavy pillow off the bed with both hands and swung it at the airborne monster. It was a good hit, solid enough to send the shrieking beast straight into the window, rattling it loudly. It got to its feet and scrabbled through the crack at the bottom a second later.

I must follow it!

Cassandra ran over to the window and looked down at the ground for a body, a blur – for anything that would indicate the next step. But there was no little beast to be seen. In the five seconds it had taken her to cross the room, the rat-thing had vanished.

"Oh God," she murmured, staring at the ground two floors below. "Oh God."

She had been stalked. She had been attacked, yet again. The monster was intelligent enough to know to search her room – was it searching for the journal? Suddenly paranoid, Cassandra ran over to her trunk. It was still firmly locked, but the lock itself was scratched, as though it had been gnawed at.

It knew she had the journal; it had searched her room… it must have been looking for the key. Cassandra laid a hand on the end of the chain around her neck where she kept the heavy key safe beside her cross, and closed her eyes with relief.

A sudden knock on her door made her startle. "Miss Wright?" It was Young Garrett. "Is everything well? Ma heard a bit of a racket, and she sent me up to make sure you're all right."

A racket… yes, being in the second fight for my life in one day would indeed cause a racket. Could the rat-thing have killed her? Cassandra didn't know, but she *did* know that sharing this information with her hosts would only cause them to doubt her.

I am, in fact, not all right, I was attacked by a tiny monster who must have scaled the walls of your establishment to get to me. I stabbed it and beat it out the window, but there is no evidence of it other than a few drops of blood, so please do not think me mad.

"Forgive me," she called out, her voice barely trembling. "I am afraid I had a bit of a nightmare. It caused me to upset a few things in here… I am well now, though."

There was a pause, then, "I'm glad to hear it. Come down if you need anything, miss, and me or Ma will help you out however we can."

"Thank you, you are most kind." The boy went away, and Cassandra bowed her head down against the top of her chest and recovered herself for a few moments.

She had fought, and *this* battle she had won all by herself. No matter what was going on, she would not allow her nerves to get the better of her.

Thomas. She would tell Thomas what had happened first thing in the morning. He would believe her, she knew he would, and he would help her to make up a plan for what to do should such a thing happen again. Together, they would discover the black heart of this plot. For her sake, for her poor fool of a father's sake, and for the sake of the girl who was destined to lose her life should they fail, Cassandra would see Mr Fraser's plots and plans go to ruin.

Cassandra got to her feet and relit the candle, then dipped a cloth in the basin of water on the vanity. Better to clean up the blood before it dried. She cleaned her hatpin first and laid it reverently beside her bed.

That, she would keep close from now on.

CHAPTER FOURTEEN

Cassandra expected to see Thomas early the next morning. Indeed, she would have welcomed his company as quickly as possible. For all her fatigue and despite her best efforts at calming herself, as well as closing the window and shutters very firmly, she was not able to catch more than a few hours of sleep. Just as the sun rose over the horizon, she gave up on the notion of any more rest and got up, dressed herself in one of her older, more comfortable gowns, put her hair up, and found a place for the pin within it.

I should have a proper knife as well. The pin had done well for her, but the idea of something more substantial was an alluring one. Even something as simple as a penknife would be an improvement, and she should be able to conceal it within her skirts easily enough. Getting it *out* again might prove a challenge… perhaps if there was a hidden slit of some kind.

Another thing to talk to Thomas about. Cassandra was quite looking forward to seeing him this morning. She took tea and a small breakfast downstairs, permitted Mrs Copeland to fuss over her a bit, assured her that her shoulder was well – in truth, she hardly felt the pain of it any longer – and waited for the gig to arrive.

And waited.

And waited.

By the time the church bells rang at ten o'clock, Cassandra had progressed from impatient to unquiet to truly worried. Something must be wrong. Had they gone out on the hunt yet again? Had Thomas been injured? Had Gilbert? Something must have occurred that necessitated his absence from her, and to receive no word from him, not even a brief note... it was not like him. It would especially not be like him on a day such as today, in the aftermath of their confrontation with the Beast of Avon Vale.

By noon, Cassandra was resolved to get to the house herself by any means necessary. She would walk if she had to, out in the bright sunlight that the beast seemed loath to enter. She resolutely buttoned her pelisse and tied on her bonnet, then headed for the inn's door.

Just as she stepped out, a carriage pulled in. It was drawn by four matched horses, all of them black and gleaming. The carriage was black as well, but heavy and well-made. *Some new guest*, she supposed. She stepped off to the side and watched as one of the stable boys ran over to help take charge of the team while a footman, dressed in white and blue regalia and wearing a curling white wig, stepped down from where he had been perched beside the coachman.

Rather than open the door to let someone out, however, he stepped forwards. "Ho the inn!"

"Coming, sir!" Young Garrett ran outside, wiping his hands off on a rag. He stuffed it into a pocket of his apron and gave a bow. "Welcome, sir, welcome to The Four Feathers! Are you looking for rooms?"

"We are looking," the footman said in a cold and detached manner, "for one of your guests. A Miss Cassandra Wright."

"Oh." The boy looked as surprised as Cassandra felt. He turned towards her, but she was already stepping forwards.

"I am Miss Wright," she said.

The coachman stared at her for a long moment, clearly barely restraining a sneer. "I see. Then this is for you." He reached within his jacket and emerged with an elegant note, which he extended towards her. "It requires your immediate answer."

Truly puzzled now, Cassandra broke the plain wax seal and pulled out the letter within the envelope. She read it, and with every word her breath seemed to congeal within her chest, until it felt as though she was attempting to breathe around a block of ice.

To Miss Cassandra Wright

Upon my arrival at Harston Hall last night, I was informed by my son of your unexpected presence in Tarryford, as well as of your recent betrothal to Mr Griffith. I was also informed of the trials you faced in Ferris Woods, and was dismayed that my son allowed you to leave without ascertaining the state

of your health yesterday. I insist on being allowed to
rectify his mistake, and look forward to renewing my
acquaintance with the beloved daughter of one of my
dearest friends.

I await your arrival at Harston today at your
earliest convenience. This coach is at your disposal.

With sincere good wishes for your health,

Mr James Fraser, Esq.

Oh, heavens. He was here. He was… here. Mr Fraser, the man who had tempted her father down the path of unrighteousness, had arrived at Harston. The block of ice in her chest became a knife, cutting into her heart, and for a moment Cassandra thought she might faint.

"Miss Wright?" Young Garrett was suddenly standing beside her, one hand extended as if he might take hold of her elbow to steady her. "Are you well? You'll have to forgive her, sir," he said to the footman, "the lady had a terrible scare yesterday."

"So my master has heard. That is, in fact, the reason behind his invitation today."

"I'm just saying, sir, she might not be up to it. Probably ought to stay in bed, 'specially since the beast ain't been found yet." Young Garrett was trying to be jolly, but his efforts fell flat.

"I'm afraid that I cannot take no for an answer," the footman said, staring straight at Cassandra now. "Your presence is both requested *and* required by my master, Miss Wright."

For a brief moment, Cassandra wondered what would happen if she refused. Would this man drag her into the carriage? Would he make trouble for Mrs Copeland and her son? Would he return with Mr Fraser to fetch her himself?

No, she would not tempt fate in such a way. Besides, she wished to go to the house anyhow; Thomas was there, and she needed to make sure that he was all right. She turned to Young Garrett with a smile. "Thank you so much for your assistance," she said, "but I am well enough for this." She knew she wasn't imagining the relief on his face at her acquiescence. No one wanted to get on the bad side of the local gentry.

Cassandra turned to the footman and lifted her chin. "Very well, sir. I will accompany you to Harston."

He didn't reply, just inclined his head then walked back and opened the carriage's door for her. She allowed him to help her into it, then sat down on one of the red leather seats and folded her hands in her lap to keep from fidgeting. The interior was huge, with room for eight to sit comfortably. It had to be Mr Fraser's personal conveyance, large enough for his wife and children to ride with him.

Had they all come to Harston as well? Were they innocent of their father's machinations? The youngest child would be only twelve now, she remembered. Just about the age of Elizabeth when…

Whether they were at the hall or not, it did not matter. All Cassandra had to concern herself with now was enduring what was to come next. To see this man after five long years, to look upon his hateful face…

I would stab him with my hatpin if I thought I could get away with it.

With four horses, the ride to Harston passed in a blur. Before she was truly prepared, they had come to a stop outside the hall. Cassandra closed her eyes and willed herself into a state of collectedness as the footman went to open the door. She stepped out and–

"Cassandra!"

It was Thomas. He had come to her first, hands lifting hers up to cradle against his chest as he drank in the sight of her. He stood in a way that blocked her view of the house, which suited her perfectly well. She let herself lean into him, let the sight of his dear face soothe her spirit. "I was worried when I did not see you this morning," she murmured.

"I am so sorry." Simple words, but she could sense the truth behind him, the regret. "I meant to come to you as soon as possible, but Mr Fraser arrived late last night, when all the rest of us were abed. Finding him here this morning was… quite surprising, and I was not able to get away." His eyes searched her face sombrely. "You look as though you haven't slept a wink."

Because I haven't. "I–"

"I understand that you and Miss Wright are betrothed," a strong, stern voice called out from behind them, "but it is impolite of you to keep her all to yourself, Mr Griffith. She is, after all, here as our guest today."

Thomas's spine stiffened so hard Cassandra wondered that the bones didn't creak, but when he spoke, he sounded perfectly steady. "Of course, sir." He gave her hands a reassuring squeeze, then moved one to the crook of his elbow before they turned and faced their host together.

She stayed on her feet, did not sway or shy away. She did not care to look at his hateful face yet, but instead glanced around and saw no sign of the rest of his family, other than Gilbert, who looked supremely uncomfortable. When Gilbert made eye contact with Cassandra, his lips twisted into a moue of discontent, as if he were sorry she was there… or perhaps in an attempt at an apology.

Ha. As if he had ever had a say in what his father chose to do.

Cassandra curtsied as shallowly as was still polite. "Sir," she murmured, then tensed as fingers slid beneath her chin and raised her gaze to the man of the house.

"There," Mr Fraser said, wearing a detestable little smile. "That is better. Welcome, Miss Wright."

Do not touch me!

Luckily he moved his hand a moment later, or she might have given in to the urge to slap his hand away. "Thank you, sir," she said. Now that she was looking at him, she could not look away. He appeared unchanged from how she remembered him: the same strong jaw, bright blue eyes, and red hair touched with grey at the temples. His form was tall, his shoulders strong and broad. He had the look of a man of power, the air of the conqueror about him. His riding jacket was black, the tails longer than most, and his boots had silver buckles polished to a brilliant shine.

"It is a true pleasure to see you once more," he continued,

nothing but geniality in his voice. "A surprise, but a pleasure. I think of your family quite frequently."

"I'm sure my father would be happy to be remembered," Cassandra said, biting it out around the anger that had lodged in her throat. "Despite how things ended between the two of you."

"Indeed. A terrible business, seeing someone you care for lose their mind in such a way. Still…" He affected a sympathetic tone, voice softening and lowering as if to keep the conversation solely between the two of them. "Byron was very dear to me," he murmured, "and one bad moment could not erase all of that. Indeed, I am grateful for the chance to renew our acquaintance in honour of his memory."

In honour of his memory. As if this odious man wasn't the reason her father was nothing more than a memory. *I could stab him with my hatpin right now.* "Thank you."

The tension was thick enough to cut with a knife, and eventually Gilbert, dull blade though he was, obliged. "Let's get you inside, eh, Cassie? The ladies are all aflutter about you. They wouldn't stop harassing us for letting you go back to Tarryford yesterday instead of keeping you here." He moved towards the door and Thomas followed, guiding Cassandra away from Mr Fraser. She was surprised at the difference a few paces made to her level of jaw-clenching fury.

"Haven't they been just wild for news of her, Thomas?" Gilbert went on blithely as he led the way to the salon.

"Rather too wild, given their propensity for avoiding

conflict themselves," he said. Cassandra's breath caught on a laugh.

"Oh, surely you do not hold their running away against them?" Gilbert chided incredulously. "They didn't even have control of the carriage they were in!"

"You would be amazed at the things I am able to hold against people," Thomas replied. "There is self-protection, and then there is cowardice, and I am very firmly of the opinion that leaving a member of your party to fend for herself in such circumstances falls on the side of cowardice."

"Well, you know... they are only women, after all," Gilbert said awkwardly before leading the way into the salon. Cassandra stared at the back of his head and recalled the very high pitch of his scream yesterday upon seeing the remains of his horse. *And you are only a man.*

"There she is!" Mrs Humphrey darted forwards, a glass in one hand, the other pressed to her breast as if barely able to contain her heart within its bounteous prison. "Oh, thank the Lord that you are well, Miss Wright! We were so worried about you yesterday, weren't we, Penelope?"

"Desperately worried," Miss Getty said, not trying nearly as hard as her sister to be convincing.

Mrs Humphrey took hold of Cassandra's arm and tried to lead her over to the couch, but to no avail. Thomas was not letting go. After a second, Mrs Humphrey seemed to receive the message and took a step back.

She was dressed, Cassandra noted, in a very fine outfit, the finest Cassandra had yet seen her in. Gold silk, lace gloves, a jewelled headdress – this was Mrs Humphrey putting her very best foot forward. Her sister and Mrs Kildeer were similarly garbed, the sumptuous fabrics clearly meant to put them on best display for the master of the house. Only Mrs Cross was dressed as she had been over the past few days, in a dark, sober green gown with minimal adornments apart from a single strand of pearls around her throat. She joined them a moment later, a look of contrition on her face.

"There is no good excuse for our actions other than to say that all of us, coachman and horses included, were spooked," she said. "By the time we got the poor things under control we could hear gunshots. I decided at that moment that it was better we continue on to the house, for nothing good could have come from us inserting ourselves into a dangerous situation such as that."

Cassandra was inclined to agree. "I understand," she said. "I did not expect you to come back for me, and as you can see, I have taken no damage."

"Oh, that cannot be," Mrs Humphrey pouted. "I was told you were injured. Reggie *specifically* told me that. Mr Humphrey! You did not lie to me, did you?"

"Why would I go to the effort?" her bored husband asked after swallowing a mouthful of port.

"Oh, Reggie!"

"Brother, really."

"The injury was not bad," Cassandra assured her. "Truly, I am quite well."

"And we are all grateful for it." And here he was once more, sliding into the room as silently as a snake. Everyone refocused every ounce of their attention on Mr Fraser. Everyone except Thomas and, she was surprised to see, Gilbert, who looked rather put out.

But of course he was. His stay had gone from a light-hearted excursion where he could play at being lord of the manor and soak up the attentions of his friends to a sharp rebuke of his efforts to be in charge. Every lie he had told himself was now shown to be just that: falsehoods that were meant to make him feel better, but not give him any sort of real respect or power. All of his "friends" flocked to Mr Fraser like bees to a rose, until the only ones not in his father's vicinity were Thomas and Cassandra.

Cassandra longed for the chance to speak to Thomas alone, but with Gilbert feeling needy it was not to be. She did her best to contain her annoyance as he addressed her.

"Well, how's this for a turn-up, eh?" He chortled weakly as he leaned his elbow against the mantel, the other hand on his hip, as though he were attempting to strike a deliberate pose: *lounging young lordling,* the picture might be titled. It was ruined by the twisted knot of his cravat and the dishevelment of his hair, made worse when he reached up and ran his hand through it yet again. "I did let Father know that we were having a bit of a slow time with the hunt, of course, but I didn't expect him to take matters into his own hands."

"Oh?" she asked with little interest. Gilbert's excuses were as old and well-trod as a Roman road.

"Mr Fraser is intent on ensuring that this beast is *captured,*" Thomas said, stepping a bit closer to Cassandra.

"Captured?" That was the last thing she had been expecting. If he had brought it into being, as she suspected, why would he need to capture it? Couldn't he just command it to do his bidding? Wasn't that the point of the sacrifice – to exchange blood for power so that whatever came into this world, it worked to the ends of the one who had summoned it, rather than striking out on its own? "Why on earth would anyone wish to capture it? It has shown itself ready and willing to hunt down people."

"I'm sure he has his reasons," Gilbert muttered, crawling his fingertips along the mantel until they grabbed a discarded glass of sherry and tipping it down his throat.

"And whatever they are, they are wrong," Thomas said, disapproval clear in his voice.

"Are they, Mr Griffith?"

How had Mr Fraser heard them from halfway across the room, with all those others chattering at him? Gilbert stiffened like a schoolboy caught dozing off at his desk, but Thomas rose to the question.

"Indeed they are," he said. "When a shepherd's dog attacks his sheep rather than herding them, that dog is put down without question. The case for killing this beast is even clearer than that, as it certainly did not get its start as a domesticated animal. Whatever it is, it needs to be ended, not captured."

"That is the answer I would expect from someone small-minded, Mr Griffith, but surely you are better than that," Mr Fraser replied, his hands folded behind his back, his expression amiable. "Consider the opportunity that has afforded itself here. Whatever this beast is, it is unique to the area, perhaps unique in all of England. This is a chance for us to study and learn, not merely to kill and discard."

"And when it succeeds in going after a person?" Thomas challenged. "What will your feelings on the matter be then?"

"That is something to deal with if and when the situation presents itself, but that is far from a certainty," Mr Fraser replied. "You yourself fired a shot at the beast which made it step away, did you not? I think there is a great likelihood that it is injured and has most probably returned to wherever it makes its den to lick its wounds. We will track it there, we will capture it, and we will decide what to do with it then."

The kernel of doubt within Cassandra began to grow. Such zeal for finding it… that he had a plan for the beast wasn't surprising, but now more than ever she wondered what she'd gotten wrong. If he hadn't summoned the Beast of Avon Vale, then who had?

"You will do as you like, of course," Thomas said. "But I will continue to carry my gun and my sword, and if I have the chance to cut this beast's throat, I will take it." He was the only man of the party not quailing under the force of Mr Fraser's regard, and Cassandra felt a surge of pride at his resilience.

"I would expect nothing less from a man such as yourself," Mr Fraser said. The words were not impolite, but the delivery was. "It takes a particularly insightful sort of mind to see beyond the veil, as it were, and to the heart of a matter as complex as this one. You never did see action in your days in the military, did you?"

Thomas pinched his lips together for a moment, then shook his head. "I was called home before that opportunity was afforded to me."

"Yes, I can tell. Those who have been responsible for the lives of others, who have *taken* lives, are much more cautious about ordering the same. I know that Colonel Cross agrees with me."

Of course he does. The colonel was clearly Mr Fraser's man. "But do you not allow for a difference in the moral weight between killing men and beasts?" Cassandra asked before she could stop herself. "Is it not a heavier burden on the soul to consign a fellow human being to death?"

Mr Fraser narrowed his eyes. "Goodness, you speak like a parson. I do not recall your father being particularly pious, Miss Wright. Have five years wrought such a change in you that you would prefer to argue religious philosophy than dance the night away?"

"Oh, yes!" Mrs Humphrey exclaimed before Cassandra could gather herself to spit in Mr Fraser's face. "Yes, we *must* have a dance! It has been so long since I heard music, I positively *long* for it. To go without it now would be the worst sort of punishment."

"What, now?" her husband asked. "You want to dance in the middle of the day? What are you, a child?"

"Reggie!"

"I agree with her inclination," Mr Fraser said then, and Cassandra shivered. "I think a bit of dancing before our midday meal would be just the thing to whet my appetite."

"Then I shall play for you all," Cassandra said quickly, for the thought of dancing with Mr Fraser left her with the feeling that she would not be able to keep her breakfast down.

"And I shall sit with you," Thomas said, then led her in the direction of the pianoforte before they could be gainsaid.

"Oh, move the table there, Reggie, move the – and the chairs, yes." Mrs Humphrey had taken charge of preparing the room, so Cassandra sat down and began to look through the pile of scores on the edge of the piano. Her hands shook so badly that she was not sure she would be able to hold them steady enough to play, especially after over a month's break from doing so.

Thomas sat down beside her, scooting in close along the piano's bench. "Do you really play?" he murmured. "I do not recall you doing so before."

"I learned as a part of my former position," she replied. She did not mention that despite her love of dancing, playing music had not come naturally to her. She could read half a dozen different languages, but reading music was a challenge that had taken many long and late hours to overcome. She had barely kept pace with the eldest daughter of the family she worked for, who was but ten when Cassandra began with them. "Not very well," she added.

"Try this one, then." He pulled out a sheet of music for a quadrille and laid it on the piano. "It does not utilise a minor key and is fairly straightforward otherwise."

"Thank you." Cassandra took a moment to focus on the music, pointedly ignoring the looks from the prospective dancers as they waited for her to begin. She flexed her fingers, took a deep breath, and began to play.

The tempo was lively but not overly fast, and despite a few fingering mistakes in the beginning, she was able to get through it passably well. The next one went similarly, and she found herself grateful for the effort playing required of her; she did not have to think about the man who was spinning about the room like he had not a care in the world.

The scotch reel was a bit more challenging, and by the stuttering end of it Mrs Humphrey and her sister were both looking annoyed. "I should have thought you equal to something as simple as a reel, but apparently not," Miss Getty said acridly. "Is there nothing else over there you can find your way through, or should we relieve you and see whether or not you can keep your feet better than your fingers?"

"I shall play the next song," Thomas said unexpectedly. "But I am afraid I cannot give up Miss Wright. I need her to turn the pages for me."

Mrs Kildeer broke into a laugh. "Sir! Am I to understand that you have some understanding of the piano? That is uncommon for a man of your station."

"Or perhaps," Mr Fraser said with a cool stare at the pair of them, "you are simply trying to excuse yourselves from polite company. Do you take some sort of issue with my hospitality, Mr Griffith?"

Thomas did not bother to reply. Instead, he laid down a sheet of music that looked far more complicated than anything Cassandra would ever attempt and immediately began to play. And play *well*. His fingers were light on the keys, his strikes precise, and there was an elegance to his execution that elevated the song from suitable for dancing to a performance. Cassandra could barely keep pace with where he was on the sheet music – indeed, she missed turning the first page, but by the end of the second she realised it did not matter. He had every note memorised.

He ended the song to lukewarm applause, and Mr Fraser disengaged from the dance to begin towards them. Whatever he had to say, however, was cut off by the sudden entrance of a servant whom Cassandra did not recognise; it might have been someone he brought along from London. No words were exchanged, but rather than continue towards them, Mr Fraser turned and excused himself from the room.

"Another dance!" said Mrs Humphrey into the awkward silence that followed their host's departure. "Let us have another dance. Play something silly, Mr Griffith. I feel positively stifled by how serious the mood has become. Gilbert, come and dance with Penelope!" Gilbert, who had been headed towards the piano with a hopeful expression, stopped abruptly, his brief lightness snuffed like a candle before he turned back towards the other guests.

Cassandra genuinely felt bad for him. It was hard not to, when she compared what he had been like before to what he was now. But she would not let her pity prey upon her, not now. She preferred to focus on the man beside her, the man who had come to her aid time and again. As he began to play, she murmured, "It was your mother who taught you, was it not?"

Thomas smiled. "You remember that?"

"How could I forget? It was the second to last ball we ever met at, and you had few kind words for the poor ladies taking their turns at the pianoforte. I called you a bit cruel, and you told me that your mother had spoiled you for anyone else's music, and that of all of her children you were the only one with her musical sensibilities."

"I am impressed with your attention to detail." His hands flowed across the keys – once more, he didn't even need to look at the sheets to know where to put his fingers. "It was one conversation out of dozens you had that night."

"I always paid attention to you," Cassandra rejoined. "You know that."

"I do," he agreed. "Though I think I have not always been worthy of those attentions."

"What do you mean?"

"I mean…" He lowered his voice. "I stood by in silence while you were courted by my friend, without speaking a word as to my reservations. I thought it did not matter, not with your families being so close and me about to go off into the army. I thought there was nothing I could do, and no hope for…" He trailed off.

"No hope for what?" Cassandra asked breathlessly.

"For–" He clamped his jaw shut and shook his head. "I cannot look back," he said after a moment. "It is too painful to me to revisit so far into the past, and it cannot be any better for you. Rather, I think it best if we turn our eyes to the future."

Cassandra sighed. "And yet the future is terribly uncertain, and not likely to be benevolent either. Thomas, there are things I must tell you ..." The song ended before she could continue, and not a moment later Mrs Humphrey came over with an air of aggression.

"What *are* you two whispering about?" she demanded. "You might be engaged, but there is no call for you to be sequestered over here like a pair of monks. Whatever you are speaking of, it is rude of you not to involve the rest of us."

"We were speaking of the Beast of Avon Vale," Thomas replied, which was as good a parry as Cassandra could have hoped for. "And how we hope that we have indeed seen the last of it for a time."

"Not likely," Mr Kildeer grunted from where he'd collapsed on one of the shifted couches. "Didn't find any body there but the horse's."

"It might have run and bled out elsewhere," Colonel Cross suggested.

"Not bloody likely though, is it?"

"It's hard to say without knowing more about what kind of animal it is." Mr Kildeer focused his narrow eyes on Cassandra. "Your previous description was terribly lacking, Miss Wright. Is there nothing more you can say about your encounter with the beast?"

Not with *this* one, at least. "It was quite dark and gloomy," Cassandra said after a moment. "I did not get a good look at it. The thing which stood out most to me was the feeling of… of malice that I detected from it."

"Malice?" Mr Humphrey laughed. "How ridiculous. Animals are not capable of malice."

"No," Cassandra agreed softly. "No, they are not." The import of what she was saying spread throughout the room, filling it with a chill silence. It was only broken when a servant – a different one this time – came to announce that lunch was served.

All of a sudden, Cassandra had had enough. She was exhausted from her disrupted night, still sore from the attack yesterday, and she wasn't sure whether her heart or head ached worse after her confrontation with Mr Fraser. She could not stay. If she stayed here, she would do something foolish, something she would regret. Something like stabbing Mr Fraser with her pin or setting the tablecloth on fire.

"Thomas," she whispered. "Please…" Her throat closed up with tension, but no more was required of her. He took one long look at her face and nodded.

"I fear we shall not be able to stay," he said briskly, standing up and offering Cassandra his hand. "Miss Wright is unwell. I am going to get her back to the inn."

"Unwell?" Mrs Cross came over to her, polite concern on her face. "I have some small skill with nursing," she said. "I would be pleased to help you, if you would accompany me to my room."

"No." Cassandra cleared her throat. "No, that is not necessary, but thank you for your kindness." *And I will be damned if I allow you to lay a hand on me again.* "I would prefer to leave."

"I- I'll get the gig brought round for you, but *Thomas*," Gilbert whined, "surely you do not need to go as well." He had the look on his face of a pup being left behind by its masters: desolate while scarcely knowing the cause.

"I would not dream of doing anything else," Thomas replied, and that was the final word on the matter. They went outside, and when it became clear that the gig had not, in fact, been sent for, Thomas took it upon himself to bring it to the front of the house. He handed Cassandra up into the seat, jumped up beside her a moment later, and had them away down the road so quickly the gravel beneath the wheels sprayed up behind them. Cassandra glanced back once they were several hundred feet distant to see the tall, imposing figure of Mr Fraser standing outside, watching them depart. His face was composed, but his hands were clenched into fists at his sides, and he was still watching them when Hartson Hall was finally lost to view.

Cassandra had the feeling that she had very narrowly evaded a very bad situation.

CHAPTER FIFTEEN

"Do I need to call for the doctor once we reach the inn?" Thomas asked, his jaw set as though he was braced for the worst.

Cassandra chuckled weakly. "Do I truly look that bad?" she teased, but he was not having it.

"You look like a woman who has not slept a wink. You look like someone who has been pushed to the very edge of what she should be expected to endure, and farther than you should ever have to. I am *worried* for you, so please... tell me something to set me at ease or allow me to follow my instincts and fetch the doctor as soon as we arrive at Tarryford." He bit his lower lip for a moment. "Is it your wound? Has it become infected?"

"Oh." In light of everything else that was weighing her down, Cassandra barely felt the scratch that she'd gained yesterday. "No, you need not worry about that, it is very minor and healing well," she assured him. "I... you are correct that I did not sleep well last night, though. I read my father's journal, and the things it confirmed to me were nothing that I had hoped for."

"I am sorry to hear that." He sounded truly sorry, too. "It is never an easy thing to have our illusions dispelled, especially when they concern our parents."

"Apart from that…" Cassandra had to remind herself that she had promised she would be honest with Thomas about this. She had to unburden her heart to *someone*, or else she would break under the weight of it. "I was attacked in my room last night."

"*What*?"

It took the rest of the drive back to Tarryford for her to explain, showing him the slight bend in her hatpin as proof and assuring him that it had not been a dream, that she would not have dreamed up such a strange creature, and that she was certain it had come from Harston Hall after what had occurred to first her and then Miss Getty in the library.

Only once they pulled to a stop outside the inn had Cassandra finally exhausted her store of words. She felt wilted, like a cut flower left out in the sun, and slumped back in the seat, unable to meet Thomas's gaze. "I know it sounds mad," she whispered as Old John ambled over to take control of the horses. "But I swear to you I am telling the truth."

"I believe you," Thomas replied almost as quietly. "I think we have much to discuss, Miss Wright. Will you allow me inside with you?"

"Please," she said with relief. She did not want to be alone. She had no idea how she was going to make it through the night, she was so ready to jump at shadows.

Young Garrett welcomed them in while Mrs Copeland fussed over Cassandra's obvious fatigue. "Let me help you up to your room," the older woman said. "You can take a rest, get some more sleep. You look like you need it, lamb."

"No, please," Cassandra said. "I need to speak with Mr Griffith. Could you set aside the small dining room for us again, as well as provide a late luncheon?"

"Certainly," Mrs Copeland said after a moment. Her eyes brightened a bit when Thomas handed over enough coins to Garrett to make his jaw drop and his eyes gape.

"Sir, this is too much for a simple lunch, even when it's Ma's!"

"The money is for more than that," Thomas replied. "I would like to let one of your rooms myself, the best of whatever you have left. I… expect my sister to arrive any day now, and I am disinclined at having her go straight to Harston Hall. Until she comes, I am going to relocate to your inn, so that I may be closer to welcome her."

The pair's expressions clearly said that neither of them believed he wanted anything other than to stay close to Cassandra, but it was a falsehood that they could accept. "There's a room just down from Miss Wright's," Young Garrett said. "I'll get it ready for you, sir."

"And I'll bring the food out," Mrs Copeland added. "The room is yours for as long as you want it."

"We shall be there for some time," Thomas said. He took Cassandra's hand and led her into the dining parlour, bypassing the table in favour of seating her by the fire.

"The name you spoke of in the journal," he began, sitting

across from her but leaning in close. "The dark god, Shub-Niggurath…"

Cassandra felt her cheeks colour. "I know, it sounds ridiculous."

"On the contrary," he said tightly. "It sounds far too plausible to me. It is, indeed, a name I have encountered before. I heard it from my own brother, David, shortly before he died."

Cassandra was confused. "I thought he died while you were with your regiment."

"No. I was sent for with that excuse, but only because his poor wife did not want to reveal his true state to anyone else."

"She found it better to allow others to believe her husband was dead, rather than give you the truth of the matter?" Cassandra asked incredulously.

"Indeed. For my brother…" Thomas slowly shook his head, as if he still could not quite believe what he was about to say. "He had lost his mind, turned into an utter raving lunatic. He had been locked into the west wing of the house, and my sister-in-law turned out almost all the servants and took over his care herself.

"She was utterly dedicated to him," Thomas continued, admiration and bitterness warring in his voice. "She was trying to preserve the dignity of our family name by spreading the rumour that he had died, but she had hoped that I would be able to find another solution for them – perhaps to put him away in a distant property where she could care for him without the pressure of a large household hanging over her."

"What happened to turn him mad?"

"She did not know for certain, but Evelyn told me that David had fallen in with a new set in London that year. Farsighted people, he described them. Men who would shape the nation. He felt honoured to be drawn into their acquaintance."

Cassandra's hand rose to cover her mouth. "Oh no."

"You can guess some of the rest," Thomas agreed. "I do not believe my brother ever met Mr Fraser, or interacted with him at all. But there are more men like him out there, men who are making contact with forces that no mortal should seek to meddle with."

The way he said it, she wondered if he had personal experience with these forces. "Did you see anything of that danger yourself?" Cassandra asked after a moment. "While you were in the army?"

"Not for myself, but some of the men who had been in longer spoke of things that defy description. Shadows come alive, bodies gnawed to bones, tentacles rising from the depths of the sea… Whatever is going on, it is not merely the folk of our isle who dabble in it."

Her heart sank. "Then there will be pressure for them to continue," she said.

"Indeed. Despite my certainty that they'll all eventually choke on their own success." Thomas's face had gone grim. "David was mad, but there was a method to his madness. He wrote constantly across the walls using his own filth and blood, and one name that was in a recognisable script. That name was Shub-Niggurath. He also drew strange, elaborate symbols–"

"I have seen them," Cassandra said. "Or things like them, in my father's journal."

"Ah." Thomas's flat, grim demeanour melted into sadness. "Then he *was* a member of the cult, like my brother."

Cassandra nodded. "Until Mr Fraser finally went too far," she said. "I think he killed someone, and my father could not abide that. He indicated in his journal that he was strongly opposed to human sacrifice – in most instances, at least." She couldn't quite bring herself to talk about the "ideal woman" her father had been resigned to killing for the sake of Shub-Niggurath. And in the end, his dismay had counted for nothing at all. His body had been found in the woods near Mr Fraser's old home, his head nearly ripped apart – something a strong creature, with knife-like claws, could do.

"I believe he tried to run," she said faintly, "and… and something much like the Beast of Avon Vale ran after him, and ended his life." She let the silence that followed this confession linger for a moment, then asked, as gently as she could, "What happened to your brother? Did you get him somewhere safe?"

Thomas shook his head tightly. "No. By the time I got there… well, there was nothing of the man I had loved and admired my whole life left in this hollow, screaming shell. No one could touch him other than Evelyn, and even then he would attack her half the time. She had to have his arms tied in front of his body in a special jacket so he would not hit her. He ate like an animal when he remembered to at all, and when he slept he fell into such nightmares that the screams reverberated through the entire manor. Only one night in and I knew I would not be able to endure a second one. I have no idea how my sister-in-law dealt with him for weeks before I got there.

"In the end, though, that one night of grace was one too many. When he fell silent in the morning, I was so grateful, I…" He swallowed hard and closed his eyes, but not before Cassandra saw the well of tears beneath his lashes. "I went to sleep," he said, his voice full of threadbare grief. "And as I slept, Evelyn went to check on him. Somehow, in the night, he had freed his arms. He grabbed her as soon as she came in, dragged her against him, and…"

He paused, then untied his cravat and undid the top buttons on his stiff, starched shirt. Cassandra did not know what to think until he turned his head to the side and, all of a sudden, she saw the blood-red scar in the tender skin of his neck. It was healed over but not old enough to have faded much, and in the light of day she could very clearly see the outline of teeth marks.

"Her screams roused me, but by the time I got there it was too late for poor Evelyn. I barely escaped with my own life."

"I am so sorry." Cassandra laid her hand on his arm, hoping that the feel of her grounded him and let him set aside the vile memories that clearly clamoured for attention in his mind.

"I had to end things then and there, before… well. It was already far too late, but there was a growing cunning to my brother's madness that I was not going to test myself against." He looked straight at Cassandra. "Do you think me a monster for what I did?"

"No," she insisted, only keeping her voice down by

force of will. How could she consider him a monster for putting a man out of what sounded like terrible misery and suffering? "No, I absolutely do not. I could *never*, Thomas, I could never think such a thing of you. You were presented with an impossible choice, and I am certain that you did the very best you could with it."

"Would that I could be so sure of myself," he muttered. "I recriminate myself for the past daily, especially with regards to Evelyn. I failed to protect her, even after she called for my aid. I failed her, fatally, and I… Cassandra." He reached out and took her hand. "I could not live with myself if I failed you as well."

His words made her heart flutter in her chest, but only for a moment. That he was devoted to her safety was an unexpected treasure, but the fact that he was so devoted out of a sense of guilt over the death of his brother and sister-in-law was less welcome.

What did you expect? For him to actually be in love with you? For him to fall for the charms of a woman with no station in life apart from what you have eked out with your wits and your hands? You two are not of the same status, and you would do well to remember that.

That he wishes to help you put an end to this vileness is enough. It must be.

"Cassandra?" She startled, realising she had drifted off for a moment. Thomas's face was nearer to hers than it had been before. "Are you well?"

"I am," she assured him, loathing her own falseness but hoping that he believed her regardless. "Ah, Mrs Copeland is here!" Cassandra had never been more grateful for an interruption in her life as she disengaged from Thomas and stood up.

"A little luncheon for the pair of you," Mrs Copeland said cheerfully as she set down a tray on the table. "Cold meats and cheeses, some bread fresh from the ovens this morning, and a pot of tea." She laid it all out for them, then vanished as swiftly as she came.

Regretfully – or thankfully, perhaps – the mood was thoroughly broken by then. Cassandra and Thomas sat and ate, and for a time she was even able to set her cares aside and devote her attention to things other than death and madness. It was delightful.

"Francine is not truly on her way here, is she?" Cassandra asked as she spread a piece of bread with butter.

"No," Thomas replied, layering his own bread with several thick cuts of cheese and ham. "Francine has been staying with our aunt and uncle in London for the past… heavens, it is two years now," he said, sounding slightly surprised by the passage of so much time. "She was, of course, staying with my brother before that, but Evelyn was wise enough to send her away when things began to be… uncertain. My aunt and uncle have no children of their own and have welcomed her into their household. She is excessively spoiled by them, I am sure."

"I remember her as such a serious, dutiful girl," Cassandra said, recalling a coltish child with the same dark hair and quiet demeanour as her brother. "I daresay she could benefit from a little spoiling."

"I confess, I contribute to the condition myself," Thomas said with a smile. "I never wanted her to feel as though she had been exiled from our family home, and yet functionally that is exactly what has occurred. Repairs are underway, but with just me there, it has been easier to restrict myself to the east wing and work with people I trust implicitly, rather than bring a larger crew of workers in to restore things. With the more parasitic members of my family flocking to the estate to 'oversee' things, I'm quite happy to be gone from the place." He shook his head. "But what of your own siblings? Your brother ended up in the navy, did he not?"

"Yes, he is a midshipman now, but he will be up for his lieutenant's exam when he comes ashore at the end of the month," Cassandra replied. "He has taken and failed it once, but he assures me that is quite normal."

"I've heard the same. It is a very challenging career, but if anyone could make a go of it, it's your brother."

"He is quite clever," Cassandra agreed. "He has always been very clever, very brave, sometimes excessively so, and I worry he passed that inclination on to our younger sister. Elizabeth does not know the meaning of fear."

"You think he is the one who passed it on to her?" Thomas laughed. "To my recollection, *you* are the one who set the example of fearlessness within your family. You were constantly putting yourself into positions where no other woman dared to tread for fear of reprisal, and you always emerged victorious."

"Oh, I was not so bad," Cassandra demurred.

"There was nothing bad about it, just... you were

startling. Your knowledge of languages, your extensive understanding of your father's library, how you were prepared to argue moral philosophy with anyone from the groomsmen to a visiting lord... Your actions always struck me as quite brave. So do not denigrate yourself as though courage is a virtue you do not possess."

Courage, Cassandra thought, could be both a vice and a virtue. She was not yet sure where it would land in this situation, but there was nothing for it but to move forward and hope for the best. "We shall have to hope we both have enough courage for what lies ahead," she said. "For I do not believe the beast is gone, nor do I believe Mr Fraser will be able to take it alive." She sighed and pushed her plate away. "I will go and fetch my father's journal, as well as my translation of it. If we are going to be partners in this endeavour, you should know everything that I do."

"Thank you," Thomas said, and she left feeling the prickling heat of his unwavering gaze upon her.

The journal was not so much a revelation as a confirmation to Thomas of the connection between the cult his brother had been a member of and the "Brotherhood of the Black Goat," as Mr Fraser had ostentatiously dubbed his group.

"This one," he said grimly, pointing at one of the larger and more complex symbols on the pages. "This was the one that my brother drew over and over again. I do not know what it is intended to do, but I have scrubbed it off enough walls to be able to see it in my sleep."

Cassandra pictured it in her mind's eye for a moment:

Thomas down to his shirtsleeves, rag in hand, furiously wiping at a wall that bore the evidence of everything that had gone wrong in his brother's life. She shook her head to clear it as quick as she could, lest the unhappiness of it drag her down. There was another aspect of this that was preying on her mind, one that she felt she could no longer ignore.

"Thomas," she said slowly, "if Mr Fraser is as deeply involved in this cult as we suspect him to be, do you think it can be possible that Gilbert is ignorant of it? After all, he is his father's oldest child, the only boy, the heir apparent."

Thomas snorted a laugh. "I believe if there is anyone capable of ignorance on this scale, it is Gilbert. Moreover, I do not think that he has the capacity for true wickedness. Heavens, you saw him during the hunt, how he screamed with fright like a child. That is what Gilbert is, what he has been enabled to remain his whole life – a child."

"However did you become friends with him?" The two men had already been close before Cassandra met either of them.

"We met at school," Thomas said, and oh, yes, Cassandra recalled that now. "Our families were not acquainted with each other, and they never bridged that gap in the intervening years, but it did not take much kindness for Gilbert to cling to me like a burr would Merlin's fur." He turned sombre for a moment. "Fools, the both of them.

"Gilbert was kind to me when I needed kindness, however," Thomas went on. "When my father died, he was the first to reach out with condolences, and he wrote to me religiously while I was with my regiment. After my brother's death, it was all I could do to prevent him from riding out to my home and taking part in cleaning it up himself." Thomas shook his head. "He thought it all merely an excitingly sordid tale of murder and suicide, of course, but I believe his heart was in the right place.

"Is he easily led? Clearly. Look at the people whom his father surrounds him with. Sycophants who have nothing in common with Gilbert but a desire to please Mr Fraser himself. But that is not necessarily his fault."

"No, it is not," Cassandra agreed. "I hope that one day he is able to extricate himself from the web his father has wound around him."

"Cassandra…" Thomas caught her gaze. "Forgive me if this is an impertinent question, but… did you love him?"

Oh, heavens… It was an incredibly impertinent question, but Cassandra wanted to answer it regardless. She felt Thomas deserved to know how she really felt about his friend, so that even if he did not suspect she was falling for him, he would at least not think she entertained any idea of resurrecting her engagement with Gilbert if they ever managed to get Mr Fraser out of the picture.

"I liked him well enough," she said honestly. "He was kind, and attentive, and I thought that was a good enough basis for a marriage to go on. He was not exactly what I had hoped for in a husband, no. I never felt more than simple affection for him, but my father was so delighted by the prospect of a match between us that I felt I would not regret it." She smiled. "Let me assure you, I would rather throw myself from the Dover cliffs than wish I had gotten the chance to marry Gilbert before everything fell apart. If I had been tied to that family permanently..." Cassandra shuddered. "It does not bear thinking about."

"I am relieved to hear that." Before she could ask anything about the nature of his relief, he moved on to asking about another section of the journal.

They spent hours poring over it together, sharing what knowledge they could. The only disruption to their day, apart from a hearty dinner, was the arrival of a footman from Harston Hall who came with notes for both of them from the master of the house.

Thomas read his quickly and tossed it aside just as fast. "What does he say?" Cassandra asked.

"He offers me a rebuke for disdaining his hospitality and requests I behave like a proper guest and return to the house at my earliest convenience. Which shall come no sooner than tomorrow," Thomas said, and Cassandra felt herself settle a bit at the reminder that she would have Thomas nearby tonight. "We cannot ignore the man entirely, but we do not need him to do our own work tracking down the Beast of Avon Vale. And you?" He gestured to her note. "What does he say to you?"

"Let me find out." Cassandra pulled out the gilt-edged paper and began to read.

Miss Wright,
*   I am told by my son that you are indisposed. I*
hope this sudden illness of yours does not continue

*long. The pleasure of your company, a memory which
had grown quite thin over the years, is undeniable.
I believe your father would wish me to show you
every courtesy, and of course my son delights in your
presence.*

*I request and require that you return to Harston
Hall tomorrow.*

Yours, etc.

Mr James Fraser, Esq.

"Require and request?" Thomas said after Cassandra handed it over to him. "Who does he think he is, the king? He does not get to require anything of you."

"And yet he attempts to do so with no sign of self-consciousness," she said wryly. "I wonder how elevated his inner circle has become that he feels he can take such a tone with people."

"How fortunate that we do not have to care." Thomas burned his note in the fireplace. After a moment's hesitation, Cassandra passed hers over and let him burn that as well, then stifled a yawn behind her hand. Lord, she was so tired. Her sleepless night was catching up to her in a final great swell, and it felt like all she could do to keep her eyes open.

"You appear very done with this day," Thomas remarked with a hint of a smile in his voice. "Shall I accompany you upstairs and see you safely to your room?"

"That would be lovely," Cassandra sighed, then shuddered with the memory of last night. "And if you would not mind – I have had the window closed all day, there should be no way my room has been invaded, but if you would not mind helping me look about and make sure the rat-thing is not there, I would greatly appreciate it."

"Ah." The edge of humour he'd acquired left his face immediately. "Of course. I cannot imagine how difficult it will be for you to face the night with the spectre of that encounter in your mind."

"I shall manage it as best I can," she said, but she already knew her sense of vigilance was going to have her waking up every hour. "If I am perfectly useless tomorrow, though, I hope you will make my excuses."

"Or you could allow me to sleep in your room."

Until this moment, Cassandra had not known that one's mind could skip a beat, much as the heart could. She stared at Thomas, utterly unable to say anything at all, and after a moment he appeared to realise what he'd just suggested.

"On the floor!" he exclaimed far too loudly. "On the floor, I – no, I was not asking to sleep in your – Miss Wright, you have my abject apologies, I never meant to insinuate that you would find it acceptable for me to – to–"

Cassandra broke into a laugh. "No, I do understand that. I was simply taken aback by your phrasing. I know you would never take advantage of me in such a way." She knew it as easily as she knew her own name. "And I believe I would welcome your presence, sir. It would ease my mind knowing that I am not alone. Or we could exchange rooms," she added, but he immediately shook his head.

"The chances that the creature would continue searching

for you until it found you alone are too high. We will be safer together."

Oh, she hoped that was true.

It would be far from the first time that Cassandra had shared a room. With her previous employer, she had shared not only a room but a bed with Mary, the chambermaid, or bedded down with one of the children if they had suffered from a nightmare. This would be no different, she told herself. No different at all.

It went without saying that they had to maintain the appearance of keeping separate rooms. Cassandra had no reputation to speak of, but she would not allow Thomas's to be besmirched. So she went to hers, searching it thoroughly for any sign of life with her hatpin in hand, and he went to his. It was not until the lights were doused and the sounds of voices had finally given way to silence that he finally came to her again.

Despite the innocence of his gesture, it nevertheless felt incredibly illicit to open the door at his discreet knock and usher him inside, especially given that he was wearing only his breeches and shirt, untucked. She had made as good a bed for him as she could on the floor, giving over her thick comforter and the extra pillow on the bed. "Will this do well enough for you?" she asked anxiously.

"It will suit me fine," Thomas assured her. "I slept far more roughly at times with my regiment. Did you inspect the room already?"

"I did. The window was still locked shut when I came in, but I looked all around just to be certain. There was nothing out of the ordinary, but you can check again if it makes you feel better."

"I have full faith in your abilities, but better to be overzealous in this case," he said gently, and proceeded to look beneath tables and chairs, shift her trunk and bed enough to peer behind them, and rearrange the bedding and curtains. "Nothing. Thank you for indulging me."

"Oh, not at all," Cassandra replied, all of a sudden feeling rather sheepish that she had invited him in so swiftly. It seemed a massive overreaction, especially considering he had found nothing of all out of place in her chamber. "I am sorry for troubling you with this. Perhaps you ought to return to your room after all."

"No, please." He stopped in front of her and reached for her hand, then seemed to think better of it. "Allow me to do this," he said. "It will make me feel far more comfortable knowing I am here for you."

How could her heart beat so quickly? When would it accept that he was not for her? "Thank you," she murmured. "Then… then I suppose I bid you goodnight."

"Indeed. Goodnight, Miss Wright."

The layer of formality, given their situation, made her grin. "You are making a bed of my floor, sir," she pointed out. "I think you may safely call me Cassandra."

"Then you must call me Thomas," he insisted. "Goodnight… Cassandra."

"Goodnight." They both bedded down, and as soon as Thomas nodded up at her, Cassandra blew out the last remaining candle. The room was plunged into almost total darkness, but she did not feel afraid this time. For all that her heart pounded, for all that she was acutely aware of the man sharing her space, Cassandra also felt a sense of pure and utter relief.

I am not alone. I have nothing to fear. Not while he is with me.

She fell asleep so fast she scarcely knew it was happening, and slept as deeply as a child who has spent all day at play.

And she was not wakened until the screaming began at dawn, just outside the inn.

CHAPTER SIXTEEN

"Mercy!" It was a boy's voice, familiar – it had to be Young Garrett. "God have mercy! Old John! John's dead!"

Cassandra, startled but still groggy, had barely lifted her head off her pillow when Thomas jumped to his feet and raced over to the window. "Do not be seen!" she cautioned him just as he threw the curtains back.

"No, of course," he agreed, and did not open the window but peered as best he could out of it. "People are gathering out front," he said. "I must go."

"Yes, go, go," she said, her heart filling with dread. "I will join you as soon as I am able."

Thomas turned and strode for the door, but a second before opening it he looked back at her. "Are you well?"

"Very well," she assured him. "You guarded my sleep impeccably."

He nodded, and – was that a hint of a blush? A moment later he left, and Cassandra hastened through changing and dressing as the entire inn – nay, perhaps the entire town – descended into an uproar.

By the time Cassandra emerged downstairs, the

beginnings of a coherent story had emerged. The cries had indeed come from one of the stable boys whose family owned a farm just north of Tarryford. He had been on his way in to work this morning when he was distracted by the buzz of flies a little way off the road – a cloud large enough that a corpse must be nearby. With all the brashness of a youth, he had run *towards* the flies, eager to see the remains of whatever cow or dog or sheep the Beast had attacked this time.

To find instead the body of Old John, "his whole middle missing!" the hysterical lad had said over and over again, had given him the shock of his life. He'd run into town, so breathless with fear that he could not even scream until he'd reached the relative safety of The Four Feathers, at which point his voice reasserted itself quite dramatically. Young Garrett seemed to vacillate wildly between both envy over the story and grief that Old John had been the Beast's unfortunate victim. Cassandra shared that grief; John had been kind to her ever since her arrival and had even warned her about the beast. To think that it had ended his life so viciously made her sick with sorrow.

Since then, two more had come to confirm his tale, and Thomas, along with one of the braver farmers who had his own wagon, had gone to see about the body. That Thomas was here, with his gleaming sword and his imperturbable gaze, was undeniably helpful. Nevertheless, after his departure there were plenty of murmurs about not only him, but the entire party at Harston.

"Useless gentlefolk," one of the men said, spitting into

the dirt nearby. "They put on a great song an' dance about bein' here to hunt this beast from hell, then spend all their time riding about with nothing to show for it!"

"And yet they expect to be lauded as heroes every time they enter the town," another man – Cassandra thought she recognised the tailor – agreed. "I shall certainly be extending no more lines of credit to them, I promise you that. They can threaten me all they like, but I won't do it."

More people spoke up, murmurs becoming grumbles becoming shouts, until they were just a few minutes away from being a mob, ready to march on Harston Hall and all who lived there. Cassandra could not allow that to happen. She readied herself to step forwards, but a strong hand on her arm pulled her back into the shadows of the inn.

"Not a good time to draw attention to yourself," Mrs Copeland said, quiet but firm.

"But–"

"Let 'em get it out of their system. They won't do anything to harm your man."

Cassandra wasn't so sure. When one of the men announced that he could see Thomas returning in the distance, a roar went up. The whole crowd moved to meet him, and Cassandra couldn't bear for him to return to such a desperate state, to people who were afraid and ready to wield their fear against him. She pulled against Mrs Copeland's grip, then froze as a voice rose in the distance.

"What is the meaning of this?"

That was not Thomas. That was Mr Fraser, and he did

not sound pleased. Nor did he sound cowed. In fact, he sounded furious.

"We bring you the body of your own departed friend, and this is the thanks we get?" he continued.

"Wouldn't be bringin' his body if you'd killed the beast already!" someone shouted. "Your people said–"

"My *people*?" The dangerous edge to his voice sharpened even further. "Do you mean my son? My friends? Perhaps you mean the lord of this place, who is *also* my friend. Shall I write to him and inform him that his land is in rebellion, and see what response that merits? Shall I have the regiments drawn away from our desperate war with France to put down an uprising in our own kingdom? Shall you people of Tarryford, too fearful to go after this terrible beast on your own, finally show the will to fight *something*, even if that means the death of every man here?"

The furore was dying down fast. Mr Fraser painted a dire picture for the people of Tarryford – to be judged in rebellion against their lawful lord would lead to swift and undoubtedly severe action by the crown.

"Help us track the beast down, and the person who leads me to it shall be given ten pounds," Mr Fraser went on, and now the murmur was back, interested this time. Cassandra had to hand it to the man; pivoting them from fear to greed was masterful. Most of these men would never make ten pounds in a full year. "Or stand in my way and be treated like the criminal you are."

There came many muttered apologies and "wouldn't dream of it, sir", and soon enough the crowd dispersed except for those who remained to see to Old John's body, which was to be taken to Upper Tarryford Church.

"The Beast has grown very bold indeed," Mrs Copeland said, staring at Cassandra's shoulder for a moment before looking up at her face. "Do you believe they'll be able to kill it?"

"I am sure of it," Cassandra replied, keeping to herself that killing it was no longer the goal. *Why does he want it captured? What does he hope to gain?*

How long has this beast even been here?

Since it was possible that Mr Fraser was not, in fact, the one who had summoned the Beast of Avon Vale here, it would serve her well to try and ascertain when the creature first came to these lands, and how.

Perhaps the parish records might be of some use to her.

Thomas finally emerged from the crowd, his mouth set in a grim line. "I must return to the house," he said quietly. "We need to organise another hunt immediately. Will you be all right here, or…" He glanced towards Mr Fraser. "Would you prefer to come with me?"

That was the easiest question she had ever been asked. "I shall stay," she said. "And, ah, should I expect to meet with you again for dinner this evening?"

"Absolutely." He looked like he wanted to say more, but a sharp shout from Mr Fraser cut him short. "I'll distract him, you go."

Cassandra nodded and went back into the inn, slowly climbed the stairs to her room, and watched from her window as the crowd milled about below, people conversing in hushed clusters as they spoke of Old John's terrible death. She decided it would be best to head out by herself in the early afternoon, once the furore had died down. There were several churches in and adjacent to Tarryford, including St. Bridget's Church, which was closest. However, it was not the "working" church of the town, the one which held the records and tended to most of the baptisms and funerals and the like. That one was called Upper Tarryford Church, and it was a fifteen-minute walk to the southwest of the town.

Cassandra made good time there, not wishing to linger in the streets even though she knew, from personal experience, that the beast did not care to be caught in the light. However, logic was not as comforting as it ought to be when one had just been confronted with the body of a man so cruelly killed.

Tears, unwelcome but impossible to stop, welled up in Cassandra's eyes as she headed down the country lane towards the steeples rising in the distance. Old John may not have been the most accomplished man in the town – certainly he was far from the soberest, even on his best days it seemed – but he had been one of the first people here to extend a hand of kindness to Cassandra. He had warned her about the very beast that had ended up killing him, in fact.

Poor man. And yet I must hope that his death was merely the work of a bloodthirsty monster, rather than part of a more sinister scheme at the hands of Mr Fraser.

Cassandra was aware that she was quite possibly giving

her nemesis too great a reputation for wicked cleverness, but in this case, she felt it better to assume the worst and be happily surprised than to be caught unawares.

After another minute of silent walking, she reached the church itself. It was a good-sized building with stained-glass windows along the sides and at the back, but apart from that it was rather humble on the inside. The pews were simple benches with no backs, and the crucifix on the wall was unpainted, polished brown wood. Despite its simplicity, it seemed like a welcoming place, and Cassandra felt her shoulders relax as she closed the door behind her. She had not even realised how tense they were.

"Hello?" she called out. The vicarage where the parish records were likely stored was behind the church, but as that was also where the reverend himself lived, she did not simply want to invite herself in.

"Good day," a voice replied from behind her. Cassandra jumped and turned in a flash, her heart pounding from the surprise of it all. Five feet away from her stood a Black man in the sober garb of a preacher, a look of polite dismay on his face.

"Oh heavens, I apologise," he said, shaking his head. "I did not mean to startle you so. I was simply replacing the candle as you came in." He gestured to the tall, white candle in the corner behind him. "I'm afraid from your angle you could not see me as you entered. Forgive me, miss…"

"Wright, sir, Miss Wright, and I confess I did not see you at all," Cassandra said, "but that is certainly not your fault." She curtsied politely, and he bowed back.

"I am Reverend Jennings," he said. "I am honoured to make your acquaintance, Miss Wright."

"And I yours." Pleasantries out of the way, Cassandra dove straight into what had brought her here. "I assume you have already learned of the terrible death of Mr…" It occurred to her too late that she did not actually know the poor man's last name. "John," she finished.

"I did indeed. Hard not to, the way people were yelling about it," he added, one hand going to clasp the cross around his neck. "What a terrible way for him to die. I do not normally offer services on weekdays, but I am planning a special one this evening for any who feel the need for comfort in this time of crisis."

"I think there are numerous folk who will take you up on that," Cassandra said.

"But not you," Reverend Jennings guessed with a little smile, which Cassandra returned.

"I am afraid not, sir. Actually, I am here today because I have an interest in looking at the parish records."

"Really?" He appeared a bit bemused by her statement. "Do you have family from this area?"

"Not precisely," she said. How did one go about explaining an interest in the strangest deaths in the area, all with the goal of discovering whether or not a cult that worshipped dark gods from another realm was new to the region or had existed in some incarnation before. "I–"

Before she could finish her sentence, the door to the church slammed open. Cassandra was surprised that anyone could move such a large, heavy door with such force, and more surprised when a tall but ascetically thin woman marched inside. She wore black, the sort of dusty shade of black that let one know her dress had been in use for many years, and on her head was a cap that was little more than a single piece of ancient black lace. The only decoration she wore was a small gold cross, but she carried herself with an air of command that would not have been out of place in a general.

"Reverend Jennings!" the woman announced in a strident voice. "I am here to plan the funeral of that wretched man."

"Ah, Mrs Hobb." The reverend didn't seem surprised by the woman's sudden appearance or outburst. "Welcome. I am gratified to hear you embrace this act of charity, but you should know that John's body was taken to St Bridget's Church rather than mine. It is entirely possible that Reverend Choke will conduct services for him instead."

"Haaa!" The older woman managed to draw the word out until it was practically haggard. "That will be the day, sir, I assure you! The Lord would sooner come down from Heaven than Choke would allow his church to be sullied with 'local riffraff,' as though he isn't anything more than a jumped-up local lad who caught the right eye. He'll send him here once he realises he won't get any more attention from having him."

Her gaze tracked to Cassandra and immediately narrowed. "I do not recognise you," she said stiffly.

"I am Miss Wri—"

"If *I* do not recognise you, it means you're not one of us," the woman snapped. "Which likely means you're one of that rich man's party. Well, let me *tell* you something, miss!"

"Mrs Hobb," Reverend Jennings said in an exasperated tone, "please desist from–"

"It is people like *you*," Mrs Hobb said – shouted, rather, in a voice that rose in volume and stridency with every word, "godless layabouts with more money than sense, who have brought evil back to Tarryford once more! At least the Northlakes had the excuse of a lengthy history in the area, although that does not excuse their *savage* ways. But to come here from your fancy 'town' and behave as though you own every man jack of us, as though we are nothing but servants to do your bidding, and to expose us to another round of your evil at the same time! It oughtn't to be born, you wretched young woman, and *you* ought to be ashamed for being party to such damnable, God-forsaken things."

Well. Cassandra could now say with some surety that looking at the parish records would be illuminating. She did rather take offence at being lumped in with Mr Fraser and his sycophants, but Reverend Jennings was there and intervening before she or Mrs Hobb could speak again.

"Madam, this is not appropriate," he said, redirecting her ire away from Cassandra firmly. "However, upon reflection I do believe you may be correct about the funeral. I would be more than happy to discuss the appropriate scriptures to read after I take care of Miss Wright, here.

"The records are this way," he said, extending his arm to Cassandra. She took it, glad for the excuse to leave this judgemental woman's company, and walked with him through a small door at the front of the church, down a hallway, and into a large sitting room. One wall was completely taken up with leatherbound volumes, none of them marked.

"I am afraid I cannot spare the time to offer you tea," Reverend Jennings said with a bit of humour, "for I have a rather pressing matter waiting for me in the church."

"I will be perfectly fine," Cassandra assured him.

"And, if I may…" He pointed at the book at the very end of the second shelf. "That one, and the one preceding it, seem most likely to have what I think you are looking for."

Cassandra found herself grateful she was working with a man with such perspicacity. "I very much appreciate your guidance, sir."

"It is no trouble. I hope you find what you are looking for." He paused, then added, "And whatever your goal is, I hope you guard yourself well. There has been a great deal of upheaval in the first families around Tarryford of late, and I would hate to see you run afoul of the same ill wind."

He inclined his head, then left before Cassandra could ask for clarification. Given that he was using himself as a human barrier between her and the indomitable Mrs Hobb, Cassandra was more grateful than regretful. "All right, then," she said, turning back to the books. "Let us discover your secrets, Tarryford."

CHAPTER SEVENTEEN

She began at the back of the most recent volume of records, where an elegant hand listed out the names of local people who had married, babies that had been born and christened, and those who had passed away – largely, it seemed, of age or natural causes such as apoplexy, typhoid, or the ever-present consumption.

There were a few accidents in there as well: a young boy run over by a cart, a man falling from the roof of the barn he was building and breaking his neck, and a woman who choked to death on a fishbone. And, oh – so many babes died during birth, and half of them took their mothers with them.

That was how Cassandra's mother had died, in agony during the birth of her fourth child. Cassandra had been nine years old, deemed old enough to help by the doctor, but her mother, in what was perhaps a prescient move, had insisted that her daughter not be allowed in the bedchamber. She had sat outside it instead, listening as her mother's pants turned to screams and, eventually, to silence. The child, another brother, had never drawn a breath.

Do not get distracted. Keep looking.

Cassandra moved backwards in time, each page a connection to the lives and deaths of the many people who lived close enough for the church to be the record of their existence. It was fascinating, even the mundanity of it – here, where a farmer insisted on a burial for his prize bullock after the creature had… had…

Had its stomach ripped from its gut.

Where had this happened? A bit of sleuthing and the discovery of a neatly drawn map of the parish framed on the wall was enough to show that the death had occurred to the north and east of Tarryford, on the far side of Ferris Woods. Cassandra skimmed the next few pages, looking for more incidents in the same area, but apparently not everyone was as inclined to mourn their livestock as this particular farmer. She had almost given it up until she saw an entry from four years ago that froze her hand in place.

John Carmichael, aged forty-two, farmhand. Died
of a dog attack, which severely wounded his throat
leading to exsanguination. The animal in question has
not yet been identified.

Was it possible that, rather than a bad dog, this was an early atrocity by the Beast of Avon Vale? Perhaps it had not yet grown confident in its hunting ability, and therefore was more tentative in its attacks? A ripped-out throat was no laughing matter, to be sure, but it was a far cry from an assault that was aggressive enough to decapitate a horse.

A few pages further, and then things became considerably more dire. *The Northlake family...* every single one of them had died following the death of the family's only daughter, Elizabeth. Cassandra could not be sure from her reading exactly what the cause of death for the young woman had been; all that was noted down was that she had not committed suicide, but her death had nonetheless been violent, resulting in her exsanguination. The day after her death, her father had apparently gone mad with the loss of his only child and burned his enormous manor house, with him in it, to the ground.

Cassandra recalled that she'd seen the ruins of a great home on her way into town, just as she crested the hill that looked down on Tarryford. None of Gilbert's party had spoken of it, and neither had anyone in town. Was that out of a sense of respect for the departed, or one of fear?

There was an addendum next to Elizabeth's name: *See century marks.* Now what could that be about? A century mark... a hundred years previous, perhaps? Cassandra turned her attention to the shelves again, searching for a volume dated to a hundred and five years ago. It took some work, but she finally homed in on the correct book. She took it out and paged through it until she found, in spidery, faded writing, the name William Northlake, aged six months, dying. That in and of itself was not terribly unusual; infants died frequently, but... Cassandra went another hundred years back.

Blanche Northlake, age 6. Accidental stabbing.

Accidental stabbing... another exsanguination. Hmm...

Cassandra checked again and was able to go another hundred years back, but this book had been damaged by damp at some point – the pages were spotted with mildew, and she could barely make out enough to verify that there was indeed a Northlake who died a hundred years previous to the last. If there had been more information once, it was lost to her now, but this was enough to send Cassandra back to the newer volumes with a more avid interest.

Delving deeper into recent years, she could see a string of deaths in the town itself around the same time, all connected to the tavern. Apparently, the incidents had been resolved, or at least ignored until they stopped. *Sleeping deaths...* what could cause such a thing? Some sort of fever?

Or something worse?

Cassandra noted all the names, dates, and places of interest in her personal journal. Some of the locations in particular held an interest for her, as they were places where strange things had happened to people – sometimes resulting in death or disappearance, as with the vanishing of Robert Williams under very strange circumstances. His sister Diana had fled Tarryford shortly thereafter, and their estate, Mortview House, was apparently abandoned.

The idea that there was a connection between the Beast of Avon Vale and the terrible things that had occurred in and around this town a few years ago was, it seemed, not so far-fetched as Cassandra thought.

She was just closing the ledger up when Reverend Jennings returned to join her. "I see you have made good use of your time, Miss Wright," he said with a smile, gesturing to the various books on the table.

"Indeed I have," she agreed. "I was just about to put them away, I promise."

"No need, I will handle that."

Cassandra shook her head. "No, I cannot allow books to remain unshelved once no longer in use. The student in me shall not allow it."

Internally, she wanted to grab herself by the arm and shake. *Why must you bring the past into this?* But the reverend didn't ask any curious questions, merely nodded and helped her put things neatly back in their place.

"If you're interested," Reverend Jennings said as he escorted Cassandra back to the front of the church, "my most dedicated parishioner and I have determined that as he has no family to step in, we shall be hosting John's funeral here tomorrow. I received word that his body has been remanded to the undertaker already, so it does not make sense to delay." *In the growing heat,* he did not say, but Cassandra could read between the lines. Her mother and the baby had been buried four days after their deaths to allow time for family to arrive, but that had only been possible thanks to the coolness of their cellars.

"What time is the funeral to be?" Cassandra asked.

"Ten in the morning."

She nodded. That was a useful time; apart from her wishing to be here no matter what the hour of the funeral was, an event in the morning would prevent her from rejoining the party at Harston. There was certainly no risk of Mr Fraser showing his face in this small, local church for the sake of a drunk old man. "I shall endeavour to be here."

"I appreciate it." He stepped outside with her, and Cassandra was surprised to find the shadows long already. She must have spent hours with those records. Reverend Jennings bowed to her. "Go with God, Miss Wright."

She curtsied back. "My thanks, sir." She paused, then added, "Be safe."

He nodded seriously. "You as well."

Good. They understood one another quite well.

Cassandra returned to The Four Feathers in a thoughtful, somewhat dark mood. A man's life had been taken, taken by a creature who may have been hiding, killing, and getting away with it for *years* now, even though Mr Fraser had only lived in the area for one. What hope did the party at Harston Hall truly have of killing it, much less catching it? How long would it be before they tired of sport with no resolution? There was nothing tying them here to this place; they could return to London or some other estate and never think on it again. Not so the people who lived in Tarryford. What could they do but endure, as they had endured for half a decade now?

Cassandra did not care for Mrs Hobb, but she had to admit that the woman's complaint against the gentry was a palpable hit.

Thomas was not waiting for her back at the inn. No matter, he would surely be along soon. Cassandra distracted herself by opening her notebook and writing out a formal timeline of events. It was now five years since the death of Elizabeth Northlake; that event seemed to be the start of all these ills, at least in this current time. She and all of her immediate family had died in that single, awful season. The sleeping sickness had not struck until the next year, but the first suspicious death among the people of Tarryford came six months before that, and continued in similar increments.

How often did the Beast of Avon Vale need to feed? To sleep? Did it have a sense of intelligence that allowed it to be cautious, or was it a ravening creature held back by something else? Cassandra found herself slightly disgusted to realise that she *agreed* in part with Mr Fraser – it would be fascinating to study such a being. That said, there was no way she could think of that would make that possible. Not without putting too many people in danger, and even then she did not want to be cruel, not to anyone or anything, if she could help it. If this beast truly was nothing more than an animal, murderous though it may be, then it did not deserve to be tortured for sport.

There was a knock on her room's door. "Miss Wright?" Mrs Copeland called. "Mr Griffith is here, and I've got dinner set aside for you downstairs."

"Oh, thank you." Cassandra locked her notes up, tucked the key to her trunk safely onto her person, then headed downstairs. Thomas, for once, was not ready and waiting for her to arrive. Rather he seemed lost in thought, standing by the fireplace and staring into the flames as though they contained the answer to a desperate question. He had changed his clothes from earlier, and his hair was still damp from the bath.

He was likely covered in blood, if he helped move poor John's body.

The thought disturbed Cassandra, and she impulsively walked over and took Thomas's hand. He startled, turning sharply towards her, but the sight of her lightened the shadows in his eyes.

"Cass," he said, his face so close to hers, body so warm from the fire… she was struck with the urge to lean in and kiss him, to lay claim to the mouth that spoke her name so sweetly. *Cass.* No one else had ever called her that; it was always Cassie when they used a diminutive. This felt like something just for them, and she wanted to acknowledge it so very badly.

You cannot be so forward with him. You shall ruin everything!

As much as she hated the voice of reason that warred with sentiment in her heart, she knew in this case that it was correct. So instead of leaning in, instead of tilting her head just right and inviting the press of his lips on hers, she squeezed his hand once, then let go and took a small step back. "Are you well?" she asked quietly.

"Well enough," he said, sounding slightly despondent. He must be thinking about the horror of his morning. "Mr Fraser and I ensured that the man's body was taken to St Bridget's Church, but the reverend there informed us that as the dead man is a *common peasant–*" he almost spat the demarcation out "*–*he is to be given to the care of the church just outside town. I have not yet visited to ensure that–"

"I was there earlier today," Cassandra said, daring to interrupt if it meant easing Thomas's mind. "Upper Tarryford Church is run by Reverend Jennings, who is prepared to conduct a funeral tomorrow. He asked if I would attend, and I believe I shall. You are under no compulsion to come yourself, but–"

Now it was his turn to interrupt. "Nonsense. I would not hear of you going alone, and it is the least I can do for the poor man after so miserably failing him."

Cassandra shook her head. "You did not fail him."

"Did I not?" Thomas laughed, but it was a bitter sound. "This hunt may not have been my idea, but I went along with it. I was excited for it, in fact, ready to occupy myself with something other than the misery of my memories and the welfare of my sister for the first time in two years. I spent three years in military service, and before that I frequently hunted alongside my father and brother. That the Beast of Avon Vale yet lives, and escaped after nearly taking *your* life as well, is inexcusable."

He sighed and pressed the heel of his hand to his forehead for a moment. "When I saw the body of that poor soul, I... he looked worse than anything I ever saw in the war. The wounds he took... my mind could not help imposing them on my image of–" He stopped himself there, but Cassandra could guess what he was going to say.

I saw you killed the same way.

Thomas had a gentle heart despite the trials he had

been through. Seeing such visions of someone he had selflessly dedicated himself to helping had to be an awful experience. Feeling very bold, Cassandra took his hand once more. "You saved me," she told him. "And I have faith that you and the others shall be able to find and kill this beast." It went without saying that killing it was preferable to letting Mr Fraser have his way with it. Judging from the nod Thomas gave her, he agreed.

Speaking of Mr Fraser, it was better perhaps not to share any of her darker revelations from her visit to the church yet with Thomas. He had more than enough on his mind.

The rest of the evening passed pleasantly, with quiet conversation and a generous meal provided by Mrs Copeland and Young Garrett, who was eager for any and all information that Thomas could give him about the beast. "Got to know what to expect, right? Where to look for it?" the boy said more than once. "If I found it and led you to it, I'd get that reward, right? That'd help Ma out for sure."

"You are a good son," Thomas said, but he had little enough to share about the hunt for the beast other than to warn Garrett that he shouldn't attempt to go after it on his own. Meanwhile, the room beyond theirs was packed with people, rowdy with drink and fear but not violent, which was a mercy. Some of them shared reminiscences of Old John, whom it seemed had fought in the French Revolutionary Wars in his youth and never come back quite right. "Did the best he could, John did," was the prevailing sentiment, and Cassandra was fortified in her decision to attend the funeral tomorrow morning.

That evening, Thomas slept in her room once more. It was not as awkward as the first night, and Cassandra fell asleep quickly, reassured that no matter what might happen, she was not alone.

CHAPTER EIGHTEEN

Cassandra had to smile to herself when she felt Thomas's small start of surprise as they walked into the church the next morning to see every pew filled with people. "I had not expected this to be so well attended," he murmured as they moved to the foremost row, where the parishioners obligingly made room for them. "I did not think the gentleman in question was so liked."

"I believe it is more that he is one of them," Cassandra whispered in reply as they sat down. "That counts for a great deal."

"Clearly." They quieted as Reverend Jennings came to the pulpit. He was not smiling, but there was something serene about his expression that made it easy for Cassandra to quiet her internal voices and simply listen to the service. It helped that it was short – it was, after all, a working day, and people had things they needed to do.

Speaking of which, where was Mrs Hobb? She had been such a commanding presence yesterday on this topic, why would she demur and hold herself back now? Cassandra knew she was not the only person who had noted her absence as well, for there was a tightness around the reverend's eyes that worsened as he got to the end of the funeral.

"I have one request before you go," he said before people began to file out of the church. "Would anyone who lives near Mrs Hobb's farm be good enough to pay her a visit?"

"Not I," a man grumbled, and the people near him laughed.

"Consider it an act of charity towards those less fortunate than yourself," Reverend Jennings said, a hint of censure in his voice. The laughter died. "If you like, I will accompany you there."

"Best you do," the man said, now sounding resigned. "So's she don't bite my head off for botherin' her in her own home."

Once they were outside, Thomas turned to Cassandra and asked, "Who is Mrs Hobb?"

"She is a local woman of very strong character," Cassandra said diplomatically, "who had a guiding hand in planning John's funeral. I met her yesterday and she seemed quite well then. It is strange indeed that she would not attend the service today."

Thomas stopped moving. "And she lives on a farm? Outside the town proper?"

"I..." Oh, heavens. Cassandra did not like the direction that Thomas's mind was moving in. "It seems so."

He let go of her arm. "Stop the reverend from leaving,

tell him to wait until I return with my gun," he said, then hurried in the direction of the inn. Cassandra, trying to quell her rising heartrate, returned to the church and caught Reverend Jennings and a severely dressed man who must be the undertaker just as they were leaving the churchyard.

"A moment, sir," she said. She explained Thomas's desire to go with them, and that he was in the process of arming himself.

"Is he truly concerned?" Reverend Jennings asked. "In all likelihood, Mrs Hobb is simply under the weather. She did not return to her home past dark yesterday, I can assure you of that."

"Might have followed her damn cat outside, though," the undertaker, a long-jawed man respectably clad all in black, said unexpectedly. "Treats that little thing like a child, she does. Last gift her husband ever gave her, a good mouser for her kitchen."

Thomas returned then, his gun under one arm and his sword at his side. "Good day, reverend," he said with a bow. "I hope you do not object to my accompanying you."

"Us accompanying you," Cassandra added.

All three men looked at her like she was mad.

"It's a fair walk to the Hobb farm, miss," the older man said.

"I shall be perfectly well."

"Miss Wright," Reverend Jennings began, "I think it might be best if you remained in town, in case of... ah..."

"Nonsense." She took Thomas's arm with a determined smile. "I do promise not to slow your pace. Shall we be off?"

"Why are you insisting on accompanying us?" Thomas asked in a low voice as the other two men pulled ahead, engaged in a conversation of their own. "It might not be safe."

"It is broad daylight right now," Cassandra replied, doing her best to sound reassuring. "The beast does not come into the direct light."

"You don't know that for sure."

Cassandra resisted the urge to snap. "I stared into its eyes not two days ago," she said instead. "Given how quickly it killed my horse, I am convinced that if it could have followed us into the light to kill me, it would have. I am not in danger right now."

Thomas was quiet for a moment, then said, "Do you blame me for wishing to keep you safe at all costs?"

Cassandra squeezed his arm, taking comfort from the strength she felt there. It wasn't his fault that she couldn't explain her motives better; she hardly knew herself why she was so intent on going along with them, but to do otherwise simply struck her as shirking a duty. "I blame you for nothing," she assured him. He did not reply, but the faint colour high in his cheeks was endearingly suggestive.

Mrs Hobb's farm was a little way west of town, with a well-tended vegetable plot out front and an expanse of freshly ploughed fields behind it. The house was small but neat-looking with nothing at all amiss – except for the front door that gaped open like a broken tooth. Cassandra shivered despite the warmth of the day.

"Perhaps she just stepped out," Reverend Jennings said

uncertainly before raising his voice. "Mrs Hobb! Mrs Hobb, are you in?" There was no reply. "Strange," he murmured, then headed for the door. So did the undertaker, and after checking in with Cassandra, Thomas, leaving her standing amongst sun-drenched vegetables listening to the sound of the wind in the trees… and something else… a buzz.

Bees? There were certainly plenty of bees around, but this was more concentrated than that. It was faint but persistent, and Cassandra turned a slow revolution, looking for the source of the sound. It seemed to be coming from a cluster of mint. She moved closer and saw a cloud of flies had descended on something beneath the edge of the plant.

There was not room for an entire person under there, but something had gotten the flies' attention.

Oh God, let it not be just a piece of her. Cassandra held her breath as she gingerly lifted the mint with her hand.

A clump of darker black amid the shadows… a tiny limb wrenched askew, and– She dropped it quickly as soon as her eyes resolved what she was seeing.

"The cat," she called out, but too faintly to be heard by anyone but herself. "I have found the cat," she tried again, and this time Thomas hurriedly came back outside and joined her. It didn't take more than a moment for him to see that finding the cat was, in this instance, a bad thing.

"Mrs Hobb is not in her house," he said grimly. "I shall tell the others what you discovered. I think it best if we get back to The Four Feathers as quickly as possible. I need to be involved in the search, and you–"

"I ought to help," Cassandra said.

"You are still recovering from your own encounter with the Beast of Avon Vale," Thomas replied firmly. "You should take the time to rest and recover yourself a bit more. Be assured, I will devote everything I have to discovering this monster before another life is taken."

Like poor Old John. Like this little cat, and my mare, and Merlin, and most likely Mrs Hobb, too.

A part of Cassandra wanted to insist that Thomas let her make herself more useful – surely there had to be more she could do – but he was not wrong that she was still fatigued, and the walk in the sun had not lessened this. Perhaps she could look through her father's journal again; there were numerous pages on sigils that she had only touched on before. She might find something of use there, descriptions of what each sigil connected to, perhaps.

"Very well," she said, and let him gather the men and take control of the situation from there.

No one back in Tarryford seemed particularly distressed by the revelation of Mrs Hobb as a potential victim, but they did as they were expected to and gathered themselves into a motley crew of men – and a few bold women as well – to help in the search for the beast, including Young Garrett, who begged his mother for leave until she finally gave in.

Thomas seemed in his element, coordinating with the most influential men in the town to form tracking groups and sending messages to Harston Hall without breaking his stride. Before he left, he promised Cassandra he would be back by that evening, and she felt the last of her unease melt away. Thomas would be safe in a party of so many other people, and he would do his best, she knew it.

Cassandra did her best to examine and read about sigils, but staring at the pictures for too long made her eyes ache terribly, so she put it aside after a few hours. After that, the afternoon threatened – of all things – to become slightly dull before Cassandra had an unexpected visitor. "Mr Fraser is here to see you, miss," Mrs Copeland told her after knocking on Cassandra's door.

Cassandra froze. "Mr Fraser…"

"The younger," Mrs Copeland added in a hurry, clearly not liking whatever look had come across Cassandra's face. "The younger gentleman, miss, not his father," she added.

"Ah." Cassandra's heart settled back into a steady rhythm. "That is… thank you, I will go to him." She followed Mrs Copeland downstairs to the private room, where she saw Gilbert in as fine and feathery a getup as he ever wore. He had never seemed like such a peacock to her before, more inclined towards browns and greys that complimented his ruddy complexion, but today he was in a bright blue and green silk jacket embroidered with the outlines of exotic flowers, as well as exceedingly tight breeches. Lord, she hardly knew where to look.

"Mr Fraser." Cassandra went to curtsy, but was surprised to find Gilbert reaching out to stop her with a hand on her arm.

"Please don't," he said, sounding wretched. "It simply seems wrong to hear such formality from you, Cassie. I feel that these last few days, we've grown close once again, and… and you cannot blame me for wanting to hear my name on your lips, can you? You did it once before."

Behind them, quietly, Mrs Copeland left the room but pointedly did *not* close the door. Anyone could walk by in the dining room and see the two of them, which was just the reassurance that Cassandra wanted.

"I'm afraid it would not be proper," Cassandra said, being careful to inject a bit of regret into her voice.

"Proper, yes." Gilbert let go of her, but his woeful expression did not change. "I have been hearing a great deal from my father of late when it comes to the subject of propriety. Do y'know, he actually told me that it was *improper* to allow you into the party? As though you were some fallen woman rather than someone who has merely fallen on hard times! It is outrageous of him, do you not think?"

"And what did you say to him on the subject?" she asked for the sake of having something to say.

"I told him just that! And that he was wrong, and, and, and that you have always been a true friend to me, and I would not turn you away for any reason."

Cassandra assumed that Gilbert was hoping for her to be gratified that he spoke in her defence, but in truth she simply felt tired by the show he was putting on. "Turning me away would also make Mr Griffith rather unhappy," she pointed out.

"My father does not care for Thomas either," Gilbert said mournfully, reaching for the drink he had perched beside the fireplace – heavens, his hand was shaking. How long had he been drinking, and how much had he imbibed? "He *never* likes who I like. I was fortunate the first time to get him to agree to a marriage between us, and now... now it is too late to contemplate such a thing, isn't it?"

"It was too late from the moment your father ended it, Gilbert," Cassandra said with as much compassion as she could muster, which was not much. There were no more reasons for her to look backwards, and nothing to regret from her time with Gilbert but that she had given him so much of it in the first place.

"But if it were not," he persisted, and all of a sudden he set his drink aside and took Cassandra's hands in both of his. His palms were clammy and damp, and Cassandra instinctively tried to pull away, but his grip on her was too tight.

"If it were possible," Gilbert repeated, his eyes shimmering with liquid courage, "that I could marry you, and we could begin once more... Cassie, I have never found another woman who could hold a candle to you, not a one. You made – you *make* – me a better person simply by your presence. I am beholden to your goodness in every sense of the word, and I would repay that goodness now if you would but let me."

"Gilbert!" She tugged on her hands again, but his hands were twice the size of hers and try as she might, she could not get away. "This is wholly inappropriate! I am engaged to another man."

"To Thomas, I know, and I know his love for you is true, I can see it in his face," Gilbert agreed miserably while Cassandra felt her heart stutter for a moment. "But he is not in a good way after the deaths of his brother and sister-in-law. His home is a mausoleum, a memorial dedicated to their memories, and if you married him, he would shut you up in it too and no one would ever see you again. I can give you so much more! I want to give you the world!"

He spoke more quickly now, breath coming in rapid pants. "I brought the barouche here today," he said eagerly. "The horses are fresh, and the driver is one of the few servants who will obey me over my father. We could have all your things packed up quickly and be off together to Gretna Green before anyone even knows we're missing."

"Your father would be furious." That wasn't the criticism that Cassandra had wanted to deliver – she had plenty more to say about the sheer stupidity of this plan – but it was the one that slipped out first. Try as she might, she could not escape the spectre that James Fraser threw over her life. To even contemplate doing something like this, defying his will in such a way… Gilbert would be fortunate to survive the effects of his father's rage, and whoever he married – and it would *not* be her – would fare even worse.

"I am his heir," Gilbert said stubbornly. "The *only* heir. He might not be overjoyed, but it is something he would come to understand and approve of in time. He knows how I feel about you, Cassie, he knows that I love you better than any other woman on this earth, and – please! Please, I shall beg if you make me, but–"

"Be *quiet!*" she hissed. "Mr Fraser, this is absolutely intolerable behaviour."

The gleam in his eyes began to fade. "But Cassie–"

"No!" She finally managed to free her hands from his grip and put herself several feet distant from him. Cassandra readied the sharp side of her tongue to put him down, but he looked so pathetic, standing there drooping like a cut flower that had fallen out of a bouquet, that she had to soften her tone. "Mr Fraser–"

"Gilbert," he insisted.

Oh, fine. "Gilbert. I am not completely insensible to your wishes, but you have to see that there is absolutely no potential for anything to come of them." She held up her hand when he began to step forwards, and to his very faint credit, he stopped. "I am engaged to another man," she said firmly, not caring that it wasn't true – Gilbert was treating it as true, and therefore so would she. It helped that she was beginning to wish it *was* true. "And I would not betray him in such a way, nor would I have betrayed you five years ago had someone else asked me then.

"But beyond that... Gilbert." Cassandra shook her head. "I do not love you. I have not loved you for many years now–" *if I even did then* "–and I shall not love you again, not beyond the bonds of friendship. I cannot be married to a man I do not love, and you should not want me in that case anyhow."

"But Cassie–"

"No." She said it with as much finality as she could muster. "I am not the wife for a man such as yourself. I have faith, however, that you shall find the woman you are meant to be with and be happy together." She smiled a bit. "As happy as I am with Thomas, whom I know to be one of your truest friends. You do not truly want to disgrace him in such a way, do you? I know that you do not."

"No," Gilbert agreed faintly. "I… of course not."

"Of course not. Therefore I shall say nothing to him of this meeting between us," Cassandra promised, and she meant it. The last thing she wanted was to drive the wedge between the two men even deeper. "I would not harm your friendship with him for the world. And in time, you shall forget whatever feelings you think you have for me and find someone appropriate to share your life with. And that is all I have to say on the matter." She folded her hands in front of her and resisted the urge to grab for her hatpin. If he didn't leave now…

But it seemed she had well and truly punctured the thoughtless, giddy mood that had taken hold of him. When Gilbert stepped forwards next, it was with a slow, heavy tread. His face sagged with sadness, and he would not meet her eyes as he said, "I shall take my leave of you then, Miss Wright."

"I thank you, Mr Fraser." He passed by her and she did not turn to watch him go, just listened to the drag of his feet and the mumble he gave when Mrs Copeland bid him farewell. Then he was gone, and Cassandra shut her eyes and let herself shudder. God in heaven, she had never thought to be on the receiving end of such a terribly awkward proposal by Gilbert again. The first time had been excruciating, and she had already decided to accept him in that instance! To be subject to it again, and with the plan of eloping on top of that… ridiculous! Absolute madness! Did he truly have so little love for Thomas, and so little regard for Cassandra's own sense of propriety, that he thought such a scheme possible? What... how...

"Are you all right, miss?"

Cassandra whirled around to see Mrs Copeland standing in the door, a pot of tea cradled between her hands. She sounded innocent enough, but there was an air of something in the way she stood and the set of her face that made Cassandra wonder how much she'd just heard.

"Fine," she forced herself to say. "I am quite well, thank you."

"I am glad to hear it," Mrs Copeland said easily, coming in and pouring a cup of rich black tea. She added a dash of milk, then handed it to Cassandra, who lifted it to her lips with shaking hands.

"This is only my third-best teapot," Mrs Copeland said in a low voice. "If he comes back and bothers you again, there is no harm in breaking it across his face if you must."

Cassandra laughed, making her tea splutter. "I thank you," she murmured, "but I have the feeling I shall not be seeing much of Mr Fraser in the future."

If she never saw *either* of them again, she would be very happy indeed.

CHAPTER NINETEEN

Cassandra's hopes that Gilbert's visit would be the last terrible thing to happen that day were dashed when the church bells began to ring shortly after the sun set. There was no service scheduled, no holy day to observe. This was a warning, and soon enough word came to the inn that a child was missing.

Not just any child, either. Young Garrett.

Mrs Copeland was beside herself with worry and clung to the maid's arm as she stared out into the growing dark. "I know he wanted to find the creature, but I didn't think he would actually be foolish enough to try!" she protested with tears in her eyes. "Ever since his da died he's wanted to do more for me an' the inn, no matter how I tell him we'll be all right. And now he's gone after that terrible beast!"

Cassandra's input, thankfully, was not required. If it had been, she'd have been hard-pressed to come up with something hopeful to say. The regulars of the pub, drunk on anger and liquid courage, were happy to step in at this point.

"Aye!"

"We'll make it pay for daring to step foot near Tarryford!"

"*Aye!*"

"Get yer guns, blades, and any fire you can find!"

Cassandra moved aside so as to avoid being trampled by the sudden flood of men out of the building. There was an intentness to their movements now that she had never seen before. Apparently, the loss of a drunk old man and a local harridan were one thing, but the potential loss of their hostess's child was something else entirely.

Young Garrett... oh, God, have mercy. Cassandra could not blame them for their upset – she was upset herself, stricken by the thought that the warm-hearted boy who had been the first person to welcome her into Tarryford might be a victim of the Beast of Avon Vale. He had perhaps been incautious, but he had been acting so for a good reason. And now, to think that he might be dead...

The men were right. This could not go on, but they were all of them stumbling in the dark now. There were simply too many places to search without knowing something of the beast's habits other than the fact that it could only live in the dark. And yet, perhaps Cassandra *did* know something of the beast's habits after all.

Nearly alone in the inn now except for its sobbing mistress and her steadfast assistant, she went upstairs and lit several candles, then pulled out the salient records she had copied at the church, including her rough sketch of the town and the surrounding area. She pored over the timeline of events at Northlake Hall, the incidences of sleeping sickness, and every suspicious death and disappearance so far. If there was a pattern here, she would find it.

It took hours, but finally a pattern *did* emerge. There seemed to be locations – loci, in a way – of dangerous activity both within and without Tarryford. Some of them were inside town, which made them poor dens for a beast, while others were just outside the town in the local countryside.

One of these places Cassandra could remove from the list of possible locations for the Beast of Avon Vale immediately. Northlake Hall was burned into utter ruins – unless the beast were in an unfound cellar, there was nowhere for it to hide. Not impossible, but not likely either.

It was the curious lives of the Williams siblings, and the death of Robert Williams, that led Cassandra to believe that she might have found the right spot to search. The focus had been to the north of town so far, which to be fair was where almost all the deaths and disappearances had originated, but Cassandra noted that the Williamses had lived in a place called Mortview House to the west of town.

That the Williams brother and sister had been involved in something dire was certain, although the extent of that involvement seemed unclear. They had not been well thought of in town, judging from the notes from their funerals, although their father seemed to have left a better impression before he died under his own set of mysterious circumstances. Unlike Northlake Hall, which had been burned, Mortview House was merely boarded up in the absence of anyone to let it.

Everyone was hunting a beast, a creature of forest and field, cavern and cave, but what if it was not living in the wild at all? What if it had found a more comfortable place to make its den, somewhere so ill-thought of by local residents that they preferred not to mention it at all, much less step foot in it?

I must go there.

Quick on the heels of that revelation was the sure knowledge that Thomas would absolutely forbid it if he was here. He would not want her to go on her own, at least, of that she was certain, but Young Garrett was missing. He might be dead, but what if he wasn't? Even if he was, the sooner solid evidence was found one way or the other, the better. Neither the boy nor Mrs Hobb had been killed where they were taken. They had to be somewhere, in whatever form that may take. Mortview House would be an excellent spot to hide them away in.

Cassandra craned her neck back, surprised at how it ached. How many hours had she been sitting here? There was silence all around her, but not the silence of peaceful slumber; all of the inn's residents had gone off to hunt the Beast of Avon Vale. There was no one left but Cassandra and Mrs Copeland and Molly, whom she could not bear to disturb with a revelation that might have no good resolution. There was no one for Cassandra to share her discovery with – certainly no one who would believe her. She could wait for some of them to return, but that might not happen until daybreak, and every moment counted.

Well then, I will go by myself.

The resolve made her shiver, but at the same time she felt a sense of familiar determination settle over her like a cloak. She had gotten this same feeling when she decided to leave her work and come south to investigate her father's death. There was a sense of inevitability to it, the knowledge that she *was* going to do it, so she might as well get started.

"All right, then," Cassandra said to herself. She would do this, but there was no need to be completely foolhardy about it. She wrote out a quick note for Thomas detailing where she was going, adding as a postscript that he might consider checking the little-disturbed ruins of Northlake Hall as well, then sealed it to be left at the front of the inn and prepared herself for her departure. She put on her hardest-wearing dress, a sturdy pelisse that would keep her warm in the cool night air, and added her hatpin. She marched downstairs and, after a moment's consideration, took one of the old, rusty swords from the crossed pair over the bar. It was unwieldy and too heavy for her to hold properly, but she made do the best she could.

Finally, she took an unlit torch and a book of matches, then stepped out into the darkness and headed for the eastern road out of town, the same road she had taken to get to Mrs Hobb's farm.

I might be deluding myself, she thought as she passed out of the bounds of the town, houses giving way to fields. Surely someone else had thought to check the Mortview property already, and yet Cassandra had a persistent sense of surety about it. One way or another, she needed to see what was there, and she needed to see it now. In all likelihood, even if the Beast of Avon Vale had made this place into its lair, it was out on the prowl tonight. Or would it rather stay home, protected from the masses of humans armed and arrayed against it?

For the first time since she got the idea, Cassandra stopped to truly ponder the foolishness of what she was doing. She was all alone, a single woman heading into the darkness against a foe she had no hope of matching. She had begun this enterprise with certainty, but the more steps she took, the more her heart began to quail inside her. It was not too late for her to go back; it was not too late for her to return to the inn and the safety, dubious though it was, of her room.

In the distance, she heard a hound howl. The rest of the pack took up the cry after that. They sounded like they were to her right; north again. Perhaps they had found something. Perhaps she was engaging in utter folly.

Yet here you are, already engaged. You might as well see it through. You never know, you may find something of interest after all, even if it is not the lair of the beast.

With a sigh at her own foolishness, Cassandra continued on.

It was close to a quarter hour before she saw the silhouette of Mortview House rise out of the shadows; it helped that the moon was so bright. In a few hours it would be dawn. Soon, if this place was the beast's lair, it would be home out of necessity.

Better pick up your pace, then.

Mortview House was not as imposing as Harston

Hall, but it was clearly of old and respectable make, with probably ten or twelve rooms within. Its two-level brick façade was nearly covered with untamed ivy, thick and twisted. It reminded her of a place out of a fairy tale, a place firmly deserted by the world yet full of untold secrets.

The front door was locked, but several of the windows on the ground floor had been broken. Cassandra lit the torch she had carried with her and, flames in one hand and rusty sword in another, she climbed through the largest hole and into the abandoned house's front hallway.

The air within smelled of rotting wood and mildew. The walls were crumbling, and the floor beneath her feet was gritty from dust and the droppings of many rodents. Cassandra screwed her face up at it at first, then realised that the dust was actually a blessing. She was not a tracker by any means, but it took next to no skill to follow tracks laid out on the ground before you. And in this case, one set of tracks was very clear.

The footprints were slightly smaller than Cassandra's, with a rougher sole. The stride was longer, though, as if the wearer of these little shoes was running. From fear? From the excitement of discovery? Either way, they were fresh enough to have clear edges – no draught had disturbed these marks.

Dare I call out to him? She did not quite dare to, not yet at least. Instead, Cassandra tightened her grip on the torch and bent forwards a bit, so she could more easily follow the path laid out before her.

These were not the only prints, she noted as she followed

them down the hall. There were others here and there, older and less delineated. Someone, or some*ones*, had been inside this place numerous times of late. Was it innocent curiosity? Were they helping themselves to whatever the previous tenants had left behind, or coming here for a more dastardly purpose? This place might make a very fitting summoning ground…

Cassandra did not see any of the massive prints that would indicate the presence of the beast, but then, she had not gone very far into the house yet either. She took a deep breath and continued her exploration of the lower level, torch held high. Grit ground against the wood floors beneath her shoes as she slowly moved from room to room, peering into the darkness for any sign that might be life. "Garrett?" she called out softly as she went. "Garrett, are you here?"

It was foolish, of course. If he was here, he would surely be calling for help unless he was bound or unconscious or… or… But it helped her to have something to focus on that was not the sound of the wind beyond the windows, or her own heartbeat pounding too bright and too hard within her chest.

"Everyone is looking for you," she murmured as she moved through what appeared to be a dining room. What a curious place – there were still dishes on the table, as though the family had been in the act of eating and might come back at any moment. Yet this place had been empty for years now. What had the Williamses been involved in, to force them to leave a place like this? What had happened to steal Robert Williams away and drive his sister to abandon their home? It must have been dire.

Yet this is a fitting place for dire things, I am afraid.

"Your mother is so worried about you," Cassandra went on, stepping into the kitchen. There was an enormous oven against one wall, and countertops covered in mouse faeces. The whole room smelled strongly of rodent, and Cassandra thought she heard one scuttling in the corners. She shuddered, too heavily reminded of the last rodent-like creature she'd encountered to be at ease, and immediately left the room.

"She wishes nothing more than for you to safely return home." It would be very hard for Mrs Copeland, bereft of her husband and with Garrett the only child who remained with her, to be alone if all this searching was for naught. "That is what I wish as well. Garrett…" She raised her voice a bit as she headed back into the hall and towards the stairs. There were a youth's footprints here, too, going both up and down. He, or another child, had been here at some point.

"Garrett?" The thought of going up frightened her a bit; upstairs there would be no easy egress, no window or door to dart for if things went badly. But she had to look. There was no other choice. "Damn it," Cassandra whispered very softly to herself. It was not polite language, but this was not a time that required politesse. "I am coming up," she said more firmly, and began to ascend the stairs.

Creeeeeak. Oh, lord, they were abominably loud. Cassandra winced with every step she took, and when she finally reached the landing, she gave a sigh of relief. Here, at least, the floor was quieter, even though the wind – which she had barely heard or felt on her walk over here – seemed louder than ever. She held her torch aloft and investigated the source of the whistling sound, stepping into a bedroom that must once have belonged to a lady. The furnishings were fine and delicate, and there was a dress crumpled at the foot of the bed that had likely once been very beautiful.

Of more interest were the loose pages that had been blown all over the room by the draught coming through the broken window. Cassandra bent down and picked one of them up, her eyes roving across the words written there. She had expected a letter to a friend, or perhaps a list of household goods that needed to be acquired or dealt with in some way.

What a lark this is! I never thought it would be so exciting to parlay with darkness so, and yet it is clear that both Robert and I have a true gift for it. This is more than mere play – this is a chance for us to elevate ourselves beyond all others. If our nerve holds true – and surely it shall, for we have seen nothing to fear for ourselves from these arts – then it is possible that we shall become two of the most powerful people in all the world.

Imagine all we could do. Imagine who we could become. Would I not make a fair queen?

Cassandra's eyes blurred as she stared at the page, pity and rage warring within her as she read the blithe words. So, the rumours were correct, and the Williamses had been as foolish as she feared. To tempt fate so, to throw themselves down such a dark path with so little apprehension for themselves or what they were doing... She reached for another page, then–

Scrabble-scritch-scrabble. That was no wind, nor was it tiny paws scuttling within the walls. That was the sound of powerful paws moving across the gritty flooring – not only across it, but up the stairs.

Oh God. Had the Beast of Avon Vale found her?

You are as much of a fool as this writer!

Cassandra straightened up, lifting the rusty sword she held out in front of her and keeping her torch close. The torch would likely be a better ally to her than the blade at this point, although neither meant much when it came to a monster like this. Her limbs began to tremble, and stars danced over Cassandra's vision as the sound grew closer and closer. Was that a growl?

Please, please, do not let Thomas be the one to find me. It would ruin him. Gasping through her fear and struggling to stay on her feet, Cassandra waited for her fate to come charging through the door. A moment later, it did so.

And ran right over to her and buried its face in her dress, snuffling enthusiastically.

"Merlin!" Cassandra dropped the sword and would have dropped the torch as well if she hadn't been concerned that the entire building might go up in flames were she to be so careless. She bent down to lavish affection on the enormous, ridiculous hound, her relief extreme. She pulled him close and buried her face in his neck for a moment. It felt like a part of her lungs had just unlocked and she could finally take a deep breath again.

"Merlin, where have you *been*?" she demanded. "Why did you act so foolishly? What are you ..." She stopped speaking as Merlin abruptly pulled away, bouncing backwards on his paws while staring at her as if to indicate that he wanted her to come with him. Surely he was not that clever, and yet he had survived chasing after the beast.

"Where do you wish us to go?" He turned and ran out of the room, then paused in the hallway and barked once. "Yes, I understand." Cassandra almost forgot to pick up the sword in her haste, and once she had it safely in hand she chased after Merlin, who moved five times faster than her as he raced down the stairs and towards the same hole that she had entered the house through.

So strange. But she would rather trust in Merlin as her guide than almost anyone. She followed him outside, relieved to be breathing fresh air once more after the still, dead air within the house. Merlin ran ahead towards a shadowy building in the distance that resolved into not a barn as Cassandra had originally thought but something far fairer. It was a tower, perhaps twenty feet tall by twenty across, that looked as if it had been built to seem older than it truly was. A ... what were they called? A *folly*. Not the main house, but another place where the family could relax and escape from the world.

Perhaps escape into *another* world, if Miss Williams' writing was any indication.

The folly had one large door in front. It was ajar enough for someone to slip inside, but when Cassandra tried to move it further, she found the wood so thoroughly swollen that she could not budge the door to open more. If this was a recent development, then someone much stronger than her must have levered it open.

Should I go and get help?

Merlin's insistent bark decided it for her. Cassandra turned sideways and slid inside the building. Her gaze was immediately drawn to the centre of the room, where a dusty Persian rug had been drawn back to reveal a hole three feet in diameter in the floor. "Oh!" She rushed forwards, her heart in her throat. *Please, please…* She didn't realise she was speaking aloud until the darkness pulled back to reveal the still, pale form of Young Garrett in the bottom of the hole, his face bloody, lying on some sort of stone slab. "No!"

But wait, no… his chest was moving. He was breathing! Garrett was still alive! "Thank God," Cassandra murmured as she fell to her knees at the edge of the hole. She had to get him out of there, but she knew she would not be able to raise him up by herself. Perhaps if she joined him down there she could rouse him, and they could crawl out of the hole together. It was not terribly deep, after all.

She should at least check on him, she decided. She could always get herself out once more and go and get help after. Cassandra set down the sword and looked for a safe place to lean the torch when Merlin began to bark once more.

"Ssshh," she cautioned the hound, but he was not having it. He stared at the door to the folly, teeth bared in a snarl as he set his shoulders like he was about to charge.

The beast must be coming at last! Cassandra felt familiar terror flood her once more, but for some reason this time she was able to bear it better. Perhaps it was because she had someone else to fight for now.

I must not let Young Garrett come to harm. She began to rise once more, her grip on the sword firm this time, prepared to meet the monster that was coming through the door.

Once again, she did not see the beast she expected to see. Instead, Cassandra saw an entirely different sort of monster.

"Mr Fraser!"

In the dim light, it was difficult to see much of his expression. Before everything that had happened, Cassandra had fancied herself rather a good assessor of people. It had been her duty to be pleasing, and in order to please she had to know what best appealed. At the time, she'd thought Mr Fraser had been a rather simple person to present to: show him deference mixed with vivacity and a bit of wit, the same as most men liked, and he was content with her.

Now she knew better. There was no reason to attempt to position herself in the best light, not when he already thought the worst of her. With this consideration at the forefront of her mind, and knowing what she did of the man, she clenched the sword in her hand even more tightly.

"Miss Wright." He tilted his head up a bit, and now she could see his expression. He was smiling, but that was no simple smile. It was perhaps one of the most menacing things she had ever seen in her life, far more so than the dog growling beside her right now. "I see you have been rather busy."

Cassandra swallowed hard. "Unexpectedly so."

"Surely not *too* unexpected. Why, look at you. Armed to the teeth." He bared his own in a rictus of a grin. "And finding lost things."

"I was looking for Young Garrett – the boy," she confessed, and added swiftly, "I told his mother, at The Four Feathers, where I was going."

"Oh, I rather doubt that." He shook his head, his grin dropping away. "A woman, out on her own in the darkness as everyone else hunts for the Beast of Avon Vale? It is unthinkable. No, I daresay that no one else knows exactly where you are right now, Miss Wright. It is, in fact, possible that no one will even miss you until tomorrow morning, when you do not respond to the knock at your door."

Cassandra affected a laugh. "And why would I not respond? I have every intention of making it back to my bed tonight, sir, after I have seen this young lad home."

His eyes narrowed as he gazed at her. "Do you, now?"

"Indeed I do." She lifted her chin. "And I believe that Merlin will be assistance enough, so do not trouble yourself to remain here on my account."

Go, go, get away from us all!

"Ah, yes. Your faithful hound." Mr Fraser turned to glare at the dog. "Let us see if something can be done about him." Unblinking, he raised his hands towards Merlin and murmured something beneath his breath. Cassandra could not make out the individual words, but the way he said them... rhythmic, guttural, accompanied by faint gestures that nevertheless chilled her... it made her think there was more going on here than she could readily see.

She was right. A moment later, Merlin stopped growling. He sat, then laid down.

"Merlin?" Cassandra asked. "Merlin? Come here, boy!" The dog whined piteously as he looked at her, but then his eyes closed and, after a few moments, he stopped moving altogether except for the slow rise and fall of his chest. "Merlin!"

"He will not wake," Mr Fraser said, taking a step forward. "That is one of the simplest invocations those of us with power learn, and only truly effective while within sight of the one to be afflicted, but by the time that dog wakes up, I anticipate that you shall be gone from this place."

"I am not going anywhere," Cassandra insisted. If he raised his hands to her, if he tried to bespell her somehow, she would have to run at him. *God save me.* She was not even sure her legs were firm enough to keep her upright for much longer, and now she was contemplating charging a man much larger and stronger than she was.

But I am armed, there is that. And if I do not at least try to save us, he shall surely kill the boy as well. For Cassandra was positive now that Mr Fraser was not here alone by accident. This was a place he knew, a place where he himself had likely laid Young Garrett down, for some nefarious purpose of his own.

"You are not the master of the Beast of Avon Vale." Cassandra wasn't sure why she brought it up, but she was darkly gratified nevertheless when Mr Fraser nodded.

"I am not, although I am not unfamiliar with this sort of… asset."

"Asset?"

Mr Fraser laughed. "And here I was beginning to think that you truly are as clever as your father always thought you to be." His tone went from jovial to as smooth as silk, wrapped around a neck. "I know what you have done, Miss Wright. I know what your clever little hands have pilfered from my library, and the things that you have seen that others haven't. I know why you are not truly surprised to see me here tonight, or shocked senseless by my display with this useless hound.

"And yet you are as naïve as your father ever was. It is the failing of your family, Miss Wright, the failing that will be the downfall of every one of you." For a moment, his eyes seemed to glow red in the torchlight. "In this world, there is no sympathy for those who are not prepared to do everything possible to elevate themselves. Whether it is winning a war or winning a higher place in society, those of us who are resolute about improving our situations will always fare better than innocent fools like yourself. In a society of sheep, Miss Wright, it is the wolves who determine who lives and who dies."

"I am no sheep to be slaughtered," Cassandra said, firming her grip on the sword. Mr Fraser was unarmed, with not even a long knife on him. She had an advantage there.

"No, not slaughtered," he told her, shifting from foot to foot with what could be eagerness. "What a waste that would be." He raised his hands and Cassandra prepared to run at him.

She got as far as moving her front foot when a new sound reached her ears. The sound of hounds baying, coming closer and closer. She watched as Mr Fraser froze, grimly calculating the likelihood of success before they were discovered. A few seconds later, he lowered his hands and took a step back.

"You would do well to hold your tongue about what has occurred here tonight, Miss Wright," Mr Fraser said quietly. "To do otherwise would put several people you care about in grave danger."

Of course he was threatening her. And, to Cassandra's chagrin, it was working.

I am safe now. Young Garrett is safe. There will be time later to make another plan, time to… to do something, to find a new way forward. It is not too late.

"Swear it," he insisted, his fingers strangely knotted. "Swear you will reveal no details of what passed between us tonight. I merely found you and the boy, and was preparing to assist you in returning him to the town."

The compulsion to agree was heavy, like she was carrying something on her back. Slowly, Cassandra lowered the sword. "I will say nothing of our conversation," she agreed, and the heaviness suddenly dissipated.

Wait, what? What just happened to me? Had he worked some sort of… oh, what had he called them… invocation on her? How dare he do such a thing! It wasn't enough to put her in fear for her life, now he had to compromise her very mind? She hid her clenched hands in her skirt.

How will I tell Thomas what happened?

It was too late for regrets, however. The sound of horses joined that of the dogs, and a few muttered words later, Merlin was back on his feet. He went straight to Cassandra and nosed at her hip, all his former protectiveness gone, as though his mind had somehow been reset.

"Miss Wright?" someone shouted from outside. No, not someone… Thomas.

"That's Father's horse there," Gilbert added, and a moment later the door was forced open and Thomas ran inside, his own sword out. He brushed straight past Mr Fraser, his eyes fixed on Cassandra, and the relief she felt upon seeing him was so great that she dropped both sword and torch in favour of reaching for him.

He wrapped his free arm around Cassandra and pulled her close to his chest. "Cass," he murmured, his voice full of some emotion that she was not quite bold enough to put a name to. "God, I was so worried for you."

"I am all right," she whispered. Gilbert and several others had joined them by then, and Mr Fraser had taken over the conversation with alacrity, describing how he had come across both Cassandra and the boy in the hole during his search. "Oh!" Of course, Young Garrett! Cassandra pulled away and pointed towards the hole in the floor. "I found him," she said to Thomas. "Young Garrett, Mrs Copeland's son. He's here. I do not know whether he is injured or not, but–"

Colonel Cross nodded to her as he walked by and levered himself down into the hole. "I'll tend to the lad," he said firmly.

"But Cassie," Gilbert said in a tone of wonderment. "How did you know he was here?"

She smiled weakly at him. "Just a fortunate guess. I... heard barking while I was out for an early-morning walk, and wondered if I might find Merlin. He found me instead and led me to the boy."

"And then Father found all of you," Gilbert said, finishing the story in the way Mr Fraser no doubt preferred. "What a happy coincidence!"

"Yes."

No. It was no coincidence, but Cassandra found herself unable to go into more details. Her tongue seemed to trip over itself the moment she tried, and she could get nothing out of her mouth but breath. Perhaps once she was out from under Mr Fraser's gimlet eye, she would have a bit more freedom. She looked at Thomas. "We must get Young Garrett back as soon as possible," she said.

"And get you back as well," he agreed. "You look as though you have been through an ordeal."

You have no idea.

CHAPTER TWENTY

Of all the things Cassandra might have expected to happen to her upon her return to The Four Feathers, handing a confused but awake Young Garrett over to his deliriously happy mother had been at the top of her list. That followed by Thomas taking her to the private dining room and then thoroughly scolding her had *not* been on it. He had never been less than the soul of courtesy to her, even in the direst of circumstances.

Apparently, the incident this evening had pushed him past his limit.

"A *note*, Cassandra!" He spun on one foot, his agitation propelling him back and forth across the floor in rapid succession. "After everything you have been through, everything you have seen, you thought it not only advisable to venture into the darkness on a whim on your own, but you left a mere *note* as to your whereabouts. It is sheer chance that I discovered it!"

"But you did," she pointed out, hoping to dispel his not-unwarranted dissatisfaction with her actions.

"Only because we had just discovered the body of Mrs

Hobb," he snapped, not even looking at her. "I thought it wise under the circumstances to get back to the inn to warn you that the people of Tarryford were *not* taking the discovery well, and that it would be wise for you to move elsewhere before the body of the boy was found."

"But Garrett is not dead," Cassandra said. "And for that, I believe I may be somewhat responsible." Well, herself and Merlin, but the point was a sound one. She was quite certain that the boy wouldn't have survived for long once Mr Fraser got back to him.

"That you put yourself at desperate risk to discover him does not sit well with me," Thomas replied. He finally stopped moving and pressed his hands against his eyes. It occurred to Cassandra that it had been many hours since Thomas had last slept. "God, if I had found *your* body, if you were harmed… I cannot even bear to think of it. Cassandra." He lowered his hands and turned to her. "There is nothing else for it. You must leave this place."

The request shocked her. "I can do no such thing."

"It is the *best* thing you can do now," he said, his voice gaining fervency. "I did not have a chance to tell you this, but the pack found the trail of the beast last night. Between them and the townsfolk, I believe we shall have it cornered in Pendlehaven Woods before another night falls. We shall kill it, and the nightmare shall be over. There is no need for you to remain for that."

"That is not the reason I remain," Cassandra insisted. "I never came here for the beast, Thomas. I came here to determine what Mr Fraser had to do with my father's death, and determine the best course of action once I knew. And after what happened with him in the folly..."

"What did happen?" Thomas asked.

"He–" She paused to steady herself with a deep breath. Then another. Then another. She wanted to speak, but she could not. The words simply would not emerge from her mouth. She could not even speak around them, could not say that she was certain it was Mr Fraser who had abducted Young Garrett, could not say that he had silenced Merlin; she could do nothing but stand there, her hands beginning to shake with rage as she was once again confronted with the breadth of her own disenfranchisement.

"I have you." Thomas settled on one knee in front of her, taking her hands in his as he had when he found her not two hours ago. "I am here, you are well. Be calm, Cass, you are well."

I am, thanks to you. She could not quite bring herself to say it, but she squeezed his hands in response before nodding and finding her voice once more. "I have not fulfilled my purpose here yet," she said, and was encouraged that she could at least talk about *this*. "As pleased as I am to hear that the hunt for the beast goes well, Mr Fraser is..." how to say it... "*up* to something, and I must discover what that something is. Otherwise, more people will be hurt, innocent people, and I cannot stand back and allow that to happen."

"Then allow me to handle this," Thomas begged. "You can trust me to act in your stead, can you not?"

She shook her head, ignoring the look of devastation on

Thomas's face. "I will not heap every responsibility on you and ignore my own. I cannot do so."

"It is my *honour* to protect you, not a responsibility."

Her heart felt like it was about to leap right through her chest, but somehow Cassandra found the will to shake her head once again. "It is likewise my honour to protect you," she said firmly. "With the help of my father's journal, I know more about what is going on here than anyone else not directly involved. I will be your equal in this, Thomas, not a lamb to be shepherded or a child to be guided.

"The Beast of Avon Vale had nothing to do with the disappearance of Young Garrett," Cassandra went on. "He was unharmed, and the place he was in was no den. I believe that the boy was put there by a person." That was as close as she could come to telling Thomas her suspicions. He was a clever man, surely he followed her and could work this next part out on his own.

Thomas's eyes narrowed. "You suspect Mr Fraser."

Cassandra nodded gratefully.

"It's entirely possible," Thomas murmured, beginning to pace once more as he thought his way through the day. "He has spent a great deal of time away from the party. We were given to understand that he was attending to business with his factor, but none of us could verify that." He looked at Cassandra. "You truly believe him capable of abducting a child? What would be the purpose of such a thing?"

"I believe…" Cassandra felt her tongue begin to cramp, and huffed a breath of annoyance as she rerouted her speech. "Mr Fraser is a man who is capable of far more than he is given credit for. Thomas, please believe me when I tell you that there is no innocence in the man."

"I do believe you," he said, and Cassandra nearly slumped with relief. He believed her. He had faith in her, trust in her abilities – at least this far.

"If he is willing to abduct a child," Thomas continued, "then there is no limit to what he might do next. Your father wrote of a sacrifice… that must still be his ultimate goal."

"Indeed. I intend to try to determine his next moves, and then to do something to stop him." Feeling daring, she reached out and took Thomas's hand in her own. "I know you fear for me," she said. It was certainly not an unfounded fear, either. "But I must be able to see this through. I could not bear it otherwise."

He closed his eyes for a moment, beaten but unwilling to acquiesce. Cassandra took advantage of his unseeing state to gaze on him, taking in the dark stains beneath his eyes and the lines of tension alongside his mouth. Thomas would work himself to the bone if she didn't stop him. He would claim responsibility for so many things that failure would become inevitable, and then… but no. She would not let that happen, would not allow him to be broken in such a way. She would be here alongside him, whether he liked it or not.

"Shall we not bring Gilbert into the fold?" he asked as he reopened his eyes. "He plays the fool, but he surely will not allow his father to go around murdering people."

Oof. "I am afraid that Gilbert and I are not on the best of terms right now," she said as obliquely as she could.

Thomas's eyes narrowed. "What did he do?" he demanded.

"Nothing that you need to concern yourself with," Cassandra replied firmly. "Nothing… untoward." Or at least, nothing so untoward that she wanted to ruin a friendship so many years in the making. "Truly, do not let any of this trouble you. I am well, and so are you, and you say yourself that you and the people of Tarryford are closing in on the beast. These are good things! Once the matter of the Beast of Avon Vale has been settled, we will be able to focus on Mr Fraser. Perhaps something will happen between now and then to make apprehending him an easier prospect than it currently seems."

Personally, she hoped that he insinuated himself into the hunt for the beast. The more she learned of his degradations, the easier it was to imagine how he would enjoy having such a creature under his power – and given what he had managed at the folly, the likelier it seemed that he actually *could* have such a beast under his control. Perhaps not this one, but… he had shown her an ability that she had never imagined.

Still, ability to control or not, any overreach on his part would sit very poorly with the people of Tarryford. Perhaps he would be run out of town, or worse.

You should not think such thoughts, no matter how good it feels.

Thomas sighed, his shoulders relaxing somewhat as he let go of his ire at last. Cassandra laid a tentative hand on his shoulder. "Will you not take a moment to rest?" she asked.

"You have been up and active for as long as I have, and you did not receive the same modicum of rest. You must be absolutely exhausted."

"I would like to," he confessed. "I have not felt this tired since I was watching after my brother just before his death, but… there is still too much to do."

"Let someone else do it for a time," Cassandra said. "Let the burden lie in another's arms for now." A vision of him upstairs in her bed flashed through her mind, and it took all of her self-restraint not to let her thoughts show on her face.

But I could make the offer to watch after him – not sleep with him, of course, but give him something more comfortable than the floor to lie on with the comfort of knowing he is being looked after…

Thomas heaved a sigh. "As soon as the beast is caught, I shall do so. For now I must give what aid I can." He gave her a small but real smile. "Trust me, I have learned my limits well. I can go on for some time as long as the cause is just. But please." He laid his hand on hers again. "Promise me that you shall not leave the inn again unless I am with you, at least not until the beast is taken care of. It may be overcautious, but I cannot feel that it is wrong to take extra care of you after what has already been done. Besides." He moved in a bit closer. "Mr Fraser cannot hurt you here. Mrs Copeland is exceedingly fond of you, especially now that you have brought her son back, and her good opinion carries great weight with the people of Tarryford. They will not tolerate you being dragged from this place by a man they neither like nor respect."

Cassandra shivered. "Do you think he would try such a blatant thing?"

"I cannot say with any certainty what he would be willing to try, but I would rather be safe."

She agreed, and that was that. Thomas left again and Cassandra, Mrs Copeland, Garrett, and the chambermaid became the only inhabitants of the inn. They were not together, though – Mrs Copeland was caring for her son, and the maid was left to work in the kitchen, providing for the occasional person who passed through. All the men were on the hunt, and there was a general feeling in the air of waiting with bated breath for news that the Beast of Avon Vale was finally dead.

Cassandra did her best to sleep and managed to catch an hour's rest here and there throughout the night, but by the time dawn came any real rest eluded her. Eventually Cassandra sat down at the table in her room and began to sketch out the beast as she remembered it. She had seen so little of it her drawing was more shadow than form, but surely she was not misremembering the enormous claws on the end of those long, rangy arms, nor the curious bend in the creature's legs. It looked made for running. And then there was its head, bald but not shiny except for glowing yellow eyes, and that jaw… she began to draw in the teeth, then stopped. It was not possible for them to be so long… or was it?

"You are going to make yourself sick trying to remember such things," she muttered.

"Trying to remember what, Miss Wright?"

"Oh!" Cassandra whirled around in her chair, coming to her feet so violently that she bumped into the table and knocked her book to the floor. In her doorway stood none other than Mrs Cross, of all people. The lady was carrying a tea tray and wore an apologetic expression on her face.

"Forgive me for startling you," she said, dipping her chin slightly. "I thought you had heard my footsteps, and as you can see, my hands are too full to knock. I was fortunate you left a crack in the door."

Had she? Cassandra thought she remembered locking it, yet how could Mrs Cross have opened it if she had? "I… that is all right," Cassandra said after a moment, although in truth it was nothing of the sort. She hadn't heard anything of the party apart from Thomas and Gilbert since she left the house, which had rather sealed the idea that she had been a companion of convenience to Mrs Cross, and no more. The thought unexpectedly hurt. "Whatever are you doing here?"

"I came to ask after your wellbeing and found the place practically deserted." She looked disapproving as she came into the room and set the tea tray down on the table between them. "It is a rather unprofessional state of affairs, I must say."

"Ah."

"But as this tray was already assembled, I thought I would take the liberty of bringing it upstairs to you."

She didn't seem to care that Cassandra was still clad in only her nightgown and shawl. "Thank you, but I am hardly dressed to be entertaining a visitor right now, and–"

Mrs Cross waved a hand dismissively. "You look modest enough to me, my dear. Besides..." She smiled, transforming her face from severe to friendly in an instant. "I confess, I was particularly eager to visit with you after what I heard from Mr Fraser this morning."

Cassandra paused in the act of pouring the tea. "What did you hear?"

"Why, that you were instrumental in the recovery of the missing boy, of course."

That I was instrumental in the disruption of his vile plot, you mean.

"I was very fortunate to have found him," was all she said in response.

"I think there is more than simple good fortune at work here." Mrs Cross took the cup of tea that Cassandra passed her, then waited expectantly for Cassandra to take her own. Cassandra felt far from thirsty, but she did what was expected and took a sip. *Ugh, too strong.* "I think," Mrs Cross went on, looking at Cassandra intently, "that you have a sharp and dedicated mind. I think that it would be a very poor idea to underestimate just how clever you can be."

"I have no idea what you might be referring to," Cassandra demurred. "I have done nothing exceptional apart from being exceptionally lucky."

"Miss Wright." Mrs Cross set her tea aside. "Let us speak plainly for a moment. Your presence here in Tarryford, and in such close connection with the Frasers, is something no one foresaw. Indeed, I would warrant that not even Mr

Griffith saw it coming with the clarity he is attempting to intimate."

Cassandra felt herself bristle. It was one thing to accuse her of poor behaviour, but quite another to bring Thomas into things. "Do not speak of things you do not understand."

"But I do understand, Miss Wright. Cassandra." Mrs Cross smiled. "I understand that you are dogged and determined to right the wrongs of your past. I know that Mr Fraser has been the architect of those wrongs, and that you are willing to do anything to set the world as you see it to rights, up to and including destroying the Fraser family. Are you not?"

How did this woman know so much? "Are you an ally of his, then?" Cassandra asked in lieu of answering her directly as she set her own cup aside. Better to have her hands free so that she could more easily grab her hatpin and defend herself.

"I find the man detestable," Mrs Cross replied, and Cassandra's rising dread stuttered for a moment. "He is the worst sort of person, to my mind – one who will do absolutely anything, who will sink to any low in order to get what he wants. And what James Fraser wants more than anything else is power, power in the name of England and power for himself."

"Then will you aid me?" It felt terribly risky to ask, but Cassandra felt now was the time to take a chance. Once the beast was gone, she would need every bit of assistance she could get when it came to cornering Mr Fraser. "Will you assist me in ensuring that he pays for what he has done?

For I am certain that my father is not his only victim, and–"

"I'm afraid I cannot."

Hearing this negative felt like being placed beneath the wavering edge of a guillotine. Cassandra stood up and stepped away from Mrs Cross, reaching for her pin... but her legs were unexpectedly wavering. *What... what is wrong with me?*

"His detestable nature aside, Mr Fraser is one of a handful of people who are actively investigating a means of improving our odds in this war," Mrs Cross went on. "For this war with France is not just about Napoleon and his ilk. It is about fighting back against powers that are so much vaster than us, it would not be incorrect to compare them to the ocean, and us to mere grains of sand. That we have gained the attention of these beings at all is... regrettable, but now that we have, we must ensure that it is our people, our island, *us*, who have greater control of them. Otherwise, we will be swept away, and the world entire might go with us.

"My husband and I have made... brokers of ourselves, you might say." Mrs Cross stepped slowly across the room towards Cassandra, who at this point was barely able to hold herself upright. "We facilitate the work that luminaries such as Mr Fraser are doing, to the best of our ability. When it became clear that he would require a virgin sacrifice in order to make his altar work, we found who we thought was a suitable candidate, one whose absence we would be able to explain away."

"It was *your* idea to capture a child?" Cassandra had not

thought the other woman capable of such evil. She tried to raise her voice to the level of a shout, but the ability to take a deep breath eluded her. "Young Garrett is much loved in Tarryford. To put him at such terrible risk only made the people who live here more inclined towards protectiveness than ever."

Mrs Cross frowned. "No indeed, *that* was a misstep that I had nothing to do with. I found a much better prospect for the sacrifice from a class of people who are as elegant as they are useless. Unmarried women of a certain age are, I am sure you know, relegated to the ranks of the forgotten and despised. It was simplicity itself to arrange a meeting between Reginald Humphrey and the Frasers and encourage enough of a friendship that they would travel here together, even simpler to ensure that Mrs Humphrey brought her unwed sister with her in an effort to capture Gilbert's heart.

"I knew she would never achieve her ends, and so arranged to have it appear as though she was carrying on an affair with one of Harston Hall's grooms. He has taken a carriage to Gretna Green with a woman of similar stature, and it shall appear to all the world as though Penelope has run off to be married."

"But she... but you..." Cassandra could no longer remain upright, and fell back against the mattress. "Why me, then?" she managed before her mouth went numb completely.

"Oh, Miss Wright." Mrs Cross brushed a stray lock of Cassandra's hair back from her face. "My high hopes for Penelope were unexpectedly dashed, which led to Mr Fraser making several rash and foolish decisions. But you... I believe that you shall do very nicely where she has failed us. Sleep now, my dear."

Cassandra knew she should not succumb. To sleep was to embrace death – she might never awake if she let herself fall now. She fought against the pull of it as best she could, but in the end all her efforts were for naught. She was pulled down into unconsciousness, and the last thing she was aware of was the chill of Mrs Cross's hand on the side of her face, like a piece of ice she could not dislodge.

God have mercy on me.

CHAPTER TWENTY-ONE

That chill was the first thing Cassandra noticed as she began to surface. It made her want to kick out at the woman touching her, until she realised that the sense of cold had seeped along the entire length of her body. If it was not Mrs Cross making her feel so cold right now, what was it? Careful to keep herself in the appearance of repose, Cassandra forced her senses to sharpen and focus on her current predicament. She needed to know where she was, how she had gotten here, and who else was with her.

Where could not be easily ascertained without opening her eyes. She would avoid that for now, but the *how…* that she was able to divine. She was lying on her back on a surface that was hard enough to make her body ache. Stone of some kind? There were variations in the surface of it, tiny dips and bulges that made her wonder if some sort of pattern was being pressed into her skin right now.

Her arms were stretched high above her head, and there was an additional sensation of weightiness and pressure around her wrists that made her think she must be bound in some fashion. The same pressure existed around her ankles, but her legs were not stretched as cruelly tight as her arms. Her shoulders were the only thing about her body that felt warm, and that was because they were hot with pain. She moved, ever so slowly and slightly, in an attempt to relieve that pain as she focused on her other senses.

It was quiet, wherever she was, but Cassandra thought she could hear movement far away, like the sound of someone walking along a distant corridor. Corridor... was she indoors, then? There was no movement in the air around her, yet there was a distinct feeling of *wildness*, somehow. And the smell...

That was the worst part, and the thing that broke her carefully studied stillness as soon as she recognised what she was smelling. The stench in the air, a mixture of effluvia and something darker, richer, was too strong to ignore. She coughed, then retched, turning her head to the other side in an effort to get away from the scent. Only then did she realise how sticky the surface she was lying on was, and how her cheek and hair clung to it as she moved.

To hell with this. She had to look, had to *know*... Cassandra opened her eyes and, after a few moments of desperate blinking and eventual resolution, gasped when she realised what she was seeing. A scream rose up in her chest, but she bit her lip, hard, to keep it from flooding out of her mouth as anything more than a whisper. Cassandra tasted her own blood, warm and metallic, and felt the first inkling of kinship she'd ever experienced with the person lying not two feet from her.

We both of us have bled on this altar now. Oh, Penelope…

For this was Penelope Getty staring at her with vacant eyes, the blood from the ruin of her throat emptied and seeped into the cracks on the stone. This was the fate of the woman who had loathed Cassandra and insinuated herself into Gilbert's company at every turn, who had tried so hard to be a woman he would want.

Cassandra wished more than ever now that she had been successful, for it might have saved her from this deadly fate.

"Ah." A voice she loathed more than anything else in this world resonated through the room, drawing her out of her helpless stare and back into the present. "You *are* awake. I thought you must be, but I'm gratified to see you open those beautiful eyes of yours."

"What have you done?" Cassandra's voice was rough with terror and whatever Mrs Cross had used to drug her. She coughed against her shoulder, her eyes juddering shut from the force of it.

"I think that, despite your attempts at appearing innocent, you know better than most what has been done here, Miss Wright." An uncomfortably hot hand turned her head to the right, away from Penelope's corpse, and Cassandra was brought face to face with Mr Fraser once more.

She blinked in shock. He looked so different from how he always presented himself. Gone were the breeches, the perfectly pressed jacket and flowing cravat. Gone were the Hessian boots and crisp white shirt, the gold accents and embroidery. Now he wore a dark robe that seemed to shimmer slightly in the light of the two torches she could see on the fractured walls. His perfectly coiffed hair was in disarray, and his face was bright with sweat and speckled with… were those spots of blood?

Now she saw the sigil on the half-fallen wall behind him, complicated and wavery, traced out in a rusty red that she was positive had been written in blood. Cassandra recognised this one from her father's journal. *He tried to open a portal with Penelope's blood.* But whatever he'd attempted to summon hadn't found Penelope sufficient to the task… *Oh, dear God. I'm next.*

"I have found that places accustomed to ancient powers respond more easily than those yet unsullied. This place, ruin that it is, will serve us very well tonight." He sighed. "You will doubtless not believe me, but I truly did not want to bring you into this," Mr Fraser noted, stroking a hand idly over her hair. Cassandra tried to pull away, but there was nowhere to flee to. "You should have stayed in service in the north. You could have lived a simple, quiet life, all danger and darkness left behind. But you couldn't leave well enough alone, could you?"

"And let you get away with murdering my father?" she demanded. Her lips were cracked, and her throat was desperately dry, but she managed to keep from coughing again by sheer dint of the force of her indignation. "He trusted you, he *loved* you, and you destroyed him and ruined all our lives!"

"Byron was a good friend to me," Mr Fraser said heavily. His hand still rested against her hair, an unwelcome weight that immobilised her even better than the ropes did. "Likely better than I deserved, and his mind! He had a near-perfect memory, did you know that? Coupled with his gift for languages and drawing, he was the ideal assistant to take note of what worked and what did not throughout our experiments." He shook his head. "If only he had been able to stomach the real work that the Brotherhood of the Black Goat is accomplishing. I feel that everything would have come together much more quickly for me if your father had not made himself expendable."

Cassandra's urge to defend her father welled up in her throat once more, but this time she did not give voice to it. After all, what could she say? She had read his journal – she knew, in his own words, the lengths he had gone to in his quest to assist this depravity. Her father was no innocent, but he was also not a murderer.

"Yes, you know the truth, don't you?" Mr Fraser smiled down at her, the kindly, avuncular smile of a man who was able to imitate softness in such a way that almost anyone else would be deceived. "How could you not? You, after all, are likely the only one able to read that cursed journal of his." He let go of her abruptly, turned and stalked over to a nearby table, and lifted a very familiar book into the air.

But how... Oh, that cursed Mrs Cross. She must have taken the key from Cassandra while she was unconscious and used it to open her chest. *And now I have no hatpin either,* she noted bitterly. Not that she could have drawn it, trussed up like she was, but having *some* sort of weapon on her would have made her feel better.

"I trusted your father like I would trust a brother," Mr Fraser said, and the kindness had departed from his voice, leaving bitterness and acridity behind. "I allowed him to be the sole guardian of the knowledge we learned, only to discover once both he *and* you were gone that he had amused himself by writing it all down in *code*!" He slammed the book down once more. "Useless!" he snapped. "So much work, lost to his petty little games!"

He stalked back over to Cassandra, malice glittering in his eyes. "I was tempted," he said unevenly, "to go after you when I learned the truth. From the moment I discovered you had stolen the journal, which you would not have bothered to do so if you couldn't read it. I thought about it for a long time, but in the end I decided to let you be and attempt to do this with Penelope."

He set his hands on the altar and leaned down until his face was just a few inches above hers. "My weak, stupid son would still have married you if I had allowed it," he hissed. "He held his affections for you close to his heart even after you left, and I know he does so now." Mr Fraser shook his head. "That is why what happens next shall be so good for him." He straightened up again, and Cassandra knew somehow that if she let him leave right now, all connection between them would be lost.

That connection was the only thing keeping her from becoming the next Penelope right now. She had to keep it alive, had to do whatever she could to keep *herself* alive, because Thomas needed time to find her.

If only I had left him another note!

But a note was not required, Cassandra was certain of it. Thomas was looking for her, she knew it like she knew the affections of her own heart. He would come to her if only she could last long enough.

"Wait, sir," she cried, leaning up as far as the ropes would allow. "Will you not grant me one boon before you kill me? I- I have desired for so long to truly understand my father's obsession with the work you two were doing. Even after reading his journal, I know I have only grasped the barest edges of the, the *enormity* of your endeavour. Will you not tell me more of it? Let me understand why it is I must die."

Mr Fraser stared at her with an expression of pity. "Ah, my dear," he said, "you are but a woman. How could you possibly understand what it is the Brotherhood is trying to accomplish?"

"You have brought other women into your confidence," Cassandra pointed out. "Mrs Cross comprehends a great deal of the, the *importance* of what you do, does she not? She is clever and useful to you. If she can understand, surely I can as well."

He pursed his lips. "Do you know," he said, "that Mrs Cross had the audacity to tell me I ought to gag you and prevent you from speaking once I got you here? She believed that your silver tongue would be able to turn my intentions towards you aside. I told her there was no need to be jealous of a poor, lost thing such as yourself, that you were more to be pitied than censured, but now I wonder whether she may not have been correct."

Oh, please no. Cassandra set aside every ounce of self-respect that she still possessed and crumpled in on herself. He could pity her? Then let him feel pity. Tears sprang into her eyes, tears that were not at all feigned, and a gasping sob escaped her lips. "I know that my fate is in your hands," she managed to mumble. "But I – for so long, I wondered about my father's fate and what he had done to deserve it. Everything you say… I merely wish to understand. I wish to know that his death, and mine, will *matter*."

Amazingly, his face softened once more. "Ah, my dear," he said. "Of course a clever young woman like you would set the edification of her curiosity before all else. Your father was so proud of you, you know. He spoke endlessly of your accomplishments. Despite the fact that Gilbert was marrying down by asking for your hand, by the end of your engagement I was beginning to think that *he* might be undeserving of *you*."

He was. He is. But Cassandra held her uncharitable thoughts inside and maintained her posture of desperate entreaty, and after a moment Mr Fraser nodded. "If you've deciphered your father's journal then you've clearly some wits about you," he told her. "And I confess, I have missed having someone to discuss more weighty matters with. In the absence of your father, I suppose a somewhat intelligent girl like yourself will do.

"The Brotherhood of the Black Goat arose in direct

response to Bonaparte's ascension to power," he said, turning and beginning to pace back and forth in front of a charred stone wall. Charred... indeed, the whole long room smelled faintly of ash. Were they in the remains of Northlake Hall?

Northlake Hall burned after the death of Elizabeth Northlake, Cassandra remembered. Everyone else in the family died in the flames. Could it be that her death was also the result of a deliberate sacrifice?

"None of us wanted to stoop to the levels we were forced to," Mr Fraser went on. "Sacrifices in blood, offerings for ancient gods – this is not anything our country has attempted on such a level since the time of the druids. They, too, were withstanding an invasion – a Roman one, and the Romans were just as willing as the French to rely on dark powers to gain a foothold here.

"But we have learned well from the mistakes of the past." He looked at her and smiled. "Your father was instrumental in translating some of the ancient texts that guide our actions today. It is safe to say that without Byron Wright, none of this would be possible."

Father, you damned fool. "But what exactly is 'this'?" she asked tremulously. "Are you bringing creatures like the Beast of Avon Vale into the world to fight on our behalf?"

Mr Fraser shook his head irritably. "That bloody beast," he muttered. "A remnant of the Northlake family's complete inability to control their own power. It came into this world by accident, and is of no more import than any other lone beast trying to keep itself alive. And yet it has come perilously close to endangering everything that the Brotherhood has worked for thanks to its hunting ability."

"You never meant for it to hurt anyone," Cassandra said soothingly, hoping to keep him from becoming distracted. The longer she could forestall what she knew he intended, the better.

"Absolutely not," Mr Fraser agreed. "I did not bring it into this world, and therefore its attacks were entirely beyond my control, I'm disappointed to say. Not that what you say is without merit. To have an army of such creatures fighting for England, well…" A smile crossed his lips. "The carnage on our behalf would be incredible. I would truly have enjoyed getting a better look at the beast, but I'm afraid it was not meant to be. The Beast of Avon Vale, whatever it is, has doubtless been slaughtered by the people of Tarryford by now."

Which meant that Thomas would be free to look for her. This news bolstered Cassandra's spirits substantially. "An unlucky chance," she suggested, and was gratified when Mr Fraser nodded appreciatively.

"Indeed. Particularly unlucky for you," he said with a sigh. "Miss Getty was the first attempt to ensure that you would not be necessary in this bloody endeavour, Miss Wright. As you can see, though, she failed us." He sneered. "It turns out that she did not have the necessary *qualities* to act as a proper portal between worlds, but even her death led to certain valuable revelations." He tapped the side of his head meaningfully. "I am learning new things all the time, my dear, and now I believe that it is indeed possible for me to not only make you into an appropriate sacrifice, but to *also* preserve your life at the same time.

"I was going to attempt this on the boy," he continued, oblivious to Cassandra's widening eyes and the way her hands clenched into fists, "and claim him as a ward of mine once we reached London. But although I was quite furious at you for finding him and interfering in my plans, now I know it to be an act of providence. A young woman such as yourself shall be of far more interest to Shub-Niggurath than a child. You will be a perfect vessel for this dark goddess, and aid me in turning more people to our righteous cause than anyone else ever could." He smiled proudly at her.

"You are going to be the bulwark that stands between England and the darkness threatening to overwhelm her," Mr Fraser said firmly. "The armies of France and Spain have chosen to call upon greater powers, but that makes them harder to contain as well. For every sea battle that one of these leviathans interferes with, it does nearly as much damage to the ships controlling it as it does to those it was intended to destroy."

Sea battles? The redactions in Samuel's last letter were making more sense to her now. As worried as she was for herself, her concern for her brother still surged to the forefront of her mind. "What sort of beasts?" she asked.

"Creatures of immense power," he said, his fingers tracing the edge of the altar she lay on as if to help ground himself. "Creatures capable of such overwhelming dominance that it is incredible that they have not laid waste to the entire world. I suppose we must congratulate Bonaparte on his ability to command these dark gods at all. The Spanish have been even worse with it. They have lost two coastal cities to summonings gone wrong, as far as we can ascertain." Mr Fraser smiled suddenly. "In this case, the enemy of my enemy is certainly my friend."

Cassandra, stricken with the thought of an entire city being laid to waste, and all by *accident*, could not be so sanguine. "But I am just one person," she said, pointing out what seemed to be a major flaw in Mr Fraser's plan. "How can one person, even one who is … is possessed by a god … do as much for England as one of the greater gods?"

"Ah, my dear. You are thinking too shallowly." He briefly caressed her cheek. "A war is more than the ability to bring weapons directly into battle. Our navy, even without leviathans on its side, is markedly more competent than either that of the French or the Spanish. What we lack is the will to make bold decisions in our own defence, if and when they become required."

"What do you mean?"

"We are primarily fighting a war at sea," Mr Fraser said. "But what about when that war finally makes landfall? What will we do when the engines of conflict must be fed with more blood, when more sacrifices are to be made on England's own soil? Bonaparte does not care for his worldly reputation and will let any stain rest upon it as long as he is winning, but our king wishes to be upheld as a righteous and God-fearing man. The court in general is filled with weakness, yet they are the ones whose minds must be turned if we are to expand England's might."

Expand its... "You believe there should be a counter-invasion?"

"If everything goes as it should," Mr Fraser said gently, "then this war marks the beginning of a new era of dominance for our nation. Consider how thoroughly we have already colonised the world, then think of what we could do with the unfractured might of the entire aristocracy at our backs. Just think." He grinned. "Your body might one day even be the queen of this great nation."

A familiar skittering sound interrupted their conversation. Tiny claws scrabbled against stone, and a second later Cassandra found herself staring into the awful, almost human-like face of the rat-thing that had snuck into her room and tormented her dreams.

She could not hold back her shriek this time, pulling away as far as she could from the tiny beast. It bared its sharp teeth at her, red eyes glinting, and snapped at her face.

"Ah ah," Mr Fraser chided it, holding out his arm. After a few more snaps, the rat-thing turned and climbed up the sleeve of his robe to sit on his shoulder. "No scaring our dear guest."

"This... this creature is yours, too?"

"A truly fortunate discovery," Mr Fraser said, stroking the little beast's bald, wrinkled head. "It was one of the first things I was ever able to call into existence. A portal for a proper god must be fuelled by a proper sacrifice, but a little thing like this in the proper location... that was much easier to come by. Working out the proportion of the things I needed to kill in order to call different creatures into being was tricky work, and something your father was a great help with."

He looked down at her placidly. "The beast that took his life the night your father died was the first one I ever called into existence with the help of a human sacrifice. It obeyed me completely, and it was responsible for ending your father's life. It's unfortunate that I was unable to keep it in this world for long, but I learned much from the experience."

Cassandra's veneer of calm finally tore completely away. "How could you?" she screamed. "How could you stand there and watch such a thing happen? How could you do this to my father? When he would have done *anything* for you?"

Mr Fraser shook his head. "Ah, my dear. I knew your acquiescence was too good a thing to be true. You are just as bold and thoughtless as Byron in the end. As for the *how* ..." He leaned down. "You read his journal, did you not?" he asked with a sneer. "You must know he harboured doubts about what we were doing. You know he doubted *me*, after swearing to our cause and becoming a member of the Brotherhood. He committed the ultimate betrayal, and his death was the smallest form of payment for that betrayal that I could extract."

His eyes were bright with a mad fervour and glinted the same red as the rat-thing that still clung to him, gnashing its teeth with delight at Cassandra's sorrow. "If I had been thinking clearly, I would have spilled his blood in a far more useful fashion. Luckily for me, I have the chance to correct that mistake with you, Byron's flesh and blood.

"And it is *my* flesh and blood that shall do the correcting. *Gilbert!*"

CHAPTER TWENTY-TWO

No. No, it was not possible. Gilbert could not be party to his father's madness, he *could not* be. Cassandra turned her head away from Mr Fraser in denial, only to be confronted with the brutal reality of Gilbert, her former betrothed and a man who had so recently declared his love for her, walking down the room towards them with a dejected expression on his face.

"Father," he said as he drew close. "I – oh god!" His steps stumbled to a stop as he caught sight of the altar. "You said she would be asleep!" he moaned. "You said she would never have to see me do this!"

"I decided that it is better for you to confront your baseless fears in this case rather than hide behind them," Mr Fraser said coldly. "Cassandra Wright is nothing to you."

"But she–"

"No, Gilbert. Cassandra Wright is *nothing to you*," he said fiercely, coming around the altar to grab his son firmly by the arm. "She is merely a body waiting to be transformed into a being who will alter the face of the entire world. The person within that frame is nothing compared to that, *nothing*, do you understand me?"

"But I didn't want her to see me," Gilbert sobbed, still staring at Cassandra. "You said she would not see me. I cannot bear the look on her face."

What look was he seeing? Cassandra wondered. What fraction of the utter disgust at the monster her former betrothed had become was showing through? Was it tempered by fear, or amplified by her horror at the situation? Whatever he saw, she hoped the sight of it tortured him.

"And you left the other one there, too. It was hard enough to kill a woman the first time, Father, why must *I* do it again?"

Wait… she was not even to be his first murder? Gilbert was the one who had killed the hapless Miss Getty? What the lady must have felt when he did it, this man on whom she had placed so many of her hopes…

"You are lower in my eyes than dirt," Cassandra said. The words came unbidden, but she was unable to stop herself from saying them as she caught Gilbert's gaze and held it as though she'd shackled him to her mind. His watery eyes widened with alarm, but he didn't look away. "You are the worst sort of man imaginable, Gilbert. Your father may be mad, but at least he is a man acting from his own twisted convictions, while *you* are nothing more than a puppet to be manipulated."

"That's not true," Gilbert whimpered. "I – you could have avoided all this! All you had to do was leave Thomas for me and I could have kept you safe! I *wanted* to keep you safe, Cassie, why wouldn't you let me?"

"You what?" his father asked, contempt giving way to astonishment.

"I love you," Gilbert went on, oblivious to the tears rolling down his florid cheeks. "I truly do! Why did you have to make me confront you like this? Why do you never make *anything* easy for me?"

"What weight does your love even carry?" Cassandra asked loudly. It was oddly comforting to hear her voice echo from the walls of this long, dark room. It reminded her that she was real, she was alive. For now, at least. "You expected me to be unconscious when you arrived! You expected to murder me in my *sleep*! What form of love is that?"

She wanted desperately to continue to decry Gilbert, to make him feel a fraction of the discomfort and distrust that she felt now in his presence, but she stopped herself. She was still alive, and if she wanted to *stay* that way, she needed someone on her side. Gilbert was her best chance.

"I want to believe in your love for me," she said, lowering her voice to something more intimate. "I want to believe that there is more good in you than even you know, that given the chance to repent, you will do what is right and–"

"Be silent!" Mr Fraser came over and slapped Cassandra hard across the face. It was impossible to dodge, and the impact of his hand on her cheek was enough to snap her head back against the altar, rendering her momentarily senseless. He quickly stepped in to fill the void left by her silence.

"Do not listen to this harlot," Mr Fraser commanded his son. "If her affections for you were true, she would have returned to you instead of forming an arrangement with your dearest friend. Neither of them are worthy of your time, Gilbert." His voice went from commanding to threatening. "And if you want to be worthy of *mine*, and prove that all the money and time I have put into you has been well spent, then you shall begin the bloodletting immediately, or *so help me*, I shall make you suffer the consequences of your inaction!"

"Father, I–"

"Now!" From under his robe he produced a black, double-edged knife that he passed to Gilbert hilt-first – *the obsidian blade*. Cassandra recognised it from her father's description in the journal. It was an ancient sacrificial weapon responsible for killing untold numbers of people, and now it would be used on her.

Gilbert looked perfectly miserable as he came over to Cassandra's side. "At least you're not really going to die," he said, as though her soul being ejected from her corporeal form to make her into an ancient god's puppet was so much better than that. "And… and this knife is very sharp, the cuts truly don't hurt as badly as they could. But if you move the wrong way, I could go too deep, so…"

She began to thrash immediately, ripping herself back and forth across the altar. He was worried about going too deep? Then she would make it impossible for him to do otherwise. She would rather her whole self died than that she died just enough for her body to go on without her and be used in his father's dire schemes.

"Cassie, stop!" Gilbert begged. "Please, I do not wish this to be any worse for you!"

"This will never be anything but the *worst* thing you could do to me," Cassandra spat at him. "Tell yourself what you like, but do not for a moment believe this is anything other than a betrayal of every decent aspect of human nature. You are *nothing* now, you have no soul! You are as cruel and unjust as your father and you are even *worse* than him, because you claim to know better!"

Gilbert looked at her with wide, wounded eyes, and Cassandra thought for a moment she might be getting through to him. Perhaps her cause was not entirely hopeless! "But you can still–"

"*Enough!*" Mr Fraser grabbed her by the shoulders and pinned her to the cold stone with one hand, the other one pressing down firmly on her mouth and nose. She tried with all her might to raise her legs enough to push him back, but they were bound too tightly. She attempted to shake her head from side to side and dislodge his hand, but the cold and the aftereffects of the drug left her too weak to do more than tremble with effort. "Do it now, Gilbert!"

The sharp admonishment was enough to galvanise Gilbert into action. Tears welled up in his eyes and spilled down his cheeks as he brought the knife to bear on the soft flesh of Cassandra's right arm. She screamed as he cut a long, thin line from just below her shoulder all the way down to her elbow before stopping.

Blood flowed out from her throbbing wound onto the altar, and suddenly the stone was no longer cold. Instead, it held a charged energy wherever her blood filled the shallow lines beneath her, warming her body with the kind of heat that bespoke a fire blazing to terrible life.

On the wall where Mr Fraser had drawn the sigil, a vortex of some kind appeared. It was no larger than the nail of her smallest finger to start, but the more her blood pulsed out with every beat of her terrified heart, the larger the swirling circle of dark energy became.

That is where your doom will emerge from to consume you if you don't find a way out of this!

Cassandra focused on Gilbert as best she could through the pain and screamed against Mr Fraser's hand, screamed until stars swam in front of her eyes and her lungs began to ache from a lack of air. As a filmy haze descended over her vision, she watched Gilbert step back and retch, heard his father begin to lambast him again, and then–

A sharp *crack* rent the cold air, deafeningly loud in this place of echoes and darkness. Cassandra did not know the cause of it at first, could barely understand what she was seeing when Gilbert took two faltering steps forwards and then fell, limp, across the middle of her own body. She did not comprehend the wetness she felt pouring from him, or the heat that responded to it beneath her.

All she knew was that Mr Fraser finally let her go, a curse on his lips and a wild look in his eyes. And that the knife Gilbert held was loose now, and within a few inches of her bound hands.

CHAPTER TWENTY-THREE

As the haze cleared from her mind, Cassandra became aware of two things. One was a fierce, persistent barking sound, and the other was a furious cry of, "*Cass!*"

Oh, thank God, it was Thomas!

Cassandra turned eagerly to look at him, but her hopes of a swift rescue turned to desperate concern as she watched another figure in a long black cloak – from the way he moved, she thought it must be Colonel Cross – pull a sword on him. Thomas was armed with a sword as well, but his movements were nowhere near as swift and smooth. How could they be? He had been labouring for two days without rest; he had to have been looking for her from the moment he heard she was missing. And now he was in a battle against a well-trained, well-rested opponent and Mr Fraser was barrelling towards him as well, fingers flared like talons as he shouted about making Thomas pay.

Merlin rushed forward before Mr Fraser could reach Thomas, though, slamming into him so hard that they both fell to the ground. Cassandra's heart soared even as she knew this was a brief respite at best; Mr Fraser had already shown how he could affect her canine protector.

I have to help them! Cassandra strained her fingers towards the knife that could be her salvation, focusing all her attention on it and trying not to feel the way Gilbert's body was still shuddering, the sound he made as his last breath left him...

The way the portal expanded far beyond what she herself had bled out.

The blood of a virgin... a proper sacrifice...

Oh God, Gilbert's blood was as good as hers when it came to the ritual! The portal yawned as wide as the altar itself, dark energy crackling around its edges. The scene within it was a dark, barren landscape where it was nearly impossible to make out the details. Something within it moved, though; something vast, something that made the very air seem to vibrate as it shifted its bulk. The tiny bit of light that existed on the other side of the portal was snuffed out, and Cassandra wondered what had blocked it.

Her unspoken question was answered a moment later as something that seemed like a cross between the thorny cane of a rosebush and the thick, muscular tentacles of an octopus reached through the middle of the portal, twining and twisting like it was seeking something.

Seeking her?

With a shout of effort, Cassandra finally got her fingers around the obsidian knife. She twisted it around and sawed at the rope that held her, uncaring of the nicks and cuts she gained in the process. More of her blood joined Gilbert's, the trickles from her wounds making the portal even wider. The first seeking tentacle was joined by another, slightly less thick but faster, and before Cassandra knew it the tentacle touched the very point of her chin.

The feel of it was cold – unutterably so, frigid in a way she had never encountered before, not even during the darkest of winter nights. A thing so terribly cold shouldn't be able to move, ought to be frozen solid until spring released it. But this creature moved fluidly, tracing a trail from her chin down across her neck, then along her wounded, stinging arm. It soon found Gilbert's body and twisted itself around the top of his head, hoisting the weight of him off Cassandra as it dragged more and more of him into its coils.

Had it accepted him as a sacrifice instead of her? Was she to be ignored by this fell creature? *Please, please, take him and leave me alone!*

The thicker tentacle found Gilbert as well, wrapping around his waist. He was dead, Cassandra *knew* he was dead, but the sight of him captured so completely made her heart hurt for him. The tentacles paused for a moment, and then–

They squeezed.

Cassandra had never witnessed such a show of force before in her life, not even when confronting the beast that had laid waste to her horse. The sheer, unrelenting pressure the creature was able to exert on Gilbert's unresisting body was enough to crack his bones into splinters. His head spun fully around, twisted so hard that after another few moments it fell to the ground completely severed. His torso followed, turned from a sturdy structure into a slurry of gore that sprayed across the room in mere seconds. His feet, the only part of him to remain unmolested, dropped to the floor with a thud, the heels of his boots clacking on the stone.

Cassandra felt as though her mind had been taken to a place far away from her body for a moment, like she was looking at the scene of Gilbert's dismemberment without actually being as close as she was to it. She sawed doggedly at her restraints, determined even more resolutely to free herself now. *There*, one hand was free! Now to get the other…

The thinner of the two tentacles found her again, climbing from her waist past her chest until it touched her face once more. Cassandra tried not to move much, to avoid anything that would provoke it as it trailed over her cheek, then her lips. It paused there.

No. No, no… surely not. She could barely breathe, she was so afraid, but her anger was even stronger. She wouldn't lie here and become this monster's next victim. She *wouldn't*.

The second it tried to enter her mouth, she bit down hard on it. Bitterness flooded her tongue, and Cassandra retched and spat to the side even as the tentacle reared back. It raised up as though it were preparing for retaliation, but she managed to bring the knife up just as the tentacle fell down. The blade was sharp and cut through the meaty flesh far better than her teeth had managed, and the tentacle's retreat was more pronounced this time, the member clearly in pain.

"Do not injure it!" Mr Fraser howled from behind her. A second later he was there, wrestling the knife from her hand. He looked the worse for wear after his encounter with Merlin, cradling one arm close to his body, but his frenzy lent him strength. "Do not injure the servant of Shub-Niggurath! Dark young, dark young, have mercy on us!"

He turned fully towards the portal as the tentacle continued to writhe. "Mercy!" he repeated. "She is a simpleton, a fool, she does not respect your power like I do! Shub-Niggurath, All-Mother, Lord of the Wood, we, your Brotherhood, offer you this young woman as a vessel in our world. Let her mortal frame shelter your greatness, let yourself become incarnate within our world as one who can walk among us. Shub-Niggurath! I beg–"

Begging, apparently, was not something that Shub-Niggurath wanted. The thick tentacle, which had retreated into the portal as the smaller one danced about in pain, shot through once more, this time grabbing Mr Fraser by the waist and holding him fast. He shrieked in fear, an act which quickly took on a bloody tinge of agony as pink foam frothed from his lips. Mr Fraser, piety forgotten, brought the black blade down on the tentacle holding him over and over, fighting to free himself.

It was startling to realise that beneath her horror, she was *glad* he was dying this way. Now, if only she could finish cutting herself loose so that she didn't die as well...

"Cass!"

Oh god… "Thomas?" She turned just in time for him to arrive beside her. He was bleeding from his head, from his arm, from his hip. "Are you all right?"

"Never mind me, we must free you at once." He used his sword to cut through the remaining rope that bound her arms, then did her feet. "Quickly now, we must–"

The second, skinnier tentacle was back, and it went straight for Thomas. It wrapped around his neck and chest, arching him backward as he strained to keep his feet. His sword clattered to the floor.

"Run!" he managed to shout. "Cass, run!"

"No!" There had to be a way to end this that would save him – she refused to leave Thomas here.

"*Nooooo! Not me!*" Wearied of tolerating Mr Fraser's attacks, the thick tentacle squeezed him hard enough it must have shattered his ribcage. He went completely limp, dropping the knife, and a second later his body was dragged through the portal. The skinnier tendril began to do the same with Thomas.

"You do *not* get to have him!" Cassandra screamed. She got to her feet, grabbed Thomas's sword from where it lay on the floor, raised it high above her head, and then swung as hard as she could at Thomas's captor. *He's mine, damn you!*

It wasn't until the third strike that she finally sheared through the tentacle. Bluish-black blood sprayed in gouts across her body, the altar, the floor, and Thomas himself as she helped him to shrug off the tentacle's restraining weight.

"How do we close it?" Thomas asked. "There must be a way to close the portal!"

"There is!" The sigil was already there. All Cassandra had to do was…

She ran a hand along her bloody arm, marched over to the summoning sigil, and slapped her palm down in the centre of it. The mark flared bright. "Begone!" she shouted. "Leave this world! We do not want you here!"

The tentacles retreated. The portal began to close. A few seconds later, it vanished completely.

All that was left was them, Merlin – who had already limped over to her and pressed his cold nose into her colder leg, dear thing – the altar, poor dead Penelope, and the varied remains of Gilbert Fraser. His father, James, was lost to the other realm.

I hope he is not dead, Cassandra thought vengefully, her mind still full of the violence she had just witnessed. Kindness was not in her then; she had lost her ability to be measured and calm. *I hope he is alive. I hope it leaves him to suffer for days and days, forever if there is any justice in either world–*

"Cass?" Warm hands found her shoulders and turned her, ever so gently, away from the wall that had just held a portal to another world. "Cass," the voice said – his voice – *Thomas*, he was still here! Yes, she had saved him, she–

"I am well," he said in calm tones. "You did wonderfully. Now you can relax a bit. Let go of the sword, darling."

"What?" she managed through numb, bitter-tasting lips.

"The sword, Cass. You can let go of it now."

"The sword…" She looked down and saw her hand clenched tightly around the hilt of Thomas's sabre. She could see that her knuckles bulged from effort, that her arm was shaking with fatigue, but it also seemed imperative that she keep holding on. "Yes, but… what if someone else comes? How will I save us without a sword?"

"You already saved both of us without it," Thomas said, capturing her gaze with his own. He looked dreadful and wonderful all at once, a mess of fluids and filth and ruined clothes, but his eyes were bright with wonder, and the smile on his face was tenderness incarnate. "You gave me the knowledge I needed to find you, and you forced the monster back into its realm.

"You have done more and better than I or anyone else could have imagined. And now it's time for you to rest, darling. All shall be well, I swear it." He stepped closer and laid his hand over her terrible grip. "All you have to do is trust me and let go."

Let go… How could she let go? And yet she did trust Thomas. She did. He was right here with her, and Merlin was here, and they cared for her. They would keep her safe.

Cassandra stared straight into his eyes and, finger by finger, forced herself to let go of the sword. It clattered to the ground between them, and Thomas did not reach for it. Instead, he folded Cassandra into his embrace, arms tight around her as he pressed his face into her hair. "Thank god, thank god," he murmured. Cassandra took a deep breath, then another, and then all at once her emotions found her again.

She fell apart, content in the knowledge that for now, it was safe for her to do so.

CHAPTER TWENTY-FOUR

The effects of Mr Fraser's deadly foolishness resonated through the remnants of the party with all the concussive force of a cannonball.

Cassandra was fortunate enough to be spared the worst of the consequences of what the magistrate, down from the county seat thanks to a plea sent days ago by Thomas, meted out amongst them. Devil worship, human sacrifice, specially trained attack animals sent to plague the good citizens of the countryside for the amusement of the gentry... it was almost too sordid to be believed. But as the reality of the situation was far *less* believable, it was accepted.

Thomas did a masterful job of laying blame where blame was due, aided by the unexpected capitulation of Mr Humphrey and Mr Kildeer, who it turned out were both considering "membership" in Mr Fraser's Brotherhood but had not yet been persuaded to lend their money and influence to the cause.

Mr Humphrey had, in fact, been the one to suggest his viper-tongued sister-in-law to Mrs Cross as a possible vessel, the revelation of which led to a shrieking attack by his wife before she collapsed in a dead faint. Mrs Kildeer professed her own innocence with great vehemence, and whether or not she was truly innocent or her husband was merely protecting her, she was not charged with anything in the end.

The true jewels of the justice's collection were the Crosses. Colonel Cross had been badly wounded by Thomas as he fought to keep the ritual from being interrupted, and he was still unconscious from blood loss. His wife, on the other hand, had been captured on the road outside Tarryford by the town's watchman, attempting to flee the scene of her many indiscretions. They were to be taken to London and evaluated for their crimes, and Cassandra was not sad to be spared the sight of that charming, genteel, dark-souled woman again.

For herself, there was comparatively little to do. That first night, after their return to Harston Hall and after the revelations that both Fraser men were dead had rippled through the staff, Thomas was accepted as the master of the house without reservation. Cassandra could understand why; for all that his appearance was ghastly after the long and bloody affair, he radiated an air of competence and understanding that people craved when confronted with the unknown. When he informed the butler that Cassandra was to be cared for, it was as good as done.

She bathed in a haze, barely able to raise her arms to help

wash her hair, much less bind her own wounds. She was silent as the maids attending her took in her wounds, and only roused when she found herself in the company of the elderly housekeeper, a gentle, soft-handed woman who reminded her of Ma Hughes.

"Ah, m'dear," the woman said as she inspected the cuts on Cassandra's arm and hands. "This has been a hard time for you, hasn't it?"

Cassandra did not mean to break down in tears; in fact, she had felt herself entirely unable to cry at all, lost in a numbing haze. But now, that one simple question, by a woman who had already been kind to her, shattered her brittle shields. She wept; the housekeeper clucked and soothed her as she bound her wounds and finally gave her a sleeping draught that would "give you rest without dreams, lass, it's the least you're due right now."

Cassandra wasn't sure how long she slept, but when she woke she felt more human than she had in… heavens, how long had she been at her self-imposed task? Had it truly only been a week since she came to Tarryford? Since she met Thomas once more and became embroiled in the ill deeds of the Fraser family? It felt like so much longer; she had changed more completely as a result of this one week than she had imagined possible, even after the great upheaval of her life upon her father's death.

Now she knew the truth. That was what she had come for and that, Cassandra knew, was where she needed to find her sense of solace from this day forward. Truthfully, she did not know what her next step would be. It had never seemed important to think beyond this moment when she was putting together her initial plan. Why distress herself with thoughts of what might come next when she did not know when this part of her life would end? She had thought it might take months to get the information she needed, or longer. And now...

And now Mr Fraser is justly dead, and Gilbert slightly less justly so, and you know that your father was less innocent and more foolish than you had ever imagined.

Coming to terms with that knowledge hurt Cassandra's heart more than she expected it to. It was one thing to point a finger at villainy easily perceived in others, quite another to find herself perceiving it in her own kin. In some ways, she felt she might have been better off not knowing the truth. It felt as though the last vestige of her innocence, of that long-gone girlhood where she had been so full of hope and contentment, was gone now.

Yet it was also freeing. Freeing, and motivating all at once.

There is nothing to bind me to any one path now but my own heart and mind. I may do with my life what I wish. And what she wished to do with it was...

A sudden knock on the door interrupted Cassandra's musings over a handsome, serious face. "Miss?"

"Come in," Cassandra called out, and one of the Harston maids entered the room with a broad smile on her face.

"You're awake! Bless me, that's good! I've been checkin' on you for the past three hours – thought you were going to sleep another day away!" the young woman said as she bustled around the room, opening the curtains and letting the bright sunlight shine in.

Sunlight... another day...

"How long have I been asleep?" Cassandra asked.

"This is the second morning since you were brought here, miss."

The second morning! Lord in heaven, she'd been sleeping for something like thirty hours. No wonder her bladder pressed at her so alarmingly. Cassandra got to her feet, ready to dismiss the maid so she could tend to her needs in private, then slumped right back down again on the bed when her legs decided to refuse her directives.

"Careful there, miss!" The young woman was by her side in an instant, one hand going beneath her arm to steady her. Cassandra hissed in pain at the pressure on her wound, and the maid drew back instantly, a shamed look on her face. "Oh, I am sorry, Miss Wright!"

"It's fine, you were only trying to keep me from falling on my face," Cassandra said with a smile. "And that is something I do appreciate."

"Aye, miss, it's just... we're meant to show you every courtesy. I'd do it anyway," she added with a firm look on her face, "even without you bein' a guest here, since you helped put an end to all the dark doings that've been happenin' to Tarryford."

Ah. "I assume you're referring to the beast," Cassandra said, testing her balance before attempting to stand again. She managed much better this time.

"Well, aye, miss, that rotten thing's been taken care of,

but also…" She lowered her voice and leaned in. "We all knew Mr Fraser was up to no good thing," she whispered hurriedly. "Nor the people he brought here. Nothing to do about it when you're a servant, but *you*, you came and everything changed. There was a darkness here, Miss Wright, a darkness that all of us could feel, an' it's gone now. And for that, we thank you and Mr Griffith so much."

Thomas. Cassandra was suddenly filled with longing at the thought of seeing him once more. "Where is Mr Griffith?" she asked.

To her surprise, the young woman laughed. "Oh, he's waiting for you, miss! Hasn't shifted from the parlour since he woke up himself yesterday, an' he will not hear of going anywhere before he speaks to you once more!" A knowing look entered her eyes. "Would you like me to help you get ready, Miss Wright? I am sure he would love to join you for breakfast."

As if conjured by the word, Cassandra's stomach rumbled with hunger. "That would be excellent," she said, then winced. "*After* I take a moment to myself."

"Of course, miss." The maid departed, and Cassandra saw to her intimate needs in gratifying solitude. She took stock of herself; her cuts were bandaged and healing, her head was clear and her body refreshed after her very welcome rest, and while her energy was flagging, she was certain a good meal and good company would restore it quickly. Altogether, she was quite pleased that her terrible time in the ruins of Northlake Hall had not left her worse off.

Of course, there was still plenty of time for that. Bitter

experience had taught her that she would likely never be free of nightmares after what she had endured, but if she were fortunate, they would not ruin her on a nightly basis.

By the time the maid – whose name, when asked, was blushingly given up as "Mary Price, miss" – was finished helping her dress and put up her hair, Cassandra was feeling very nearly like her old self once more. It had been a long time since she had had assistance with getting herself ready for company, but given that she could not raise her own arm above her head to help put her hair back without pain, she was grateful for it. Once she was done and dressed in her most comfortable gown, she let Mary guide her to the drawing room where Thomas was waiting for her.

He was slumped in a chair by the fireplace, unmoving, and for a moment Cassandra's breath caught in her throat. Then she noted the movement of his chest, and took in the improved but still present circles beneath his eyes, and realised that he was simply exhausted. *He has not had the leisure of sleeping the worst of the aftermath away as you have.*

"Oh, miss," Mary said quietly behind her. "Shall I wake him for you?"

"No," Cassandra said, "I can handle that, but if you would call for a fresh pot of tea as well as some breakfast to be brought here, that would be lovely."

"Of course, miss!" She vanished down the corridor and Cassandra let herself into the room, closing the door behind her in near-silence. She slowly walked over to Thomas's side, taking in every inch of him. She noted the new thickness around his middle which spoke of bandages there, as well as a cut just beneath his hairline that she could recall from the battle they had waged. His hands were also heavily bandaged, and while he was not wearing his sword, it lay less than a hand's length away on the table beside the chair. There was an empty glass that might have held wine but, knowing Thomas, was more likely to have contained water, as well as a book that had failed to hold his interest long enough to keep him from sleep.

Cassandra felt a bit guilty about waking him, but she also desperately wished to speak to him. She had to know for certain that he was all right. Also, he was the only person here whom she could speak to about her... other concerns. And there were many of them.

Mostly, though, she simply found herself craving his company for her own sake. She reached out and laid a gentle hand on his arm. "Thomas," she said softly. "It's Cass." She squeezed lightly, and then—

She drew back quick as a flash when he came awake with a gasp, his hand going to a dagger she had not even seen at his belt as he lunged to his feet. Cassandra was rather surprised she had managed to evade him. "Thomas," she said, louder this time, more firm. "Wake up, my dear. All is well now."

He stared at her for a long moment before saying, hoarsely, "Cass."

"Yes."

He looked from her to the dagger in his hand, then threw it aside with disgust before coming to her. "God help me, I could have – are you all right? Did I hurt you?"

"Not at all," she assured him, holding her hands out for him to take. His grip was warm despite his pallor. "I should have been more cautious with waking you. I do know better, I assure you, so this misunderstanding is entirely my fault."

"No." Thomas held on to her like she was all that tethered him to the ground. "No, none of this is at all your fault. I–" He closed his eyes for a moment. "Allow me to begin again. Are you well?"

"Quite well," she assured him. "I am only sorry that I slept for so long. I understand that you've been waiting for me to wake for some time now."

He shook his head. "No apology is required. Your body simply took what it needed."

"And yet yours has not, clearly," she said, trying to be delicate about it. "Is there a reason you would sooner fall asleep in a chair in this room than take to a bed for what must surely be better sleep?"

He laughed, heavy and sardonic. "I have rested when I could, but there has been too much to do. The beast's remains had to be properly disposed of, for one. It took a great deal of persuasion to convince the townsfolk to burn the corpse in its entirety right there in Pendlehaven Woods rather than take teeth and claws as keepsakes."

Ah, now they were getting to it. "What was it?" Cassandra asked.

"I think it was a gh–" He stopped as Mary reappeared at the door, a tray of food and tea in hand and a cheerful smile on her face. "Oh." His stomach rumbled audibly, and Cassandra laughed.

"We have neither of us eaten for some time," she said. "Come, sit and eat with me while we continue." She was loath to remove her hands from his, but it was the only proper thing to do now, especially while they ate. Luckily, Thomas seemed no more inclined to want distance than she did, and drew their chairs scandalously close together at the table, so close that their knees touched as they began to eat.

"I believe it was a ghast," Thomas said once they were alone once more. "A name I was only able to put to use thanks to your notes on your father's journal. I did not realise he was acquainted with such creatures."

"I… do not know that he *personally* was," Cassandra said, her momentary high spirits dipping low once more. "He knew enough to be able to depict them, but nothing in his journal speaks of using them himself, although, given how he died, I would not be surprised if Mr Fraser set one on him."

Thomas shook his head. "I am sorry for that."

"It's in the past," Cassandra said firmly. Even the pain she had feared to feel when she spoke of her father was somewhat removed now. "And I would sooner put it behind us entirely. Tell me what else has happened. What has become of the rest of the party?"

Thomas's glower returned. "The Crosses are missing."

"What?" The tip of Cassandra's spoon clacked loudly against the inside of her teacup, almost shattering the poor piece of crockery, but she had no attention to spare for chips. "How can that be? They were a part of this plot from the beginning! You yourself ensured they were delivered to the magistrate to be taken to London and put on trial!"

"I did," Thomas agreed darkly. "But it seems that the Crosses have better friends than any of us foresaw. The carriage carrying them to London was found not two hours ago, abandoned by the road. The Crosses were gone, as were the horses, the driver, and the guards."

Oh, damn. "You think someone in a position of power is protecting them, I assume?"

"They are certainly not victims of the Beast of Avon Vale," Thomas replied. "Whether or not they survived their rescue is another question. Colonel Cross was badly wounded after our altercation, and it is often easier to silence conspirators than it is to deliver them to safety."

Cassandra thought about that prospect for a moment. She recalled Mr Fraser's ability to put Merlin to sleep, and his insinuation that anyone with power could do something similar. Was that how Mrs Cross had helped their carriage evade the Beast of Avon Vale the night they were attacked? Had she done something similar this time?

It hardly matters at this point. She is gone… hopefully for good.

"I suppose it is possible that I am destined for Hell," she said at last, "because the prospect of someone finding their bodies in a ditch does not distress me in the slightest."

Thomas's lips finally turned up in a smile. "In that case, I shall join you there."

"You very nearly did." Unable to stop herself, she reached out to hold his hand once more. "I cannot believe you risked yourself for me when you could have been dragged into another world!"

"What is so hard to believe about that?" Thomas asked blithely, using his free hand to butter a piece of bread. "Apart from the actual dragging; I suppose that most people would be hard-pressed to imagine such a thing."

"Stop being so dismissive!" Cassandra's heart raced just to think of what might have become of Thomas if she had been the slightest bit slower cutting him free. "You have done nothing but aid me from the very beginning of this monstrous hunt of mine. To think that I might eventually have repaid you with the loss of your life to a hideous, otherworldly creature in your efforts to save me… it does not bear thinking about. You should never have risked yourself in such a manner."

Thomas's smile was gone now. "Do you truly think it was any different for me? That I could have stood by and allowed everything that makes you yourself to be killed, so that there would be room inside you for a dark god like the one Mr Fraser was trying to conjure? Do you think there is any way I could have abided such a fate without *wanting* to throw myself through that portal, just to put an end to my failure?"

He looked at her with eyes full of tenderness, an emotion that she surely did not deserve and yet there it was, unasked for, unearned, but even more precious because of it. "Cass. Have you not yet discerned the truth within my heart? I have not spoken it because I could not allow it to become a distraction as we sought the truth, but now… now, surely, you must realise that I love you."

"I…" Cassandra pressed her hand to her chest, where

her heart was beating rapidly enough to *hear*. "But I… it does not seem that…"

"Cassandra." He was holding both her hands once more, bending forwards in his chair so he could meet her gaze at the same level as hers. Whatever he saw in her face must have alarmed him, because his words began to flow more quickly, rushing out like a river.

"I should have made sure you knew, I see that now. Hell with it, I should have told you of my love for you five years ago, and never let that wretched Gilbert trap you in an engagement. But I was too afraid to speak to you back then and make my affections known to you. And then it was too late, for you and your family were gone. I regretted that, Cassandra, regretted it desperately. Too late did I realise that I had allowed you to slip through my fingers by never declaring my love for you."

"Oh." Even as stunned as she was, she could not bear to see him put himself through the pain that these recollections were bringing him. "No, please, do not distress yourself with wondering what might have been. It was… the situation was a terrible one for us all, and as to your – your affection for me, it – I – I was engaged to Gilbert, and both our families were in favour of the match, and – and–"

"And you would have turned me down," Thomas said. He did not seem hurt or surprised by the revelation, though. "I understand that, I do. I know that you are too faithful and proper to do otherwise, despite how much – or how little – you may have actually felt for your betrothed."

Cassandra knew her cheeks were flushing now, the dull

red that always suffused her face when she was caught in a truth she did not care to acknowledge. "In the end," she whispered, "despite everything that happened, I was... grateful not to be married to him."

"And despite losing you to the north, I was grateful that you *were* not married to him," Thomas said. "But please, if you – if you have the slightest feeling for me, if you believe that you could grow to love me, I beg of you, give me the chance now to win your heart." He smiled crookedly. "As you have seen, I can scarcely bear the thought of being parted from you for the time it takes to change your gown, much less stand you leaving the county entirely. Please, stay. Stay and let me attempt to win you properly." His voice dropped as the heat in his eyes rose to a smoulder. "Stay and give me the chance to prove my love to you, and persuade you to give me your hand in marriage."

Prove his love? Cassandra laughed a bit wildly. "I cannot find myself in doubt of your affections," she confessed breathlessly. Her racing heart made it hard to speak, and yet she was filled with an exhilaration that she had never felt before. "But I must doubt your powers of comprehension if you believe *me* to be anything other than utterly lost to you, Thomas."

His breath caught. "Does that mean..."

"Of course I love you," Cassandra said, meaning every word of it. "But that does not mean I would make you a good wife! There is much about me to object to, from my fall in status to my father's regrettable associations. Surely your family will object to a marriage between us."

"Who is to object?" Thomas asked fervently. "My parents are dead, my brother and sister-in-law as well. My sister has always adored you. As for my various aunts and uncles, they will find themselves cut off from the family fortune if they so much as turn their noses up at your choice in bonnet.

"I loved you five years ago, but now I adore you beyond all measure. My heart is entirely yours, and even if you find that you cannot accept me today, I will remain true to you until I can convince you of my sincerity. Your grace, your intelligence, your fierce fight for the truth – I love everything about you, and there is nothing anyone can say that will turn me away from you. If you agree to marry me, I will be the happiest man on this earth."

What could Cassandra say to that, except finally give in to the urges of her heart and accept him? "Yes," she said, beaming, and was graced with the sight of Thomas beaming right back at her. "Yes, then, with all my heart, I accept. I love you, and I will marry you."

"Cassandra…" He gave her the lightest of pulls downwards, and when their lips met in a kiss it was the most perfect thing she had ever experienced in her life. She laid a hand against his face, partly to steady herself, partly just to feel the glorious warmth of his skin and savour the man who had raised her hopes from nothing into a life that she would be most happy to live.

"You have saved me," she finally said once they broke apart. "You have been saving me from the moment I arrived in Tarryford, and you are doing so yet again today. I do not know what I did to deserve your devotion, but I swear to you that I will always cherish you."

Thomas turned his face and pressed his lips to her palm, his eyes drifting shut for a moment. "You saved me, too," he told her. "Or have you forgotten who sliced through a tentacle as thick as your waist to keep me from being pulled into an abyss?"

Cassandra laughed. "Ah, but I did not do it very well," she confessed. "It took me several tries to get all the way through it, and I feared for a moment that my arm was unequal to the task. In fact, if you have a mind to give me something special for our wedding, I would *greatly* appreciate learning more swordplay. For it seems that our lives are likely not meant for quietude."

Thomas was silent for a moment before saying, "Then you mean to pursue this? To pursue the matter of Shub-Niggurath and the Brotherhood?"

"How can I do otherwise?" For a second it was as though Cassandra were lying on the altar once more, cold and wet with sticky blood, the cloying smell of death thick in her nose as the end of her life reached for her with a thick, grasping tentacle. "It is plain there are more people involved in this degradation than I foresaw, but knowing what I do now, I cannot imagine allowing it to continue unchecked when I might do something about it instead. Even if my contribution is only to inform the authorities of what I know."

She took a deep breath and braced herself for the worst. "Of course, I understand if you do not wish to further your involvement in such things. You have already experienced so much pain at the hands of these cultists, even your own poor brother, and I would not force you to relive it. Please know that I hold you under no obligation to me, and you may–"

"Stop." She stopped. "I am not afraid for myself," Thomas told her very seriously. "Only for you. But if this is a cause that you mean to devote yourself to, then I shall of course stand with you. And in that case, I agree, teaching you to wield a sword and fire a pistol are absolute necessities, although you have not done so badly for yourself with your hatpin, have you?"

Cassandra laughed with relief. "No, I haven't," she agreed. "I wonder whatever became of it." *And what became of the mannikin.*

"It ought to be with your things. I had them all brought here from the inn."

"It was not. The last I remember having it, Mrs Cross had just served me poisoned tea." Cassandra shook her head. "But if it is lost now, it certainly served me well in the interim."

"That it did." Thomas kissed her hands again, then her lips. One kiss became many, and by the time they were finally ready to turn their attentions once more to breakfast, the tea had long since gone cold.

And neither of them minded a bit.

EPILOGUE

What a marvel a wedding could be.

It was not the ceremony itself that was due to contain anything particularly marvellous. Weddings, and their corresponding sermons, generally followed the same somewhat solemn lines they had since time immemorial, and as far as Cassandra was concerned, that was something more to be endured than enjoyed. No, she was not overly excited by the wedding itself; she and Thomas already belonged to each other in nearly every way that mattered. Rather, it was everything leading *up* to the wedding that had her spirits at a peak.

Informing her siblings of the impending marriage was a joy and learning they were both able to attend was nearly enough to send her into raptures. It had been so long since the three of them had been together.

Naturally, her maternal aunt did her absolute best to talk Cassandra out of it once she heard. The letter that she sent while Cassandra and Thomas were still housed at Harston

Hall was nothing short of condemnatory, full of scarcely-spoken-around accusations of entrapment and insinuations of using her body in a less-than-appropriate manner.

Cassandra had huffed a laugh to herself as she read that part of the letter. Thomas, sitting near her – they had made a habit of being near to each other these days whenever they could – turned her way. "What is it that amuses you?" he'd asked.

"Oh, my aunt," Cassandra said with a grin. "She believes I have captured your attention in 'illicit ways' and hints that she is sure I have been indiscreet with you. And she is true, to some degree," she allowed. "It was certainly not the most discreet thing ever to be bound to an altar in my nightgown in front of you, but I scarcely think I can be blamed for that."

"Certainly not," Thomas said, his cheeks darkening.

"There was nothing indiscreet about it," Cassandra went on blithely.

"No."

"Rather, it is a memory we would prefer to forget entirely."

"Ah…"

Oh, he was so easy to tease! It was still a bit difficult for Cassandra to believe how enjoyable it was to tease Thomas, and how lively he became teasing her back. Even now, he rallied admirably and said, "Your aunt sounds like nothing short of a harridan, and I hope she does not expect to attend the wedding."

"Mm, no, she does not. Although she does try to threaten us with the absence of my sister, but Beth has assured me that she will hire her own carriage if she must in order to be here for the happy occasion."

Deciding to get married out of Harston Hall was not the easiest choice to make, not after it had been the source of so much grief for both of them. But the truth was, there were few other appropriate options. Thomas had been empowered by Mr Fraser's grieving widow to utilise the services of the family's lawyer and find a buyer for the estate, and to avail himself of it while he did so. Meanwhile, his own home had not been entirely restored yet, although the tradesmen he employed assured him that it would not be long. Thomas had visited once already to see for himself that he was not being deceived, and had returned sombre but hopeful.

"You will love it there, I think," he said after spending some time in quiet contemplation. "Love it as it will be, returned to how it was before my brother's madness."

"It will have you in it," Cassandra replied. "Therefore I know I shall love it."

Being married out of Harston Hall was additionally advisable because the entire town of Tarryford was, it seemed, heavily invested in their happiness. Mrs Copeland had set herself up as Cassandra's stand-in for a mother, acting as chaperone when needed – which was almost never – and ensuring they both received the best of everything the town had to offer.

Young Garrett often came with her, always full of stories and forever asking to play with Merlin, who was only too happy to go and romp across the fields for a while. The servants of Harston were obliging to a fault, and eventually the only thing they were waiting on was the arrival of their siblings.

Francine arrived first, and not without an arch glance from Mrs Copeland and a murmured, "Heavens, took your pupil long enough to get here, aye?" to Cassandra, who flushed when she remembered the tale Thomas had told her about Cassandra being a tutor.

"It is better to be late than to never arrive at all," she rejoined, and Mrs Copeland laughed and moved back inside as Thomas went to help his sister from the carriage.

Francine Griffith was every bit what a young woman of the gentry should be: pretty, composed, and elegantly attired. She greeted her brother with a smile and a kiss, then turned to Cassandra, who had readied herself for everything from polite condemnation to a warm welcome to the family.

She was not expecting Francine to squeal, throw up her hands, and embrace Cassandra like she was a long-lost sister. "I cannot believe it!" Francine exclaimed. "When Thomas sent word that you two were to be married, I was so astonished I could barely hold myself together! I remember how sorely he pined for you, and for everything to be working out so well in the end, truly, it is just – and after what happened to David – and – and–"

Her enthusiasm quickly descended into becoming overwrought, for which there was no cure except the copious application of tea and cake and ready assurances from Cassandra that truly, all was well. She and Thomas shared a look over Francine's head while in the drawing room and silently assured each other that they would *not* be sharing any of the more salacious details of their time in Tarryford with her. The poor young woman was alarmed enough.

Beth arrived next, not in a proper carriage but in a gig that she apparently hired "from the nicest gentleman I met on the road, I swear, he was quite lovely except for not knowing his left hand from his right. It was rather a bumpy ride as a result because the horse was quite stupid and didn't know how to keep itself out of hedgerows, so finally *I* took the reins and did a much better job getting us here in one piece, and now, well… here I am!"

Yes, here she was, all of sixteen years old, with no gloves, a mismatched dress and pelisse, mud-stained shoes, and a bonnet that had several ribbons dangling haphazardly from it – likely one of Beth's own efforts at decorating, Cassandra thought. Her hair was the colour of chestnuts, her eyes as blue as cornflowers, and her smile as bright as the sun.

Cassandra had not realised just how much she missed her little sister until she had her in her arms once more.

"Look at you," she murmured once the hugging had relaxed to the point where she could breathe again. "Five years older and still as wild as ever."

And as tall as me now. Heavens, you've grown so much, and I did not get to see any of it.

"*Independent* as ever," her sister corrected her, pulling back to beam. "That's what Aunt Morrel says – when she's feeling indulgent, at least – that I am distressingly independent." She reached up and framed Cassandra's face with her hands, her gleeful look momentarily dimming into something a bit deeper and more introspective. "You have not had an easy time of it lately, have you?"

Cassandra did not give in to her urge to hide the truth. She would keep her sister innocent for her whole life if she could, but ignorance would not keep her safe. "No, I have not," she said instead.

"But Mr Griffith has been good to you, hasn't he?"

Cassandra took a deep breath. "He saved my life. More than once, in fact."

Beth's eyes went wide. "Saved it how?"

"I will tell you once Samuel arrives." For Cassandra wasn't sure she could bear to tell the story more than once, and her brother deserved to be informed at least as much as Beth did. "In the meantime–" she turned Beth towards Harston Hall "–you shall be able to work to great effect here. Francine needs a companion closer to her age–"

"But Cass, she's so *proper*!" Beth moaned.

"–and I require someone closer to my size to practice swordplay with," Cassandra went on. Beth grabbed her arm and pulled her around so that they faced each other.

"You are not joking?" her sister asked hopefully. "Tell me you are not joking!"

"I am not joking," Cassandra assured her. "Thomas is teaching me, but he thinks I will be well-served having someone else to work with so that he may observe and offer guidance from an outside perspective."

"You never showed any interest in learning this sort of

thing before." Beth narrowed her eyes. "When is Samuel getting here?"

"He ought to be here by the end of the week, why?"

"Because I am not sure I can wait so long to figure out what has changed you so much."

More than you can imagine. Cassandra merely smiled. "Come. Let us go and greet the Griffiths."

"Ugh, must we?"

"And then we shall have lunch."

"Excellent, I'm starving!"

Beth was a breath of fresh air in Harston Hall, full of enthusiasm and vigour, loud and boisterous and not afraid to show it. She allowed Francine to tempt – "coerce" as she put it – her into redecorating their bonnets exactly once before dragging the other girl outside with her. "It has been forever since I saw so much space without buildings mucking it up," she marvelled. Clearly, London was not her favourite place to be.

Despite their differences, the girls got along better than Cassandra had hoped, and Beth even made inroads with Merlin and Young Garrett before the week was over. Now all that remained was to wait for Samuel to arrive.

That he might not be able to make it was understandable. Her letter had been brief, and his reply had been but a single line letting her know when to expect him. The navy was an uncertain career at the best of times, and after what Mr Fraser had said about France summoning monsters from the deep, it would be reasonable, even expected, for Samuel to miss their nuptials. Yet as much as Cassandra might wish to delay things, the banns were set to be published and Upper Tarryford Church had been booked. Her wedding would happen on Saturday morning with or without her dear brother. She prayed it was with him.

"He will come," Thomas assured her on Friday morning as Cassandra paced in front of the windows facing the road. "And whether he is in time to see you in your wedding finery or not, we will wait for him here until you are together again."

Cassandra stopped pacing and smiled at him. "You must not make it a habit to read my mind *too* readily, my dear Thomas. A woman needs a few secrets, after all."

"Never fear," he assured her, his gaze soft. "There are aspects of you that shall forever be a mystery to me. But surely you can agree that in this instance, you're not making much of an effort to hide your thoughts."

"I suppose not."

The day wore on in excessive tedium; Cassandra had to force herself not to count the passing minutes, and her anxiety made it impossible to truly enjoy the last of the wedding preparations, although she did her best to keep her chin up for Mrs Copeland and speak enthusiastically with Reverend Jennings. By the time the remnants of dinner were taken away, Cassandra's plate was nearly untouched.

Beth, with the sort of delicacy she rarely displayed, did not say a thing about it directly, nor did she mention anything about the wedding, which it now seemed likely her brother would not attend. Rather, she leaned over to kiss Cassandra on the cheek, then took a curious Francine by the hand and led her out of the dining room with promises of "the most exciting game, you shall *love* it, I even have a knife you can borrow!"

Francine shot a tremulous look over her shoulder at Thomas, who sighed and got up to ensure that his sister was not about to be accidentally stabbed. "I shall return momentarily," he promised Cassandra before going after the girls.

Cassandra got to her feet and returned to the room she had been in all day – the south-facing drawing room. She stood in front of the windows and stared out at the darkness, her hands absently wringing the ends of her shawl, and tried to come to terms with the fact that her brother would not make it. Her mind refused, however.

Marriage felt like moving on, entering an entirely new stage in life. But how could she move on when her mind was still so mired in the past? How could she look to the future without the people she loved most around her, and the promise of their togetherness throughout life? Moving to Northumberland had felt, in many ways, like a death; not a new stage so much as an end simply waiting to be reached. But now…

Wait…

Was that a light on the road?

Cassandra did not wait to confirm it; she raced for the front of the house, past several startled servants, and threw herself out of the doors and onto the gravel path. "Samuel!" she called out, and a moment later she heard her brother's beloved voice.

"Cassandra!" The light in the distance began to bob, and soon thereafter resolved into her brother, still dressed in his uniform, carrying a pack over one shoulder and a lantern in the other hand. He set both down just before she reached him and opened his arms in an embrace.

Ah, he was here. Her little brother was here at last. The final knot in Cassandra's heart eased, and she laughed so hard she began to cry.

"Ah, no cause for that, is there?" Samuel pulled back and squeezed her shoulders. God, he looked so grown now; his youthful, lanky frame had filled out from years of hard work, and his skin was tanned from the sun, but his beaming smile was just the same. And his eyes … those were their mother's eyes, warm hazel, looking out at Cassandra from his face. "No more tears, sister, or you'll make your betrothed think you're not happy to see me."

"Thomas shall think no such thing," Cassandra assured him. "He will be as excited to see Midshipman Wright as I am."

"Lieutenant now, thank you." Samuel proudly tapped the gold epaulet on his right shoulder. "Just passed before coming here. It's how I was able to get the time away. And *Thomas*, is it?" he teased, picking his things back up. Cassandra wound a hand through his arm and they walked back towards the brightly lit hall. For a place that had caused her so much dismay, she was surprised to realise it had become a true source of comfort to her now. "Not Mr Griffith? Have you already lost your sense of propriety with him?"

"It is hard to call someone by their surname after the

events he and I went through together," Cassandra said. Samuel's smile fell away.

"You didn't say much in your letter, but… you solved Father's murder, didn't you?"

"I did," she said, then sighed. "And it was not a pleasant revelation, but I promised Beth I would tell you both at the same time."

"Must you tell her?" Samuel asked with a pained look. "She is still so young. I was able to meet with her last year, and despite how worldly she would have us believe she is, there's still such an innocence about her."

"I know," Cassandra said, her voice heavy. "And I do not relish the thought of diminishing that, but the things that happened here… I cannot see any other way of keeping her safe."

Samuel pulled Cassandra in a bit closer. "If what you saw was half as bad as some of what I have seen at sea," he murmured, "then I do not blame you."

Their arrival at Harston was met with all the joy of the occasion. Samuel was greeted warmly by the Griffiths, and Beth was over the moon to be with him once more. He was fed, and they all took their time renewing their acquaintance in the drawing room before Francine finally went off to bed. She seemed surprised that Beth was not also withdrawing, but a nod from her brother was enough to allay any suspicions.

"*Finally*," Beth said, plopping herself down on the footstool in front of Cassandra's chair. "Now will you tell us what happened here? I have been half out of my mind wondering about it, and the servants have nothing to say but the wildest stories!"

Naturally she had already spoken to the servants about it. Cassandra shared a look with Thomas, then said, "What I am about to tell you must not leave this room." She waited for confirmation from her siblings before starting at the beginning of her story – her arrival in Tarryford.

She left none of it out. She told them of the hunts, of her encounter with the beast, of the mannikin which had crept into her room at The Four Feathers. She told them of Thomas's aid – and their mutually agreed-upon deception – and of finding the journal. Unflinchingly, she told them of their father's foolishness, and the horrors he had participated in. Finally, she told them about the portal to the other realm and the monster that had come through it, and nearly taken her and Thomas back again.

"I am telling you both this so that you will be careful," she finished. "I do not know how far this rot has spread in England, but I fear that nowhere is truly safe."

"The seas are as rough as they say." Samuel spoke up at last. "I have seen evidence of some of these sigils written on the ruins of French and Spanish ships. Our navy does not use them, as far as I know, but our battles have been… chaotic." He frowned. "There have been storms rising up out of nowhere, and entire ships pulled into the water without rhyme or reason. It is only due to the swiftness of our ships and the rigor of our sailors that we haven't lost the seas entirely. As things stand right now, the odds of our maintaining naval superiority are… not good."

"I think I have seen something of this myself," Beth mused, startling all of them. "What? You think I do not see things? There is a particular style of cravat that has become quite popular in town lately, and some men have taken to fixing it with a very flashy pin. I did not think much of it until now, but I know that the pin cannot be bought. It can only be *gifted* from one wearer to another."

A chill went through Cassandra. She wasn't ready for this fight, not yet, and she had no desire for either her dear brother or her precocious little sister to throw themselves into the fray either. Samuel she could not help, as he was bound to the navy, but Elizabeth...

Judging from the look on her face, she was already getting ideas. "You know, I am certain I could sneak into some of the salons where–"

"No."

"No!"

"Absolutely not!"

"Fine," she said sulkily. "But then what shall I do when I return to town?"

"Why return at all?" Cassandra asked.

"You mean..." Beth's eyes went wide. "I could stay with you?"

"I would love it if you did, but if you are not inclined, perhaps we can–"

Beth cut her off by leaping at Cassandra and holding her around the neck so tight she could barely breathe. "Of course I am inclined! I would give *anything* not to sit through another lecture on 'ladylike comportment' from

Aunt Morrel, and my cousins are so dreadful. Francine is much more tolerable," she assured Thomas, who looked bemused.

Cassandra patted her sister on the back, then eased her grip away. "It is decided then," she said. "And Samuel, how long can you stay?"

"Not long," he said apologetically. "Only until Sunday. Then I'm back to my ship before the next week is through."

"You'll move faster in a private carriage," Thomas said.

"Aye, but–" Samuel finally figured out what Thomas was offering and ducked his head gratefully. "Ah. Thank you. Then I believe I can remain until Tuesday."

Four whole days with her brother, with her family altogether once more, and Thomas and Francine as well. It felt like an unbelievable luxury, like the greatest of gifts. Once she was joined in matrimony with Thomas, her happiness would truly be complete.

She did not expect so many people from Tarryford to attend her nuptials the next day, but when Cassandra entered the church and saw the extensive garlands, heard the cheers from the folk she had grown so fond of, and finally stood beside Thomas as a joyful Reverend Jennings began the ceremony that would legally bind them as tightly as their love already did...

Well. It seemed that the wedding ceremony was quite marvellous after all.

ACKNOWLEDGMENTS

Huge thanks to the team at Aconyte, especially my editor Lottie, who thought I'd be a good fit for this and was SO RIGHT! And thank you to Chaosium Inc. for providing the backdrop for a truly fantastic world to write in.

ABOUT THE AUTHOR

CATH LAURIA is a Colorado girl who loves snow and sunshine. She prefers books to TV shows, has a vast collection of beautiful, edged weapons, and could totally survive in the wild without electricity or running water, but would really prefer not to. She loves writing speculative fiction of all genres, and has a long list of publications under her belt as romance author Cari Z.

authorcariz.com // @author_cariz

When two spiritist
swindlers accidentally
summon something horrific
from beyond the stars, they must
thwart a sinister time-spanning plot,
in the first novel set in Chaosium's
CTHULHU BY GASLIGHT

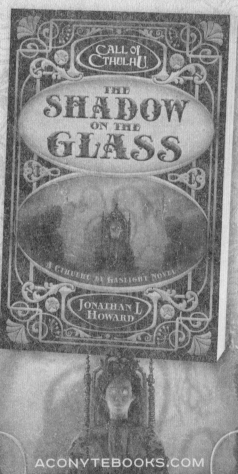